Beautiful
SACRIFICE

ALSO BY JAMIE MCGUIRE

Providence (Providence Trilogy: Book One)
Requiem (Providence Trilogy: Book Two)
Eden (Providence Trilogy: Book Three)

Beautiful Disaster
Walking Disaster
A Beautiful Wedding (A Beautiful Disaster Novella)

Beautiful Oblivion (Maddox Brothers: Book One)
Beautiful Redemption (Maddox Brothers: Book Two)

Red Hill
Among Monsters (A Red Hill Novella)

Happenstance: A Novella Series
Happenstance: A Novella Series (Part Two)
Happenstance: A Novella Series (Part Three)

Apolonia

Beautiful
SACRIFICE

JAMIE McGUIRE

Visit my website at www.jamiemcguire.com

Cover Designer: Sarah Hansen, Okay Creations, www.okaycreations.com

Editor and Interior Designer: Jovana Shirley, Unforeseen Editing, www.unforeseenediting.com

ISBN-13: 978-1511847506

For my European ambassadors—
Jasmin Häner, Kateřina Fojtů, and Nina Moore

CONTENTS

CHAPTER ONE

TOO MANY PEOPLE IN A SMALL ROOM sounded a lot like the roar of a fire—the high and low inflections, the constant and familiar hum that only became louder the closer you got. In the five years that I'd waited tables for Chuck and Phaedra Niles at The Bucksaw Café, being around that many impatient, hungry people day after day made me want to torch the place at times. But the lunch crowd wasn't what kept me coming back. It was the comforting drone of conversation, the heat of the kitchen, and the sweet freedom from the bridges I'd burned.

"Falyn! For fuck's sake!" Chuck said, trying not to sweat in the soup.

He reached out his hand and stirred the broth in a deep pot. I tossed him a clean rag.

"How is it this hot in Colorado?" he complained. "I moved here because I'm fat. Fat people don't like to be hot."

"Then maybe you shouldn't be working over a stove for a living," I said with a smirk.

The tray felt heavy when I lifted it in my arms but not as heavy as it used to feel. Now, I could carry it with six full plates, if necessary. I backed into the swinging double doors, bumping my butt against them.

"You're fired," he barked. He wiped his bald head with the white cotton cloth and then tossed it to the center of the prep table.

"I quit!" I said.

"That's not funny!" He leaned away from the heat radiating from his station.

Turning toward the main dining area, I paused in the doorway, seeing all twenty-two tables and twelve barstools filled with professionals, families, tourists, and locals. According to Phaedra, table thirteen even included a bestselling author and her assistant. I leaned over, compensating for the extra weight of the tray, and winked in thanks to Kirby as she opened the stand next to the table where I would set my tray.

"Thanks, lovey," I said, pulling the first plate.

I set it in front of Don, my first regular and the best tipper in town. He pushed up his thick glasses and settled into his seat, removing his trademark fedora. Don's khaki jacket was a bit worn, like the dress shirt and tie he wore every day. On slow afternoons, I would listen to him talk about Jesus and how much he missed his wife.

Kirby's long dark ponytail swished as she bussed a table near the wall of windows. She held a small tub full of dirty dishes against her hip, winking at me as she passed through to the kitchen. She was gone only long enough to drop off the pile of plates and cups for Hector to wash, and then she returned to her hostess podium. Her naturally wine-stained lips turned up at the corners as a light breeze blew through the glass entrance door, propped open by a large geode, one of hundreds Chuck had collected over the years.

Kirby greeted a group of four men who'd walked in as I attended to Don.

"Would you cut open that steak for me, handsome?" I asked.

Don didn't need a menu. He ordered the same meal at every visit—a house salad swimming in ranch, fried pickles, a medium-rare New York strip, and Phaedra's turtle cheesecake—and he wanted all of it at the same time.

Don complied, tucking his tie between the buttons of his shirt, and with his shaking thin hands, he sawed into the juicy meat on his plate. He looked up and offered a quick nod.

While he prayed over his food, I left him for just a moment to swipe the pitcher of sweet sun tea off the bar counter. When I returned and picked up his cup, I held the pitcher sideways, so plenty of ice poured out with the light-brown liquid.

Don took a sip and let out a satisfied sigh. "As I live and breathe, Falyn. I sure love it when Phaedra makes her sun tea."

His chin was attached to the bottom of his throat with a thin flap of loose skin, and his face and hands were dotted with liver spots. He was a widower, and he'd lost weight since Mary Ann passed.

I offered a half smile. "I know you do. I'll check on you in a bit."

"Because you're the best," Don called after me.

Kirby guided the group of men to my last empty table. All but one man was covered in soot smeared with a day's worth of sweat. The clean one seemed to just be tagging along, his freshly washed hair barely long enough to hang into his eyes. The others looked pleased with their exhaustion, a hard, long shift behind them.

Only the tourists stared at the ragged men. Locals knew exactly who they were and why they were there. The men's dusty boots and the three bright blue hard hats sitting on their laps, bearing the Department of Agriculture's emblem, made their specialty easy to guess—a hotshot crew, likely the Alpine division out of Estes Park.

The spot fires had been particularly relentless that season, and it seemed like the Forest Service had dispatched their interagency crews from every district, some as far as Wyoming and South Dakota. Colorado Springs had been hazy for weeks. The smoke from the fires in the north had turned the afternoon sun into a glowing bright red ball of fire. We hadn't seen stars since before my last paycheck.

I greeted the men with a polite expression. "What are we drinking?"

"You sure got pretty hair," one of the men said.

I lowered my chin and cocked an eyebrow.

"Shut the fuck up and order, Zeke. We'll probably get called back out soon."

"Damn, Taylor," Zeke said. His frown was then targeted in my direction. "Get him some food, will ya? He gets cranky when he's hungry."

"I can do that," I said, annoyed with them already.

Taylor glanced up at me, and for just a moment, I was captured by a pair of warm brown irises. In less than a second, I found something familiar behind his eyes. Then he blinked and returned to his menu.

Although usually cute, mostly charming, and always with a respectable amount of muscles, men who blew through our town with a dusting of ash on their boots were only to be admired from afar. No self-respecting local girl would be caught dating one of those fascinating, brave tanned young men for two reasons. They were seasonal, and they would leave you behind, pregnant or heartbroken. I'd seen it so many times, and not just with the hotshot crews, but with the airmen passing through, too. To the young men my father referred to as vagrants, the Springs was a buffet of young girls just desperate enough to be fooled into loving someone they knew wouldn't stay.

I wasn't one of them even if, according to my parents, I was the most educated whore in Colorado Springs.

"Let's start with drinks." I kept my tone pleasant and my mind on the decent tip the hotshots would usually leave on the table.

"What do you want, Trex?" Zeke asked the clean one.

Trex looked at me from under his damp tendrils, all emotion absent from his eyes. "Just a water."

Zeke put down his menu. "Me, too."

Taylor glanced up at me again, the white of his eyes practically glowing against the dirt on his face. The warm brown in his irises matched the buzzed hair on his head. Although his eyes were kind, the skin on both of his arms was crowded with various tattoos, and he looked like he'd been through enough to earn every one of them.

"Do you have sweet tea?" Taylor asked.

"Yes. Sun tea. Is that okay?"

He nodded before expectantly watching the man in front of him. "What do you want, Dalton?"

Dalton sulked. "They don't have Cherry Coke." He looked up at me. "Why doesn't anyone in the whole goddamn state of Colorado have Cherry Coke?"

Taylor crossed his arms over the table, the muscles of his forearms sliding and tightening under his ink-covered skin. "I've accepted it. You should just accept it, man."

"I can make you one," I said.

Dalton tossed his menu on the table. "Just bring me a water," he grumbled. "It's not the same."

I took their menus and leaned in toward Dalton's face. "You're right. Mine is better."

As I withdrew, I heard a couple of them giggling like boys.

One of them said, "Whoa."

I stopped at Don's table on the way back to the drink station. "You all right?"

Don hummed, "Yes," while chewing on his steak. He was nearly finished. His other plates, all but the cheesecake, had been scraped clean.

I patted his bony shoulder and then made my way around the bar. I filled two plastic cups with ice water and one with sweet sun tea, and then I began making Dalton's Cherry Coke.

Phaedra pushed through the double doors and frowned at the sight of a family standing near Kirby's podium. "There's a wait?" she asked. She dried her hands on the dishtowel she had tied around her waist as an apron.

Phaedra had been born and raised in Colorado Springs. She and Chuck had met at a concert. She was a full-fledged hippie, and he tried to be one. They would sit in on peace rallies and protest wars, and they were now the owners of the most popular downtown café. Urbanspoon had listed The Bucksaw Café as its number one pick for lunch, but Phaedra would take it personally when she noticed waiting customers.

"We can't have great service *and* no wait. Busy is good," I said, mixing my special cherry syrup into the Coke.

Phaedra's salt-and-pepper long hair was parted in the middle and pulled back into a wiry bun, and her wrinkled olive skin weighed down her eyes. She was a wisp of a woman, but it wouldn't take long to learn she could be a bear if you crossed her. She preached peace and butterflies, but she'd put up with exactly zero shit.

Phaedra looked down as she said, "We won't be busy for long if we piss people off." She rushed off to the front door, apologizing to the waiting family and assuring a table soon.

Table twenty had just signed their check. Phaedra rushed over to thank them and bussed their table, quickly scrubbing it. Then she motioned for Kirby to seat the family.

I loaded up the drinks on a tray and then carried them across the room. The crew was still looking at the menu. I inwardly grumbled. That meant they hadn't decided.

"Do you need a minute?" I asked, giving each man his drink.

"I said a water," Dalton said, holding up his Cherry Coke with a frown.

"Just try it. If you don't like it, I'll bring you a water."

He took a sip and then another. His eyes popped open. "She wasn't kidding, Taylor. It's better than the real stuff."

Taylor looked up at me. "I'll have one, too, then."

"You got it. Lunch?"

"We're all having the spicy turkey panini," Taylor said.

"All of you?" I asked, dubious.

"All of us," Taylor said, handing me the laminated long sheet.

"Okay then. I'll be back with your Cherry Coke," I said before leaving them to check on my other tables.

The dozens of voices in the packed café bounced off the windows and came straight back to the bar where I was mixing another Cherry Coke. Kirby rounded the counter, her shoes squeaking against the orange-and-white tiled floor. Phaedra was fond of random—fun portraits, trinkets, and off-color signs. They were all eclectic, like Phaedra.

"You're welcome," Kirby said, tucking her shirt into her skirt.

"For the tray stand? I already said thank you."

"I'm referring to the gaggle of hot firemen I seated in your section."

Kirby was barely nineteen, baby fat still plumping her cheeks. She'd been dating Gunnar Mott since her sophomore year of high school, so she took extreme pleasure in trying to fix me up with every halfway decent-looking man with a job who walked through the door.

"No," I said simply. "I'm not interested in any of them, so don't even try your matchmaking crap. And they're hotshots, not firemen."

"Is there a difference?"

"Yes, a big one. For starters, they fight wildfires. They hike for miles with huge packs and equipment; they're on the job seven days a week, twenty-four hours a day; they travel to wherever the fire is; and they saw through fallen timber and dig fire lines."

Kirby stared at me, unimpressed.

"Do *not* say anything to them. I mean it," I warned.

"Why not? All four of them are cute. That makes your odds fairly fantastic."

"Because you suck at it. You don't even care if they're my type. You just set me up with guys, so you can date them vicariously. Remember the last time you tried to set me up with someone? I was stuck with that slimy tourist for an entire evening."

"He was so sexy," she said, fantasizing in front of God and everyone.

Beautiful
SACRIFICE

"He was boring. All he talked about was himself and the gym … and himself."

Kirby ignored my resistance. "You're twenty-four. There is nothing wrong with putting up with an hour of boring conversation to experience three hours of amazing sex."

"Ew. Ew, no. Stop." I wrinkled my nose and shook my head, involuntarily imagining dirty talk that included the words *repetitions* and *protein*. I put Taylor's cup on a tray.

"Falyn, you're up!" Chuck called from the kitchen.

I swung by the food window, tray in hand, seeing that table thirteen's order was sitting on the shelf cut out of the wall separating the bar from the kitchen. The heat lamps above warmed my hands as I grabbed each plate and placed them on the tray, and then I rushed the food to the table. The author and her assistant barely noticed as I placed the beef and feta cheese salad and chicken club on the table.

"Does everything look all right?" I asked.

The author nodded her head, barely taking a breath while she chatted away. I carried the final Cherry Coke to the hotshot crew, but as I walked away, one of them grabbed my wrist. I looked over my shoulder, glaring at the man with the offending hand.

Taylor winced at my reaction. "A straw?" He loosened his grip. "Please?" he asked.

I slowly pulled one from my apron and handed it to him. Then I spun around and checked on the rest of my tables, one after another.

Don finished off his cheesecake and left a twenty on the table, as he always did, and the author left twice that. The hotshot crew's signed receipt was merely rounded up to the next dollar.

I tried not to wad it up and stomp it into the ground. "Dicks," I said under my breath.

The rest of the afternoon was nonstop, not unlike any other afternoon since the Urbanspoon app had decided to put The Bucksaw Café on the foodie map. As the hours passed, I served more firefighters and hotshot crews, and they all left decent tips, as did the rest of my tables, but I couldn't shake the bitterness for Taylor, Zeke, Dalton, and Trex.

Fifty-one cents. I should hunt them down and throw the change at them.

The streetlights shone down on those walking past the diner to the two-story country-western bar four buildings down. Young women, most barely twenty-one, trotted along in groups, wearing short skirts and tall boots, as they enjoyed the summer night air— not that August had the corner on skin-baring clothes. Most locals would shed their layers for anything over forty degrees.

I flipped the sign on the door, so the word *Closed* faced the sidewalk, but I leaped back when a face loomed over me from the other side. It was Taylor, the hotshot crew guy and piss-poor tipper. Before my brain had time to stop my expression, I narrowed my eyes and sneered.

Taylor held out his hands, his voice muffled from the glass. "I know. Hey, I'm sorry. I was going to leave cash, but we were called out, and I forgot. I should have known better than to come into town while we were on call, but I was sick of the food at the hotel."

I barely recognized him without the seven layers of grime. Wearing clean clothes, he could have been mistaken for someone I might actually find attractive.

"Don't worry about it," I said, turning for the kitchen.

Taylor pounded on the glass. "Hey! Lady!"

Deliberately slow, I faced him, craning my neck. "Lady?" I nearly spit the word.

Taylor lowered his hands and then shoved them in his pockets. "Just open the door, so I can tip you. You're making me feel bad."

"You should!" I spun around in a huff to see Phaedra, Chuck, and Kirby behind me, all far too amused with the situation. "A little help here?"

They all shared the same smug expression, and I rolled my eyes, facing Taylor once again.

"I appreciate the gesture, but we're closed," I said.

"Then I'll tip you double when I come back."

I dismissively shook my head. "Whatever."

"Maybe I could, uh ... take you out to dinner? Kill two birds with one stone."

I arched an eyebrow.

Taylor glanced from one side to the other. Passersby were beginning to slow, so they could watch our exchange.

"No, thank you."

He puffed out a laugh. "You're acting like I'm a weapons-grade asshole here. I mean, I might be—a little. But you ... you're ... distracting."

"Oh, so it's my fault you didn't leave a tip?" I asked, touching my chest.

"Well … kind of," he said.

I glared at him. "You're not an asshole. You're a cunt rag."

Taylor's mouth slowly turned up into a broad grin, and he pressed both palms against the glass. "You've gotta go out with me now."

"Get the hell out of here," I said.

"Falyn!" Phaedra screeched. "For God's sake!"

I reached up and switched off the outside light, leaving Taylor in the dark. The mop and yellow bucket I'd just filled with soapy hot water before I had been so rudely interrupted was still waiting.

Phaedra clicked her tongue at me and then took my place at the front door, turning the key in the lock until it clicked before letting the metal fall into her apron. Chuck ducked into the kitchen while Kirby and I cleaned the dining area.

Kirby shook her head as she swept under table six. "You're going to regret that."

"Doubtful." I reached into my apron and popped a large chunk of bubble gum into my mouth.

Kirby's face fell. I couldn't tell if she felt sorry for me or if she was just tired of arguing.

My trusty old earbuds fit snugly into my ears, and the lead singer of Hinder crooned through the wires running from my cell phone as I pushed the mop around on the tiled floor. The wooden handle would usually leave at least one splinter in my hand a night, but I would be glad to have that rather than mandatory three-days-a-week piano lessons. It was preferable to reporting my whereabouts every few hours or else risking public reprimand and far better than going to med school.

I loathed being sick or being around the sick, bodily fluids, and physiology in its most basic form. The only people who thought it would be a good idea for me to go to med school were my asshole parents.

During the two-second pause after "The Life" ended, I could hear knocking on the glass panes that made up the front wall of The Bucksaw Café. I looked up and froze, pulling on each wire hanging from my ears.

Dr. William Fairchild, the former mayor of Colorado Springs, was standing on the sidewalk, tapping his knuckles again even though I was looking right at him.

"Oh, shit. Shit … Falyn," Kirby hissed.

"I see him … and her," I said, narrowing my eyes at the petite blonde nearly hidden behind the portly doctor.

Phaedra immediately went to the front door and jammed the key in the lock, twisting it. She pulled but didn't welcome the people standing on the sidewalk. "Hello there, Dr. Fairchild. We weren't expecting you."

He thanked her, taking off his cowboy hat, before attempting to walk inside. "Just needed to speak to Falyn."

Phaedra put her hand on the doorjamb, barring him from taking another step. "Sorry, William. Like I said, we weren't expecting you."

William blinked once and then glanced back at his wife.

"Falyn," she said, peering over her husband's broad shoulder.

She was wearing an expensive gray sheath dress with matching shoes. By her attire and his suit and tie, I guessed they had come downtown to meet someone for dinner.

She sidestepped, so she could face me head-on. "Do you have time to talk?"

"No." I blew a large bubble and let it snap back.

The double doors swung open, and Chuck arrived from the kitchen, his hands and forearms still wet and covered in suds. "Dr. Fairchild," he said. "Blaire."

Blaire wasn't pleased. "Also Dr. Fairchild," she said, attempting to sound casual but failing.

"No disrespect," Chuck began, "but you can't come here, unannounced. I think you know that. Now, why don't you call the next time? It would cause less stress for everyone."

Blaire's eyes targeted Chuck. She was already planning on making him regret standing up to her.

"There's a young man outside. Is he here to see you?" William asked.

I dropped the mop and rushed past Phaedra and my parents to see Taylor standing with his hands stuffed into his jeans pockets, leaning against the corner of the building, just beyond the glass wall.

"What are you still doing here?" I asked.

Taylor stood up straight and opened his mouth to speak.

William pointed to him. "Is he one of those damn provisional Land Management trash?"

The redness in William's cheeks and the sudden gloss in his eyes filled me with a satisfaction only true spite could produce.

Taylor took a few steps in our direction, completely undeterred by William's anger. "This must be your dad."

I chomped the wad of gum in my mouth, annoyed with the unexpected introduction.

Blaire looked away in disgust. "Really, Falyn, you look like a cow chewing its cud."

Blowing a large bubble and letting it snap back into my mouth was the only response I could muster.

Taylor held out his hand with confidence. "Taylor Maddox, sir. US Forest Service trash."

The hotshot lifted his chin, likely thinking this would impress the pompous ass standing in front of him.

Instead, William shifted his weight, incensed. "A vagrant. Just when I thought you couldn't sink any lower. Christ, Falyn."

Taylor pulled his hand back, again shoving it into his jeans pocket. His jaw tightened as he was clearly trying to resist the urge to retort.

"Bill," Blaire warned, checking to see who was within earshot. "Not the time or the place."

"I prefer the term *seasonal*," Taylor said. "I'm with the Alpine Hotshot Crew, stationed just up at Estes Park."

His bulky shoulders rose as he pushed his fists further into his pockets. I got the feeling it was to keep from connecting one of them with William's jaw.

Taylor's movement caused my father to notice his arms. "Hotshot crew, eh? And part-time doodle pad by the looks of it."

Taylor chuckled, glancing down at his right arm. "My brother's a tattoo artist."

"You're not really dating this deadbeat, are you?" As usual, my father's question was more of a demand for an answer.

Taylor looked at me, and I grinned.

"No," I said. "We're in love." I strolled over to Taylor, who looked as surprised as my father, and I planted a soft kiss on the corner of his mouth. "I get off at eight tomorrow night. See you then."

Taylor smiled and reached around my middle, pulling me to his side. "Anything for you, baby."

William sneered, but Blaire gently touched his chest, signaling for him to stay quiet.

"Falyn, we need to talk," she said, her eyes making note of every tattoo on Taylor and every frayed edge of every hole in his jeans.

"We've talked," I said, feeling confident while being hugged to Taylor's side. "If I have anything else to say, I'll call you."

"You haven't spoken to us in months. It's time," she said.

"Why?" I asked. "Nothing has changed."

Blaire's eyes fell from my face to look down my body and then came back again. "Quite a lot has changed. You look atrocious."

Taylor held me away from him, gave me a once-over, and then made a show of his disagreement.

Blaire sighed. "We've given you space and time to figure this out on your own, but enough is enough. You need to come home."

"So, his upcoming campaign has nothing to do with it?" I nodded toward my father, who puffed out his chest, indignant.

His audacity to even pretend to be insulted made it almost impossible for me to keep my cool.

My face contorted. "I want you both to leave. Now."

William angled his body and stepped forward in an offensive move. Taylor steadied himself, ready to defend me if necessary. Chuck had stood up to my parents before, but standing next to Taylor was different. He barely knew me, yet there he was, in a protective stance in front of me, glowering at my father, daring him to take another step. I hadn't felt that safe in a long time.

"Good night, docs," Phaedra said in her shaky Southern twang.

Taylor took my hand and led me past my parents into the dining area of the café.

Phaedra shut the door in my father's face and cranked the key in the lock as Blaire watched. As Phaedra turned her back to them, my parents continued on to their original destination.

Chuck crossed his arms, staring at Taylor.

Taylor looked down at me even though I could claim all of five feet nine inches. "You did that just to piss off your parents, didn't you?"

I flattened out my apron and then met his eyes. "Yep."

"Do you still want me to pick you up at eight?" Taylor asked. "Or was that just for show?"

I glanced at Kirby, who looked entirely too happy about the situation.

"It's not necessary," I said.

"C'mon"—Taylor flashed his teeth, a deep dimple sinking in the middle of his left cheek—"I played along. The least you could do is let me buy you dinner."

I blew my bangs out of my eyes. "Fine." I untied my apron as I left him for home.

"Did she just say yes?" Taylor asked.

Chuck chortled. "You'd better take it and run, kid. She hasn't said yes to anyone in a while."

I jogged up the steps to my apartment above the café, hearing the front door click after someone had let Taylor out. After taking just a few steps to the window overlooking Tejon Street, I watched as Taylor walked to his pickup truck in the parking lot.

A long sigh separated my lips. He was too cute and too charming, and he was on a hotshot crew. I was already one statistic. I wouldn't let him turn me into another. One dinner wouldn't be hard, and I sort of owed him for playing along while I'd pissed off my parents.

I was well practiced in walking away though. One dinner, and we'd be done.

CHAPTER TWO

My FINGERS FLITTED UNDER THE COOL WATER gushing from the showerhead. The pipes sang a sad song, expanding and trembling within the thin white walls of my quaint two-bedroom loft above The Bucksaw Café. It seemed like it was taking forever for the hot water to kick in.

The carpets were worn, and it smelled of grease and mildew when a candle wasn't burning, but for two hundred dollars a month, it was mine. In comparison with other apartments in the Springs, the loft was practically free.

Leftover decorations from Phaedra's eclectic collection hung from the walls. I had left home with nothing but the clothes I wore and my Louis Vuitton purse. Even if I had wanted to take some of my things, my father wouldn't have let me.

Dr. William Fairchild was feared at the hospital and at home but not because he was abusive or ill-tempered—even though he was the latter. William was a renowned cardiologist in the state of Colorado and married to Dr. Blaire Fairchild, one of the best cardiothoracic surgeons in North America, also known as my mother ... and queen bitch of the universe by some of her nurses.

My parents had been made for each other. The only person who didn't fit into our family was me, and I was a constant disappointment to them both. By my junior year of high school, I had been introduced to my favorite friend, my secret comfort, the promise of a stress-free good time—cheap beer. The more obsessed and well-known my parents had become, the more I'd nursed my loneliness and shame—not that they'd noticed.

The water began to turn warm, bringing my thoughts to the present.

"Finally," I said to no one.

The button of my jeans easily popped open, the slit worn and a bit stretched out. I unzipped my pants and then realized, with the millions of thoughts swirling around in my head, I'd forgotten an important part of my nightly routine. I swore aloud while rushing to my bedroom closet. Bending down, I uncovered a size-nine shoebox. I carried the cardboard to the kitchen and set it next to my apron on the counter.

A thin stack of twenties and fewer small bills peeked out from the apron that was folded neatly on the speckled gray-and-rose Formica. I removed the lid from the box that held over five years of letters, pictures, and cash instead of Adidas. I carefully placed half of my tips inside, and then I hid it back in the dark corner of my closet.

I returned to the kitchen to tuck the rest of the money inside a plain black wallet that I'd purchased from the local discount store shortly after I'd sold the Louis Vuitton online. One hundred and eleven dollars in cash fit right in with the rest of the stack. I would have rent by the end of my shift the following day. With that thought, I smiled and tossed the wallet onto the counter on my way to the bathroom.

My T-shirt was stuck to my skin from sweating throughout the day. I peeled it off and easily kicked off my ratty white Converse high-tops, and then I maneuvered my way out of my skinny jeans, pulling them down over my ankles and tossing them to the corner.

The large pile of dirty clothes made me happy, knowing that would never have existed in my former life. With a houseful of staff—Vanda, the housekeeper, and the three maids, Cicely, Maria, and Ann—overlooked laundry at the end of the day would have meant somebody's termination. My bed had been made the moment I climbed out of it, and my clothes had been laundered, pressed, and hung up by the next day.

I let my panties fall to the floor, and I pulled off my damp socks with my toes. I stepped under the steaming uneven spray. Once in a while, the water would become ice cold and then turn scalding before returning to normal, but I didn't care.

The trash was full, the laundry was a week behind, and dirty dishes were in the sink. And I would go to bed without giving any of it a second thought. No one was there to yell at me, to obsess over order, or to chastise my untucked shirts or untamed hair. I didn't have to be perfect here. I didn't have to be perfect anywhere anymore. I only had to exist and breathe for no one but myself.

The yellow wallpaper in the bathroom was peeling from years of steam filling the room, the paint in the living room was chipped and scuffed, and the ceiling in my bedroom had a large water stain in the corner that seemed to get worse every year. The carpet was matted, the furniture older than me, but it was all mine, free of memories and free of obligation.

Once I'd scrubbed the grease and sweat from my skin, I stepped out, wrapping myself in a fluffy yellow towel. Then I began the nightly routine of brushing my teeth and moisturizing my body. I slipped on a nightgown and watched exactly six minutes of the news—just long enough to catch the weather. Then I crawled into my full-sized bed and read something completely and utterly trashy before falling asleep.

Breakfast at the Bucksaw would begin in ten hours, and I would repeat my day like every other day, except for Sundays and the occasional Saturday when Phaedra would insist I find somewhere else to be. Only, the next day would be different. I would have to survive dinner with the interagency oaf, likely listening to how cool axes and tattoos were and being just bitchy enough that he'd steer clear of me until he went home to Estes Park.

A knock on the door startled me, and I leaned up on my elbows, looking around the bedroom as if that would help me hear better.

"Falyn!" Kirby said from the other side of the door. "Gunnar is going to be late! Let me in!"

I groaned as I crawled off the comfy mattress, and I crept out of my room and across the living area to the front door. Just after I rotated the dead bolt, Kirby pushed through the door, still in her apron and holding a to-go cup half full of soda.

"Is it possible to love everything about someone, except for everything about him?" she growled, slamming the door behind her, narrowly missing my face. She sipped on her drink and leaned against the closest thing to the door, the side of my refrigerator. "This is the second time he's been late this week."

"Maybe you should stop letting him borrow your car," I said.

"His truck is in the shop—again." Kirby's eyes scanned over my purple cotton nightgown, and she puffed out a laugh. "What a sexy nightie you have, grandma."

"Shut your face," I said, taking a few steps to face the large mirror on the wall. It was basically an oversized T-shirt. There was nothing grandma about it.

I padded across the worn carpet, inviting her to sit. I grabbed a section of my still damp hair, mindlessly using both hands to twist the ends. My hair was camouflage, falling in soft waves over my shoulders, long enough to cover my breasts if I were ever stranded in a lagoon without clothes. It would keep my hands busy when I was nervous or bored. It was also a cloaking device. With just one tuck of the chin, a tawny veil would be lowered between me and an unwelcome stare.

Whether a man would mention my hair or my eyes first was a toss-up. My eyes weren't as closely set as Kirby's, but they were the same almond shape, only slightly hooded. No matter how many YouTube makeup tutorials I'd watched, eyeliner was a waste of time. Makeup in general was a waste of time because I had never mastered the art, but for some reason, the shape of my eyes plus their bright green color were something my regulars would comment on often. That was only slightly more frequent than the mentions of the splash of freckles over my nose.

Kirby made herself at home, sitting on my sofa and leaning back into the cushions. "I love this old thing. I think it's older than I am."

"Older than both of us put together," I said.

The loft had come furnished with all but the bed. I'd slept many nights on that sofa until I could save up enough to buy a frame and mattress. I deemed a headboard unnecessary. My tips were spent only on the bare essentials.

I sat in the scratchy orange swivel chair beside the sofa, watching Kirby frown as she sipped from her straw.

She turned her wrist to glance at the delicate black leather watch on her wrist, and then she heaved a dramatic sigh. "I hate him."

"You do not."

"I hate waiting. I feel like that sums up my entire relationship with Gunnar—waiting."

"He adores you. He is taking all these classes to get a good job and give you everything you want when you're his wife. It could be worse."

"You're right. He is the hottest thing in town—besides your new toy. Are you really going to let him take you to dinner?"

"A free dinner? Of course."

"You can eat for free downstairs," Kirby deadpanned, the tiny diamond stud in her nose glinting in the light.

Kirby's dainty nose went with the rest of her petite features, including her size five-and-a-half feet. She was built like a high school cheerleader and smiled like Miss America. She could be a model or an actress, but instead, she was a waitress in the Springs.

"Why are you still here?" I asked, ignoring her point.

She made a face. "God, Falyn, sorry. I'll wait downstairs."

I reached out to her as she stood to leave. "No, dummy!"

I pulled her down, and she sat with a frown.

"I mean, why haven't you bounced out of this town yet?"

Her face smoothed. "I like it here," she said, shrugging. "And Gunnar is still in school. His parents will foot the bill as long as he stays home and helps with the ranch."

"He's still going to apply for the physician's assistant program in Denver?"

"That's why he's staying close to home, doing his prerequisites for pre-PA at UCCS, and then he can transfer super easily to CU Denver."

"You mean, he's staying close to you."

"Just to save money. Then we'll move to Denver. Hopefully, I can find something there that's flexible like this job, so I can work while he is in class."

"I bet you can. Denver is … well, Denver. You'll have options."

Hope widened her eyes. "Where did you go? Not around here."

I felt my expression involuntarily turn in. "I was premed at Dartmouth. Well, that was the intended direction anyway."

"You didn't like it?"

"It was a great year."

"Just one year? You act like it was a lifetime ago."

"Just one. And, yes, it feels that way."

Kirby fingered the edge of the plastic lid on her to-go cup. "How long has it been since you left? Two years?"

"Four."

"I've been working with you all year, and you've never talked about it. It has something to do with your parents, doesn't it?"

I raised an eyebrow. "I'm surprised it's taken you this long to ask."

"By the time I thought we were close enough for me to broach the subject, I was afraid of what you might say."

"There's nothing to talk about."

"Are you just saying that to make me feel better?" she asked. "Because if something happened to you there, you can talk to me. You know I won't tell anyone, not even Gunnar." Her perfect features were even more stunning when she was sad, her bottom lip even fuller when she pouted.

"Nothing bad happened to me at Dartmouth. I told you, I liked it there, but my tuition came with conditions I couldn't agree to anymore."

"Oh," she said, a bit relieved. "Your parents."

"Yes. Them."

A knock on the door sounded again.

Kirby yelled, causing me to jump, "Come in!"

The knob turned, and in walked a mammoth man-child with the sweetest baby face and more muscles than his T-shirt could handle. He flipped his trucker hat backward with a quick motion, and caramel wisps fanned out in every direction from beneath the black mesh, refusing to behave. He rushed to the sofa to sit next to Kirby. "Damn it, baby, I'm sorry. Fucking night class and fucking traffic."

She leaned over with a stoic expression, letting him kiss her cheek. She batted her long eyelashes.

She wasn't fooling anyone. He was already forgiven.

He peered over at me. "I apologize for the language."

I waved him away, dismissing his apology. "There are no rules here." I looked around my loft with a grin. "That's part of its charm."

"How was work?" Gunnar asked, his eyes bouncing between Kirby and me. His tongue fell just behind his teeth when he spoke, causing the slightest hint of a lisp that I found undeniably adorable.

Gunnar was naturally polite and considerate, yet when I joined him and Kirby on nights out, his foreboding glare would keep any unwanted male attention at bay. On many occasions, Kirby had mentioned what being the love interest of a superhero felt like, never feeling afraid or worried because Gunnar had it handled at all times. Although he spent his time in the gym when he wasn't studying or with Kirby, Gunnar didn't have the girth of a serious bodybuilder, but he was tall and just bulky enough to be intimidating. His only fault was that he was too nice, trying to be everything for everyone, often making him late and overwhelmed in the process.

Exhaling, Kirby stretched her legs over her boyfriend's lap. "It was wonderful. Falyn has a date."

Gunnar looked to me for confirmation.

I shrugged. "My parents showed up. They were there when he asked. I kind of had to say yes."

He shook his head with a smile, already knowing where the story was headed. "Poor guy."

"He knows," Kirby said.

"Oh. Then it's his own damn fault," he said.

I pulled a throw pillow from behind my back and hugged it to my chest. "It's just dinner anyway. It's not like I'll break his heart."

"That's what I said when Kirby asked me out," he said, chuckling.

Kirby yanked the pillow from my grasp and chucked it at Gunnar's head. "Stop telling people that! They're going to think it's true!"

Gunnar was still grinning when he plucked the pillow off the floor and playfully tossed it back at her. "Maybe I want you to believe it. That version at least makes it seem like I haven't been chasing you the whole time."

Kirby melted.

With little effort, Gunnar pulled Kirby onto his lap and gave her a quick peck on the mouth. He stood up, lifting her with him, before quickly setting her on her feet.

"I'm glad you're leaving," I deadpanned. "PDA makes me nauseous."

Kirby stuck out her tongue, letting Gunnar lead her by the hand to the door. He stopped, and she did, too.

"Good luck tomorrow," Gunnar said.

Kirby's features sharpened into a mischievous grin. "The guy is the one who needs the luck."

"Get out," I said.

I reached over the arm of the sofa and snatched up the pillow, throwing it at the door. At the same time, Gunnar pulled Kirby through, closing the door behind her. The pillow bounced off the old wood and fell to the tan carpet below.

My entire body felt heavy as I pushed myself up off the chair and trudged to the bed. The covers were already pulled back from when I'd crawled in earlier. I sat down and slipped my legs underneath, pulling the blanket up to my chin and snuggling with myself and the empty space around me.

I took a deep breath, breathing in my freedom after five full years of dealing with my grief and guilt on my own terms. I might have let my parents make one too many decisions for me, but against all reason and fears, I had liberated myself. Although my parents would stop by on occasion, they couldn't hurt me anymore.

My eyelids grew heavy, and I blinked a few times before letting myself nod off to sleep with no nightmares about bright lights, white walls, strangers grabbing at me, or screaming in the distance. Those hadn't happened since a month after I moved into my tiny loft. Now, I would imagine omelets and cheesecake and sun tea along with Chuck's expletives over the stove and Phaedra's insistence on seating patrons. *Normal* came with the absence of suffocating impossible expectations.

I took a deep breath and exhaled, but I didn't dream of the Bucksaw.

I dreamed of Taylor.

CHAPTER THREE

THE ALARM BLEATED, yanking me out of unconsciousness, and I reached over to smack the snooze button with my palm. The sheets were wrapped around my legs, and the blanket had fallen to the floor like it did every night.

I stretched and slowly sat up, squinting at the bright sun pouring in through the bedroom window. The white walls made it even more severe, but I wouldn't dare ask Phaedra to change a thing. She and Chuck had already given me this loft apartment for nearly nothing, so I could save money.

I dressed in one of the dozen or so V-neck shirts stored in my tiny closet and stepped into my favorite jeans that I'd found at the local ARC Thrift Store. The faded skinnies were the pair I'd purchased just a couple of days after moving into the loft, after my first paycheck from the Bucksaw, and after Phaedra had found out I was sleeping in my car, exactly ten days before my parents had towed and sold it.

Even though I'd had a bedroom full of designer clothes and shoes at my parents' house, my closet in the loft still had plenty of space. Aside from the things I had stashed in a bag—like toiletries, water, snacks, and the shoebox—before my getaway, all I'd had was my car and the clothes on my back. Five years at the Bucksaw had gained me five more pairs of jeans, three shorts, and a dozen or so shirts. It was easy to do without when you had nowhere to go.

I pulled back the top section of my hair into a clip, letting my bangs fall, which would catch my eyelashes every time I blinked.

Always in my damn eyes!

The time for a haircut at The Falyn Salon was overdue. I glanced down to the drawer that held the scissors and decided against it since it was just before my infamous date with a cute but decidedly unlucky hotshot. There was no way he would be able to compete with my perfect dream version of him, who could make me orgasm with just a side glance, so my mind had already written him off as a disappointment.

After scrubbing my face and completing the rest of my morning routine, I grabbed my apron and pushed open my door. With a quick flip of the wrist, I locked the door behind me. After just a short jaunt down a narrow hallway and fifteen stairs, I was in the Bucksaw again.

Chuck was at the prep table, and Phaedra was counting the cash in the register, the morning sun highlighting the silver strands in her hair.

"It's like I never left," I announced.

"You say that every morning," Phaedra called back to me.

"It feels like that every morning."

"You say that every morning, too," Chuck said. He placed a plate of pancakes drowning in syrup, topped with a small swirl of whipped cream and a sliced strawberry, onto the counter in the window between the kitchen and the main dining area.

"For the record, I can think of only one other place I'd rather be," I said, taking my plate.

"You'll get there," Chuck said.

"So, the kid," Phaedra began, a hint of warning in her tone. "He's awfully cute."

"Nothing I can't handle." My words were garbled around the forkful of pancake I'd just shoved into my mouth.

"He's picking you up here?" Chuck asked, crossing his arms over the window counter that sat just below chest level for him.

The space was big enough to place at least five plates of food when we were busy.

He looked to his left when Hector pushed through the double doors leading into the kitchen.

"Morning," Chuck said.

"Hello, Mr. Chuck," Hector said, sitting on a stool at the end of the bar. He prayed over the omelet he'd brought from the kitchen before shoving a fourth of it into his mouth.

Ten feet behind where Hector sat was the stairway that led to my loft.

"Whatcha lookin' at, Falyn?" Phaedra asked.

"It used to bother me that anyone inside the Bucksaw could walk up those stairs."

"Until you realized that I have no patience for curious patrons."

Chuck laughed. "Not even kids. Remember the time you made the Morris boy cry?"

"Jumpin' jacks, Chuck, he's in middle school now. Are you ever going to let that go?"

"No," Chuck said. "Because I love the look on your face when I bring it up."

From his spot in the food window, Chuck faced forward, staring down the long bar lined with stools. It separated the cash register and a couple of drink stations from the main dining area. To Kirby and me, that narrow space felt like home base, a place where we could have a few seconds to gather ourselves before heading back out into the trenches.

I sat on one of the barstools, happily chewing my bite of pancake drenched in syrup.

"You dodged my question, Falyn," Chuck said.

I wasn't particularly in a rush to swallow the sweet goodness of the spongy pancake to answer Chuck, but I didn't want to be rude. "I'm not sure if he's picking me up here. I haven't heard from him."

"He'll come by I bet," Phaedra said, closing the cash register drawer. She crossed her arms. "Now, if he is anything but a gentleman—"

"I know," I said. "I'll punch him in the throat."

"Good girl," Phaedra said, punching the air. "They hate that."

"She's right," Chuck called from the kitchen. "We do!"

I laughed once, knowing Chuck would rather cut off his stirring hand than do anything to a woman to earn a throat-punch.

Chuck disappeared from the window and then pushed open the swinging doors. He wiped his hands on his pristine apron, leaving orangish-brown streaks behind.

"Uh-oh," I said mid-bite, noticing Chuck's expression. "You're not going to give me the talk, are you? Please don't."

"What about this boy? I'm concerned about your motivations, but I'm even more concerned about his intentions," Chuck said.

Phaedra beamed at her husband, like forty-six years of love had just been doubled with one question.

I finished chewing, and then I dabbed my mouth with a napkin. I wadded it up and let it fall to my lap.

Blaire's soothing but firm voice echoed in my head.

"Incorrect fork, Falyn."

"We do not collect our soup that way, Falyn."

"Stand up straight, Falyn."

"No man worth having will want you if you're not behaved, Falyn."

"We do not discuss vulgar topics, such as your opinion, at the dinner table, Falyn."

When I was compelled to use the manners so forcefully imposed on me, even after my liberation, I would use bad manners just to spite Blaire. Even if she couldn't see it, rebellion would make me feel better.

Nearly five years after I'd left, it still made my blood boil that those habits wouldn't die—just like my parents' need to control me, to make me fit into their perfect mold of how Colorado's first family should be.

"Falyn?" Phaedra said, her comforting gravelly voice bringing me back to the Bucksaw and away from my childhood. "Are you all right, kiddo?"

I blinked. "He's, uh … it doesn't matter what his intentions are. I just said yes to rile William."

"Then why follow through with it?" Chuck asked.

"Because he played along when I lied to my parents," I said with a grin. "He doesn't care anyway. He's just looking for an easy lay."

Chuck stared at me with a blank expression, and then he slowly backed toward the double doors until he was out of sight.

Phaedra burst out laughing. "You're going to be the death of that man. He loves you like his own. Let him believe you're a virgin." As soon as the words had left her mouth, she froze, and her eyes widened. "Oh, honey, I'm so sorry."

"I think he already knows I'm not," I said, making a show of dismissing her apology.

Noticeably shaken, Phaedra went back to preparing her world-famous sun tea.

I stood up and walked around the end of the bar. I hugged her from behind, resting my chin in the crook of her neck. "It's okay," I said softly.

"Damn my big mouth"—she sniffed—"and damn my small brain."

I turned her around, waiting until her eyes met mine. "Damn your soft heart."

Her bottom lip quivered, and then she pulled me to her chest for a quick squeeze. Her wrinkled hand patted my back. "We don't have any of our own. You and Kirby are it. Now, get out of here. Get some work done, for Chrissakes," she said, returning to her pitcher of tea.

I reached back for a napkin and handed it to her. She held it to her face, dabbing her eyes I imagined since her back was still turned to me.

"I said, get," she said.

"Yes, ma'am." I rushed around the bar and picked up my plate. I stuffed the remaining pieces of pancake into my mouth while walking toward the kitchen.

Pete—round, bald, and frowning—stood next to Chuck, helping with anything else prep-related as he did every morning.

Hector was already at the sink, polishing the silverware. "Good morning, Miss Falyn," he said, taking my plate. He pulled down the sprayer and rinsed off the round white plate made of something between glass and plastic.

"For the hundredth time, Hector—"

"Don't say, Miss. I know," he said with a sheepish grin.

Pete smiled. He was marinating chicken, keeping to himself.

The three of them, in addition to Phaedra whose creations had made the Bucksaw famous, made up the kitchen staff.

Chuck was mixing his special sauce with a blank stare, his mind somewhere far away. He wiped his wet cheek with the back of his wrist and continued chopping. He glanced at me then and shook his head. "Damn onions," he said, wiping the other cheek.

"Uh-huh," I said, dubious.

Phaedra wasn't the only softy in the family.

With a wry smile, Pete glanced over at his boss and then continued with his duties.

I helped Hector roll silverware. Then I refilled the Coke syrup in the soda fountain behind the bar, cleaned the windows, and double-checked that the dining area was sparkling clean.

Gunnar dropped Kirby off at eight o'clock sharp, and she stood at the front door with her arms crossed, like she did every morning. I wasn't sure why she insisted on coming in so early. We didn't open until nine.

I opened the door and then locked the door behind her.

"I'm here!" she announced as she walked across the dining room, another thing she did every morning.

"I'll alert the media," Phaedra deadpanned.

Kirby stuck her tongue out at Phaedra and then winked at me as she pushed through the double doors, letting them swing violently behind her.

"You're gonna break those damn doors one of these days!" Phaedra called.

"Sorry." Kirby was rushed but sincere, her dark ponytail swishing as she carried the salt and pepper canisters.

As she began to refill the shakers on each table, they exchanged knowing smiles.

"I've known that brat since she was a latchkey kid," Phaedra said, shaking her head at Kirby.

"I can hear you," Kirby called back.

"Good!" Phaedra snapped. "I'd make myself a grilled chicken panini with pickles and chipotle mayo every day, right about the time Kirby would pass by on her way home from Columbia Elementary."

Kirby smirked. "And she'd always magically lose her appetite."

"Just because I knew you'd be ravenous by the time you poked your little crow head into my door," Phaedra said, her tone a mixture of sass and silly. "She would talk nonstop with her mouth full, carrying on about her day, while she annihilated my poor panini, and then she wouldn't even say thanks before wiping her mouth with her sleeve and walking the few blocks to Old Chicago where her mom waited tables."

Kirby screwed on a saltshaker lid. "That isn't entirely accurate."

"Okay," Phaedra spit. "She used a napkin. Sometimes."

Kirby shook her head and chuckled as she detached the pepper shaker lid.

Noticing the time, I began unscrewing lids for Kirby, and she picked up her pace.

"Kirby is the only person in the world, including Chuck," I said, nodding toward the kitchen, "who could get away with sticking her tongue out at you and live to tell about it."

"No. I have two girls, and I take shit from both of them," Phaedra said, arching her eyebrow at me.

I swallowed back the lump that had formed in my throat. Phaedra had a way of making me feel like family when I least expected it and always when I needed it the most.

She picked a hand towel off the counter as she approached me. She swung it over her shoulder and then glanced at her watch. She turned me to face the wall of glass, toward the three parked cars full of people.

She raised my hand with the open saltshaker still in my grip and began to recite her favorite sonnet, "Mother of Exiles! From her beacon-hand! Glows world-wide welcome; her mild eyes command!"

After each verse, she would shake my elevated hand, salt falling over our heads like an erratic blizzard.

"Give me your tired, your poor, your huddled masses!"

After Phaedra finished, she let go of my hand, and I shook out the white specks from my hair.

Phaedra sighed. "No one talks like that anymore."

"You do," Kirby said.

"God, do I love my country."

Kirby made a face. "Anyone would know that after seeing your arrest record from participating in sit-ins. What does that poem have to do with anything?"

Phaedra looked dumbstruck.

"It's Emma Lazarus," I said.

Kirby's expression didn't change.

I continued, "That sonnet is on a plaque at the Statue of Liberty."

When recognition finally hit, Kirby's mouth formed an O.

Phaedra rolled her eyes. "Dear Lord Jesus, help us all."

"I'll get the broom," Kirby said, dashing to the back room.

Phaedra grumbled all the way to the kitchen. Failure to know important pieces of history, or ignorance of common knowledge in general made her temper flare.

Kirby reappeared, broom and dustpan in hand. "Shit. I've tried to forget all of that since graduation. It's summer break. You'd think she'd cut me some slack."

"It's going to be a long day," I said, fetching the broom.

Kirby and I worked to clean the mess, and she rushed to the trash can with the dustpan while I flipped it open. People inside the three parked cars in front began to stir, and by the time Kirby returned from taking the broom to the back, the customers were waiting to be seated.

"I didn't finish the shakers," she whispered to me.

"On it," I said, rushing to finish her job.

I looked at the clock, wondering how we'd gotten so far behind schedule. Usually, we'd finish with ten minutes to spare.

Phaedra didn't reveal her mood to the customers, but Kirby and I had to work extra hard to keep her smiling. An entire pitcher of sun tea crashed to the floor, Hector broke a stack of plates, and I didn't get one of the saltshakers screwed on tightly enough, so Chuck had to make a Philly cheesesteak sandwich on the double to replace the one with more salt in it than what had been in my hair.

Kirby seated the author and her assistant, their second visit in as many days.

"Afternoon," I said with a smile. "Back again, huh?"

"It's so good," the author said. "I wanted to try the Cuban before we left."

"This is not what I ordered," a man said loudly to Phaedra.

Dwayne Kaufman was sitting alone in the corner, licking his thumb after tossing the top bun of his burger to the floor.

"Uh-oh," Kirby whispered in my ear. "Dwayne's been drinking again. Should I call the police?"

I shook my head. *Who gets drunk before noon?* "Let Phaedra handle it."

"I said, no ketchup! And it's fucking cold!" Dwayne yelled.

"My apologies, hon," Phaedra said. "I'll get that fixed right away, Dwayne." She scooped up his plate and rushed through the double doors.

"I'm not your hon!" he called after her. "Piece-of-shit café."

I walked over to Dwayne and smiled. "Can I get you a coffee while Chuck grills that up for you?"

"Fuck off," he grumbled, facing me but keeping his eyes on the floor. "I just want a fucking burger the way I ordered it. Is that so hard?"

His cup of tea was over half full, but I wanted to keep him occupied until Phaedra returned. "She's working on it. Let me get you more tea," I said, picking up his cup.

He grabbed my wrist. "Get your tater-tot tits outta my face!"

The liquid sloshed from the cup onto my shoes as I tried to pull away, and then it happened again when another large hand encompassed Dwayne's wrist.

Dwayne froze, and so did I.

Taylor had suddenly appeared next to me. "What did you just call her?" His voice was low and ominous.

I began to speak, but Dwayne let go of my hand and laughed nervously.

"I don't want more tea," he growled. "I want to be left alone!"

Taylor let go of Dwayne's hand and stepped back, making way for Phaedra.

"Here you are, Dwayne. Cheeseburger straight off the grill, no ketchup. So sorry," Phaedra said, louder than necessary.

She put her body between Dwayne and me, and I took another step back.

"How does that taste? Better?" she asked.

He took a bite. Closing his eyes, he chewed like a wild animal, bread and a piece of onion falling from his mouth. "Yes. Took you long enough."

Phaedra motioned for me to get busy, and she shot Taylor a look, but I wasn't sure what it meant.

I escorted Taylor back to his table. He was sitting alone this time.

"You okay?" he asked.

"Yes, I'm fine," I said. "What can I get you to drink?"

"I'll have one of your famous Cherry Cokes, please."

"Coming right up," I said through my teeth.

"Hey," he said, tapping the bottom of my elbow before I took a step, "are you mad?"

I paused, glancing over at Dwayne. "I had it covered."

"I believe you."

"So, you didn't need to step in," I hissed.

"Probably not."

"Stay out of my business. I don't need your help. Ever."

He relaxed back in his chair, unfazed. "Okay."

"That's it? Just okay?"

He chuckled. "I understand."

I could feel him watching me as I made my way to the drink station.

"I'm sorry," I said, stopping at the author's table. "What can I get you to drink?"

She shook her head, her eyes bright. "This is the most fun I've had in weeks. I'll have an orange juice."

"I'll have the mango sunrise," her assistant said.

I nodded and continued my trek. Dwayne held out his cup in front of me, and I plowed through it, spilling tea all over him and me.

Instinctively, I raised my hands, palms out, and stopped on my tiptoes even though it was already too late. "Oh my gosh, I'll get you another one right away."

"Goddamn it, you bitch!" he yelled at the same time. His chair complained against the tiled floor as he stood, towering over me.

"All right, now, you've pissed me off." Taylor's strained voice carried from his seat across the room.

In the next moment, he was next to me. He put Dwayne into a headlock and guided him toward the door.

"No! Stop! Please!" I begged.

Each word was mixed with Dwayne's protests.

Everyone in the room was frozen, staring at Dwayne flailing his arms and trying to push Taylor back but to no avail.

I covered my mouth, and Kirby watched helplessly from her podium. Just before Taylor made it through the door, Phaedra blew her famous two-fingers-in-the-mouth whistle, one that could be heard even in the high school football stadium full of people. I winced at the shrill noise.

"Knock it off!" Phaedra commanded.

The room was silent. Both Chuck and Hector were staring from the window. Dwayne stopped struggling, and Taylor released his neck.

"No one throws my customers out but me!" She marched over to Dwayne, narrowing her eyes. "Did you just verbally abuse my server?"

"She spilled my fucking tea all over me!" Dwayne said, pointing at me.

"This is a family-friendly establishment, and we do not say fuck!" Phaedra said, practically yelling the last part. "Come back when you get some manners, Dwayne!" She turned. "You know what? Not even then!" She looked to Taylor. "Take the trash out, kid."

Taylor crossed his arms, glowering. Dwayne didn't put up a fight. Instead, he walked out, ashamed.

Phaedra faced the rest of the café with a bright smile. "Does anyone need anything?"

Most people shook their heads. The author and assistant sat silently, looking so gleeful that I thought they would break into applause at any moment.

I retreated to the bar.

Kirby followed me. "Whoa. Shit, that was hot," she said, turning her back to the side of the room where Taylor was. "Are you rethinking your plan to kick him to the curb before he's even on it?"

"Yes," I said, making the worst Cherry Coke ever. I took the cup around the bar and marched it over to him before setting it hard onto his table.

Taylor looked amused, which only made me angrier.

"I need to cancel tonight," I said.

"Did you forget about a prior engagement?" he asked.

I blinked. "No."

"Family emergency that can wait until you're off work?"

I frowned. "No."

"Then why are you canceling?"

"Because you're a bully."

He touched his chest. "I'm a bully?"

"Yes," I said through my teeth, trying to keep my voice down. "You can't just manhandle our customers like that."

"I just did." He leaned back, too pleased with himself. "Didn't you hear your boss? She told me to."

I snarled my lip, disgusted. "And you enjoyed it. Because you're a bully. I don't go out with bullies."

"Great."

"*Great?*" My voice rose an octave.

"You heard me." Taylor crossed his arms, the polar opposite of annoyed, offended, or angry.

I had hoped my public rejection would rob him of that smug smile. "Then why are you smiling?"

He touched his thumb to his nose, the muscles in his arm flexing as he did so. "I think you'll change your mind."

I took a step and kept my voice low as I said, "Not even if I wanted to, and at this point, I certainly do not." I spun around and minded my tables.

The pace picked up as the afternoon wore on, and when it was time to check on Taylor's table, I noticed he was gone, a twenty-dollar bill left behind. I held it up. He'd only ordered the crappy Cherry Coke, so he'd left a seventeen-dollar tip.

I swallowed back my surprise and appreciation and shoved the money into my apron before clearing his table. I took the cup to Hector and then washed my hands.

"Do you think maybe you were a little harsh?" Chuck asked.

"With who?" I asked.

"You know who."

"He's a jerk. I told him I had it handled. He made a huge scene."

He waved me away. "Dwayne deserved it. Phaedra's been wanting to kick him out of here for years. Right before you started, he turned over a table."

My mouth fell open.

The sprayer silenced, and Hector spoke, "That's not like Mrs. Phaedra to let someone do that and keep coming back."

Chuck shrugged. "He hasn't always been like that. His wife left him a few years back. He started drinking all the time. Phaedra's put up with his tantrums because she felt sorry for him, I guess."

Hector and I traded glances.

"And you don't think Taylor's a bully for throwing him out like that?" I asked.

He shook his head. "I've daydreamed about doing that same thing."

"But she's your wife. You'd just be protecting her honor. I get that," I said.

He pressed his lips together. "You're right, but you're wrong."

I furrowed my brow, confused.

"I don't think that Taylor kid is looking for anything easy. Just the opposite. And I think he knows he's found it."

"What does that mean?" I asked.

"It means you'd better hold on tight. Guys like him don't give up easily once they've found a girl like you."

I laughed once. "Let him try."

Chuck smirked, returning to the food on the stove.

CHAPTER FOUR

"You'd better skedaddle, kiddo," Phaedra said. "You've got to get ready, don't you?"

I looked down at my clothes. "For what?"

"Are you going out with that boy in your apron?"

"No. I'm not going anywhere with *that boy.*"

Phaedra shook her head and tended to her last table of the night. Only a few chairs were still occupied. It was a few minutes past closing time. Kirby had already swept, and she was now breaking down the ice cream machine.

Phaedra's table signed their check, and she waved as the small family left together to their car parked out front. I sat on the stool at the end of the bar, counting my tips. Kirby happily took a small stack of bills—her percentage for bussing tables and for her excellent hostess skills—as she passed by on her way to meet Gunnar at the door. He bent over to hug and kiss her, wrapping his giant arms around her tiny frame.

"Good night!" Kirby said.

"Night," I said, barely above a whisper.

Phaedra and Chuck waved to the couple before Gunnar held open the door for his girlfriend. She passed him, and then they walked together to wherever he'd parked her car. I thought about them walking alone in the alley behind the restaurant and how Kirby probably wouldn't think twice about it.

The door chimed again, and I looked up, half-expecting to see Kirby and Gunnar. It wouldn't be the first time she'd forgotten something. Instead, I saw Taylor standing next to the hostess podium.

"Why are you here?" I asked.

The double doors swung a few times before they stilled, a sign that Phaedra had excused herself to the kitchen.

"I came to take you to dinner."

"I canceled," I said, stuffing my remaining tips in the pocket of my apron.

"I know."

I lowered my chin, already annoyed. "What is it with you civil servant types? You think that because, historically, women have somewhat romanticized your line of work that you're automatically guaranteed a date?"

"No, I'm just hungry, and I want to hang out with you while I eat."

"We're closed."

"So?" he said, genuine in his cluelessness.

"So, you have to leave."

Taylor shoved his hands into his jeans pockets. "Trust me, I want to. I'm not oblivious to the fact that you sort of hate my guts. Inherently bitchy women don't appeal to me."

"Right. You prefer the easy ones who pretend to be progressive by going Dutch, and then they are all too eager to fall in line with the hotshot-groupie stereotype by the end of the night in hopes that they'll somehow hook you with their impressive blow jobs."

Taylor choked, stopping just short of where I sat, and he leaned his back against the bar. "You've got me all figured out, don't you, Ivy League?"

"Pardon?"

"Were you a psych student? Are you trying to maybe shake me up a bit by analyzing my violent temper and then throwing in a few Freud quotes for good measure? Trying to make me feel inferior with your academic prowess? Let me guess. You went to Brown? Yale? Big fucking deal. I might not have a graduate's degree, but I went to college. You don't scare me."

"Dartmouth. And community college doesn't count."

"I wholeheartedly disagree. I have a bachelor's in business and a master's in women's studies."

"That's insulting. You haven't been within a hundred yards of a women's studies course."

"That's just not true."

Beautiful SACRIFICE

I blew my bangs away from my face, exasperated. "Women's studies?"

He didn't flinch.

"Why?" I seethed.

"Because it's relevant."

My lips parted, but I snapped my mouth shut again. He was serious.

"Okay, I was kidding about the master's, but I have taken a couple of courses geared toward women's studies. I've found the reading material is on the right side of history."

I raised an eyebrow.

"I might be a civil servant type, but I'm educated. I went to Eastern State University in Illinois, and it's a damn good school for its size."

"Wait. Did you say Illinois?" I swallowed away the sudden tightness in my throat.

"Yes, and you're right. I also have a doctorate in bullshit, and I saw you coming a mile away."

"Where is Eastern State University from the town of Eakins?" I asked.

Taylor grimaced, unsure about where I was going with my line of questioning. "ESU is in Eakins. Why do you ask?"

My heart sped up, booming so hard against my chest that my head began to throb. Breathing was no longer on autopilot. I sucked in air and then blew it out, trying to remain calm. "So, do you go back there very often? Reunions maybe?"

"I'm from there, so I go back all the time. You didn't answer my question."

By his expression, I could tell that he knew something was up. The entire tone of our conversation—along with my attitude—had changed.

I watched him watching me. I tried to keep my face smooth and the truth from reflecting in my eyes.

All the cash in my shoebox upstairs was to pay for a plane ticket to Chicago, a rental car, and a hotel room in Eakins, Illinois. It couldn't just be a coincidence that this guy had breezed into my café and taken an interest in me.

"Just curious."

His shoulders relaxed, but a spark still smoldered in his eyes. "I'll tell you all about it. Let's go."

"I'm not going anywhere with you tonight," I said. "You're trying too hard. You could be a serial killer for all I know."

"The Forest Service doesn't employ serial killers."

"How do I know you really even work for them?"

Taylor sighed, reached into his back pocket, and produced his wallet. He picked out his driver's license and Alpine Hotshot Crew ID. "Is that good enough?" he asked.

I tried not to take the cards too quickly or look too interested before glancing over his ID card and then his license. His driver's license was Illinois issued. He really was from Eakins.

"You never changed your license over?"

"It expires next month. I'll get a Colorado one then. My boss has been on me about it, too."

I held my breath as I poured over his address. He was telling the truth.

"Holy shit," I whispered.

His address was on North Birch. I held out the cards, slowly returning them.

"What?" he asked, taking them from my fingers.

"Your driver's license picture is atrocious. You look as bad as a hatful of assholes."

Taylor laughed. "Whatever. I'm a fucking ace."

I clicked my tongue. "Whoever told you that needs to get out more."

His eyebrows pulled together, and he tucked his chin. "You're either a liar or a lesbian. Which is it?"

Taylor was my way to Eakins. Quelling the urge to scream, laugh, cry, or jump up and down felt like holding on to a wild animal covered in grease.

I cleared my throat. "I need to lock up."

"Okay. I'll wait for you outside."

I had to play it just right. Taylor was only chasing me because I was running. I couldn't appear too eager.

I sighed. "You're not just going to go away, are you?"

One corner of his mouth curled up, a dimple sinking into his left cheek.

Taylor was unquestionably attractive. The butterflies I felt in my stomach when he looked at me were undeniable, and I wanted to hate the way I felt, even more than I wanted to hate men. His delicious full lips, a needless decoration for his already perfect features, only added to how ridiculously good-looking he was. The symmetry of his face was flawless. His chin and jaw had just the right amount of stubble—not clean-shaven and not yet the beginning of a beard. His warm chocolate eyes were intermittently hidden behind a thick line of lashes. Taylor had all the makings of an underwear model, and he knew it.

"You're enjoying this, aren't you? You like watching me assess your looks to decide if I'm going to let that overshadow the fact that you're a cunt rag."

"I'm not that bad," he said, trying to suppress the odd amusement the words brought him.

"What is the name of the last girl you slept with? Just the first name."

He mulled over my question, and then his shoulders sagged. "Okay, I'm kind of a cunt rag."

I glanced down at his arms. They were both covered in neo-traditionalist tattoos. Bright colors and thick black lines displayed an eight ball, a fanned-out hand of aces and eights, a dragon, a skull, and a woman's name.

"I'll go away, but I don't want to." He glanced up at me from under his brow, turning his charm on full throttle.

Any other girl might have melted, but all I could think about was how hard fate had just slapped me in the face.

"Who's Diane?" I asked.

He looked down at his feet. "Why do you ask?"

I nodded toward his arm. "Is she an ex-girlfriend? Are you a scorned man, sleeping your way through debilitating heartbreak?"

"Diane is my mother."

My mouth immediately felt dry, my throat like I'd swallowed hot sand. I blinked. "Shit."

"I prefer shit to sorry."

"I don't apologize … anymore."

He grinned. "I believe that. Listen, we got off on the wrong foot. I'm a little overprotective when it comes to men getting aggressive with women. I can't promise you that it won't happen again, but I can promise that it won't happen tonight. So"—he looked at me from under his lashes, exuding the full force of his magnetic charm—"let's go."

I pressed my lips together. Now that I needed him, the game had become particularly risky. I had to be stubborn but not impossible. "Nope."

His face fell, and he walked away, but then he came back, frustrated and flustered. "Goddamn, lady, quit busting my balls!"

I raised an eyebrow. "Why do you want me to go out with you so badly? Did you make a bet or something?"

"Because you keep telling me no!"

I offered a half smile. "So, if I go, you'll leave me alone?"

"Why would I ask you out again? You think I enjoy getting shot down?"

"You must."

"It just ... doesn't happen ... to me." The thought simmered. He was clearly unhappy.

"Now, I really want to tell you to kick rocks."

"Lady," he said, struggling to rein in his temper, "just have a couple of drinks with me. I won't even walk you home. I swear."

"Fine." I reached behind me, pulling my apron tie loose with one tug. I wrapped the strings around my tips and then put it behind the counter. "Let's go enjoy our last night together."

He held out his hand. "It's about fucking time."

I let my hand fit snugly inside of his as he led me through the front door. His skin on mine made me feel warm all over, soaking into my pores, thawing a part of me that had been cold for a long time.

A quick glance over my shoulder, I could see Phaedra and Chuck waving good-bye with matching devilish grins on their faces.

Taylor pulled me across the street, not even mentioning my thrift-store jeans or the fact that I smelled like the Bucksaw. I stepped up onto the curb and continued half a block to a growing line in front of Cowboys, the country-western bar.

"Really?" I complained.

Taylor gestured to a guy at the entrance and then pulled me past the more appropriately dressed women who weren't lucky enough to know the bouncer.

"Hey!"

"No fair!"

"That's bullshit, Darren!"

I tugged on Taylor's hand, forcing him to stop.

Beautiful SACRIFICE

"Darren Michaels," I said to my former high school classmate.

"Falyn Fairchild," Darren said. His body nearly filled the entire doorframe, his too-small black shirt stretched over the muscles hiding under his tanning bed–browned skin.

"I didn't know you worked here."

Darren chuckled. "Since I turned twenty-one, Falyn. You really should leave the Bucksaw once in a while."

"Very funny," I said as Taylor pulled me past Darren into the bar.

We passed the windows where women were taking money for the cover charge. One of the women behind the counter saw us but didn't even attempt to get Taylor's attention, instead looking to the next people in line.

"Are you using your frequent-flier miles?" I asked loud enough for him to hear me over the music.

Taylor smiled, and I pushed down the ridiculous fluttering in my chest.

"Want a beer?" he asked.

"No."

"Oh, don't tell me you're a wine-cooler girl." When I didn't answer, he continued, "Cocktail? Whiskey? I give up."

"I don't drink."

"You don't … huh?"

His confused expression made me grin.

"I don't drink," I said, enunciating each word.

"I don't understand."

I rolled my eyes.

"I drink," he said. "I also smoke. But that's one thing they won't let me do in here."

"Disgusting. I'm even less attracted to you than before."

Taylor was unfazed, leading me to a tall table. He waited until I climbed onto a stool.

"I'm going to grab a beer," he said. "You sure you don't want anything? Water? Soda?"

"I'll take a water. What are you smiling about?"

"You just said you were attracted to me." His self-satisfied smile was contagious.

"Yeah, but that was before you spoke."

Taylor's smile immediately vanished. "You're so fucking mean. It's disturbing that I like it so much."

He approached the bar, my insults not affecting his arrogant swagger in the least. Music heavy in steel guitar and twang filled the entire space of the two-story dance hall. I let my chin rest on the heel of my hand as I picked out the people I knew from the tourists. Then I observed Taylor chatting up Shea, who had graduated a couple of years after I had and had been tending bar at Cowboys since the day after her twenty-first birthday. I waited for Taylor to flirt with her or do something else that would help solidify my initial opinion that he was a total slimebag.

Shea cocked her head and looked completely smitten, but then they both turned to me. There was no point in looking away. I had already been caught.

I waved, and they waved back.

Shea popped the cap off of Taylor's beer, and then she filled a plastic cup with ice and water. She patted his shoulder just before he carried the drinks toward me.

"Shea," he said.

"I know her."

"You asked me for the name of the last girl I bagged. It was Shea."

I made a face.

"It was my first weekend here. She's a sweetheart ... and wild as hell."

"*Bagged* her? What does that even mean?" I asked, already wishing I hadn't.

"Intimate relations. Intercourse. Coitus. Doing the deed. Nookie. Fornicating. Laying pipe. Screwing. Sex. Tapping that ass. Fucking. Need I go on?"

"Please don't." I sipped my water.

"I'm a vagrant, as your dad put it." He lifted his bottle and took a swig. "There is little else for us to do between calls."

"Only if you have no imagination."

"What do you suggest?"

"Oh, I don't know. August is a good time to summit Pikes Peak. The Garden of the Gods. Manitou Springs. The zoo. The Fine Arts Center. Seven Falls. The Air and Space Museum."

"Okay. Let's knock those out. How about this weekend? We'll start with Pikes Peak. That sounds fun."

"This is our last night together, remember?"

"Not at all," he said.

I rolled my eyes and then tried to find something interesting on the dance floor. There were several sights to choose from. I saw a father-and-daughter couple … at least that was what I'd thought until he tried to give her vertical mouth-to-mouth. A man was attempting to get rejected by every female standing within three feet of the dance floor. A woman in head-to-toe black fringe was two-stepping backward by herself—and quite possibly starring in a Broadway musical playing in her own head.

Taylor pointed at her with the mouth of his bottle. "We call her Cat Woman. She's just getting warmed up."

"Who's we?" I asked.

"Me … and them," he said, pointing to the two men walking toward us.

Zeke and Dalton were shaking their heads in disbelief.

"Un-fucking-believable," Zeke said. "I'm disappointed in you, Falyn."

Both men reached into their pockets, and each one handed Taylor a twenty-dollar bill.

I looked to Taylor. "I was wrong. You're worse than a cunt rag."

Zeke looked to Taylor, genuinely concerned. "What's worse than that?"

Taylor held up his hands, palms out, in surrender even though he was clearly still amused. "Just because I bet them I could get you here doesn't mean I didn't want you to come with me. Besides, I can't pass up a lock bet."

I shook my head, confused.

"Oh!" Taylor said, even more animated since his friends had arrived. "Can someone write this down? Ivy League does not understand my vernacular!"

"You mean, your verbiage," I deadpanned.

Dalton's mouth curved up into a half smile.

Taylor leaned in toward me. He smelled like cologne and cheap body wash with a hint of mint and sweet tobacco on his breath. "A lock bet is pretty much a sure thing." His voice was low and smooth.

"Yep," I said, "that's my cue." I stood up and headed for the door.

Dalton and Zeke made a fuss, yelling, "Oh!" at the same time.

Within seconds, Taylor's fingers gently encompassed mine, slowing my progress to a stop.

"You're right. That was a very douche-like thing for me to say."

I spun around, crossing my arms. "I can't really blame a dick for making a dick move."

Taylor's jaw flitted under his skin. "I deserved that. I was just screwing with you, Falyn. You haven't made any part of this easy."

I glared at him for a moment and then relaxed. "It's late. I have to work in the morning anyway."

Disappointment weighed down his shoulders. "C'mon! It's not that late! And you promised me drinks—plural."

"Do waters count?"

"Let's dance."

"No!" I said so loud and shrill that I surprised even myself.

Taylor was a bit stunned as well. "Whoa. Calm yourself. It's just dancing. I won't even grab your ass."

I shook my head and took a step back.

"Why not?" he asked.

"I don't know how to dance … like that," I said, pointing to the couples twisting and spinning on the dance floor.

He laughed once. "Two-stepping?"

"Precisely."

"Can you count?"

I narrowed my eyes at him. "That's insulting."

"Just answer the ques—"

"Yes! Yes, I can count," I said, exasperated.

"Then you can two-step. C'mon, I'll teach you." He walked toward the dance floor, tugging me by the hand.

Despite my repeated refusals that turned into fervent begging, he pulled me onto the wooden rectangle in the center of the building.

I stood, frozen.

"Relax. I'll make you look good."

"I don't like country music."

"No one does. Just roll with it."

I sighed.

Taylor put his right hand on my hip and gripped my right hand with his left. "Put your other hand on my shoulder."

I looked around. Some men had their hands on the shoulders of their partners. Some women were too busy spinning in circles to put their hands anywhere.

"Oh God," I said, closing my eyes. I didn't like doing things I didn't already know I was going to excel at.

"Falyn," Taylor said, his voice calming and smooth.

I opened my eyes and tried not to let the dimple in his cheek distract me.

"I'm going to take two steps backward with my left foot. You're going to step forward with your right. Two times, okay?"

I nodded.

"Then I'm going to step backward once with my right foot, and you'll step forward with your left foot. Just once. The count is two quick, one, two quick, one. Ready?"

I shook my head.

He laughed. "It's really not that bad. Just listen to the music. I'll take you around the floor."

Taylor stepped, and I went with him. I counted in my head, trying to mirror his movements. I wasn't completely ignorant in the realm of dancing. Blaire had insisted on ballet lessons until I was thirteen, and it had become obvious that no amount of instruction could teach me how to be graceful.

Two-stepping, however, seemed to be fairly painless, and Taylor was actually pretty good. After a few laps around the dance floor, he let go with one hand and spun me once. When I returned to the original position, I couldn't help the smile erupting across my face.

The song ended, and I huffed. "Okay, so it wasn't awful."

Another song began, this one a bit faster.

"Then let's go again," he said, pulling me with him.

Beads of sweat began to form on his forehead, and my back was feeling damp as well. Halfway through the song, Taylor twirled me around, but instead of bringing me back into his arms, he spun me the other way. By the end of the song, he added a turn where he let go, and my hand slid across his back, and then we ended up two-stepping again.

After the third song, I retreated to our table.

"You're pretty good!" Dalton said.

"She is, isn't she?" Taylor said, his eyes bright. "Do you want another water? I'm going to grab another beer."

"Thanks," I said, watching Taylor leave.

"Boy, for someone who wants to hate him so much, you sure are staring at him," Dalton said.

"Habit," I said, watching as Shea filled a cup with water.

Taylor took his beer and my water, and he carried them back toward us before setting my cup on the table.

"Damn, Taylor," Zeke said. "She's making sure you're not slipping something in her drink."

Taylor looked at me. "No. Seriously?"

"I don't know you," I said.

"Does that happen a lot around here?" Zeke asked, a little disturbed at the thought.

"It's happened," I said.

Taylor gritted his teeth. "I'd better not catch anyone doing that shit. That's grounds for an ass-beating."

"It ain't because she don't know you," Zeke said. "She just needs an excuse to watch you when you're with the hot bartender."

"I'm not with the hot bartender," Taylor told his friend.

"I'd like to be with the hot bartender," Zeke said. Smiling at Shea, he took a sip of his beer.

"She has a name," I said. When Taylor didn't seem to remember, I reminded him, "Shea."

He tried to look sorry but failed. "I know your name."

"I'm honored," I deadpanned.

"Quit acting like we're strangers. I'm not going to put anything weird in your drink. I've never had to drug anyone to get laid, and I'm not going to start now."

"I still don't know you."

He nudged me with his elbow. "You know I'm a good dancer."

"You're a decent dancer."

Dalton and Zeke busted into laughter again.

Taylor lowered his head, laughing. "Cruel. She's gone and insulted my dancing skills!"

I took a big gulp of ice water and set it down, the cup half empty. Droplets of sweat were skipping down my back into my jeans. I dabbed my forehead with my wrist. "I really should go."

A new song boomed through the speakers, and everyone cheered and headed toward the dance floor.

"One more!" Taylor said, tugging on my hand.

I pressed my lips together, trying not to smile. "Okay, but then that's it! I've got to work in the morning."

"Deal!" he said, leading me by the hand from the tightly woven carpet to the wooden dance floor.

Taylor spun me before we began our counted dance. We fell in line, dancing counterclockwise like everyone around us. Couples were spinning and laughing, and if they missed a step or messed up, they only laughed harder.

I was amazed at how quickly I had caught on, and I could even anticipate what Taylor was going to do next. That was, until the height of the song when he did something new. This time, he pushed me away from his body and crossed our arms, pulling me close to him, and then in the next moment, I was in the air, upside down, until I was back on my feet, two-stepping again.

I was cackling like a maniac, unable to control my laughter.

"Did you like that?"

"I'm not even sure what happened!"

"I flipped you."

"Flipped me? I just did a flip? In the air?" I asked, using my index finger to make invisible little circles.

"Yep. I've ruined you for all other first dates. Admit it."

I missed a step as I looked down and then back up. "This isn't a date."

"Okay, I'll buy you dinner. What's open?"

I stopped dancing. "This isn't a date. If anything, we're friends."

Taylor leaned in, his nose caressing the edge of my ear. "That never works out for me."

I stepped back. The feeling coming over me was more than just a tad alarming. I waved at him and began to walk away, but he tugged on my shirt.

Then his hands fell to his sides. "C'mon, Falyn. You weren't serious about that, were you? We were having fun."

"It was fun. Thank you."

I stepped off the dance floor and waved to Dalton and Zeke. Then I pushed through several people to get to the exit. I escaped through the door and walked into the warm summer night air, taking a big breath.

He is going to appear in three, two—

"Falyn!" Taylor said from behind me.

I suppressed a smile. "You said you wouldn't even walk me home, remember?"

Disappointment darkened Taylor's eyes, but he kept his expression smooth. "Whatever you say, Ivy League."

It was a risk. If his ego weren't as durable as I thought, he'd never speak to me again. But of all the arrogant bastards I'd ever come across, Taylor Maddox surpassed every one.

Still, I had to toss him a bone. I leaned up on the balls of my feet and kissed him on the cheek, letting my lips linger on his skin for just a second longer. Taylor came closer, drawn to my mouth, his face turning less than a centimeter toward me. I backed away, but when our eyes met, he looked completely different. I couldn't pinpoint it, but something had changed.

"Good night."

"Night," he said softly.

I began my return home, pausing at the stoplight to press the button for the crosswalk. Tejon Street had moderate traffic for a weekend night, not that I had much to compare it to. Usually, by this time, I would be lying on my couch, eating cheese and crackers while reading one of the trash mags Kirby loved to bring to work to read on breaks.

"Hey!" Dalton said, running up to me.

I raised an eyebrow. "What?"

"He promised he wouldn't walk you home. But he didn't promise he wouldn't make me walk you home."

I shook my head, trying to subdue the victory welling up inside of me. "I can handle walking across the street."

"Just pretend I'm walking in the same direction then."

I sighed. "Are all hotshots this difficult?"

"Are all Ivy League grads this difficult?"

"I'm an Ivy League dropout."

Dalton smiled. "You're all right, Falyn."

I smiled back.

The light changed, and Dalton and I silently crossed the street, passing two businesses before we reached the front door of the Bucksaw. I pulled the key ring from my pocket and stabbed the dead bolt with one of the two keys hanging from the ring.

"You live here or something?"

"Upstairs."

"That's convenient," Dalton said.

"And cheap."

"I can relate. Night, Falyn."

"Take care, Dalton. It was nice meeting you."

He nodded, returning to Cowboys. The dance club was across the street and another two doors down, but I could see Taylor and Zeke standing together on the sidewalk, smoking, chatting, and intermittently checking my progress.

I pulled the door open before closing and locking it behind me. The blinds were drawn, and the lights were off in the dining area. I fumbled around until I found the stairs leading to my loft.

The second key fit in my door. I turned the lock until I heard a click, and then I twisted the knob to my empty apartment. Most Friday nights, I could hear the throbbing bass from Cowboys as I lay in bed, and this night was no exception. But this time, I looked through the letters in my shoebox, my eyes watering at the return address on all the envelopes, with the possibility of being in Eakins soon becoming a reality.

The feeling was so surreal—being hopeful for the first time since I'd lost hope.

CHAPTER FIVE

"ORDER UP!" Chuck yelled from the window in an authoritative deep tone that he only used for that purpose.

It was a gorgeous Saturday afternoon, the normal river of voices louder and more animated. Families occupied almost every table with babies crying, a toddler running in circles around his table, and teenagers hovering over a single cell phone and then bursting into laughter.

Hannah, the high schooler who would help on the weekends, checked on each table, stopping briefly before moving on like a hummingbird in a field of flowers.

"Oh! I'm sorry!" Hannah cried, nearly mowing over the two-year-old who had been a moving obstacle since his parents were seated.

"Jack! Get your heinie over here now!" his mother growled.

Jack ran toward his mother with a smile on his face, knowing that he hadn't yet completely worn out her patience.

"Jeebus," Hannah said, blowing away a few long golden strands that had fallen into her face. "It's not even a holiday weekend."

"Thanks for coming in," I said, pouring sun tea into four tall cups. "I know you had volleyball practice early."

"I'll be a senior this year. I can't believe it." She sighed. "What are you going to do without me next summer?"

"You're not coming back to work?"

She shrugged. "Mom said she wants to travel together all summer before I leave for college."

"That sounds fun," I said with a polite smile.

"You're lying," Hannah said.

"You're right. Traveling with Blaire for an entire summer sounds like a form of punishment."

Hannah pressed her lips together. "I'm sorry you don't get along with your parents. You're so nice."

Hannah didn't have the impossible-to-satisfy, overbearing evil queen that was Dr. Blaire Fairchild.

"Blaire would lose her shit if a pant leg was peeking out of the dirty laundry hamper, and being forced to wait in any line would turn her into an even worse version of herself. Amusement parks were out of the question. I'm glad you're doing that though. With your mother, I'm sure it will be fun."

Hannah's grin disappeared. "Crap, I need to get the Ashtons cashed out. John Delaney just came in with his munchkins."

"All five of them?" I asked, turning to see the answer.

John was loaded down with two baby carriers holding his twin sons. His wife, Marie, readjusted their three-year-old daughter on her hip and then leaned down to say something to her two school-aged daughters.

John used to be the girls' lacrosse coach, but he was now a salesman at a Ford dealership. He was distracted by his children, and I tried my best not to look too long in their direction.

"Oh, wow. Marie's a champ," I said.

"Or nuts," Hannah said. "Didn't they almost get a divorce a few years ago, right before he quit coaching?"

"I don't know," I said. "I don't pay attention to the gossip."

With a bright smile, Hannah rushed the black leather bill presenter to table eight. I filled a small bowl with lemons and then took the drink tray to table twelve.

"Are you all set to order?" I asked, readying my pen and pad.

"How's your dad doing, Falyn?"

I glanced at Brent Collins, who had clearly asked the question with an agenda in mind. No longer the Snickers-eating pudgy classmate I'd graduated with, Brent was now the CrossFit instructor down the street.

"He's been busy," I said. "You should try the roast turkey. It is exceptionally amazing today."

"I don't eat meat. I'll have the kale salad. What happened to you? Weren't you in med school or something?"

"Not really."

"You didn't go to Dartmouth?" he asked.

"I did. So, you're a vegetarian? So, no egg on the salad? Dressing? Phaedra makes a homemade green goddess with vegan mayo that is pretty badass."

"Perfect. Dusty, didn't you hear that Falyn went to Dartmouth?"

Dusty nodded, sipping his tea. Both men were with their girlfriends. All of them had either graduated with me or the year after.

"Nice ring," I said to Hilary.

She patted Dusty on the arm. "He did good, didn't he?"

Dusty smiled. "I sure did, baby." He looked at me. "She doesn't know that she's way out of my league, so I had to put a ring on it, right?"

I grinned. "Right."

Two bacon cheeseburgers and two kale salads later, I was dropping off a new table's order sheet at the window and picking up an appetizer to table one for Hannah.

"Thank you!" Hannah called as I served her table.

I liked Hannah, but I barely knew her. She was still in high school, so she was worlds away from where I was in life. She had every opportunity still in front of her. I was running away from anything that remotely resembled a future—at least a set one.

"Just seated table three for you," Kirby said as she grabbed more menus from behind the bar.

I looked up, and I had to harness the smug smile trying to erupt across my face. "Thank God," I whispered.

"So, you had a good time with him then?" Phaedra asked, dropping off clean menus.

"He's from Eakins, Illinois."

Phaedra blinked. "What did you say?"

"Taylor. He's from Eakins."

Phaedra paled. "Did you tell him?"

My nose wrinkled. "Of course not."

"Tell him what?" Kirby asked.

"It's personal," Phaedra snapped. "She'll tell you if she wants to, but don't bug her about it."

"All right," Kirby said, her eyes bulging for half a second, as she raised her hands, palms out.

"It's nothing," I said.

Kirby looked at table three and then back at me. "They specifically asked for you."

"Good," I said, letting them get settled before heading over.

"Falyn!" Brent called.

I stopped at their table. "Sorry. I'll be right back to top off your drinks."

"What happened with Dartmouth?" he asked. "Your mom told mine you were kicked out. Is that true?"

"Stop it, Brent." Hilary frowned.

My words were stuck in my throat. It had been a long time since someone asked about my past. "No. I left."

"Why?" Brent asked.

I swallowed.

"Leave her alone," John said, turning around in his chair. His cheeks instantly flushed.

Brent made a face. "Hey, Coach Delaney. Funny seeing you here."

John glanced at me and then returned his attention to his wife, who was unaware, still fussing over the babies.

Phaedra cupped my shoulders, smiling at Brent. "I'll just get your check, if you're in a hurry to leave."

"No, thank you," Brent said, stumbling over his words. "We'll just, um … I'm sorry. I was rude. If it's okay, we'd like to stay."

Brent's girlfriend and Hilary were clearly angry with his behavior.

"Good idea," Phaedra said before walking away.

I bit my lip, feeling a bit nauseous, and I retreated to the drink station.

Dalton, Zeke, and Taylor were reading over their menus, once again covered in soot and sweat, each hooking his hard hat over his knee.

"So, my mom wants to start the trip at Yellowstone," Hannah said, putting miniature lids on tiny cups for Delaney children. "We've been there at least a dozen times, but she wants to start there, so that's that. I want to go down the whole West Coast and see what LA is like."

"Have you ever been?" I asked, distracted by the dirty men near the window. I would have to win them all over, not just Taylor.

Hannah shook her head, waiting for me to answer my own question.

"Yes," I said, remembering my own trip to LA, "with Blaire."

"See? You can travel with her."

"It was for a medical conference. I spent all day in the hotel room. I think she only brought me to help her with her bags while she shopped."

"Oh. That sounds kind of ... awful. But at least, if you got sick, she could take care of you. She's a doctor, right?"

"A cardiothoracic surgeon. She's rated as one of the top five in the country."

"Wow. That's pretty amazing!"

"She is an amazing surgeon."

"Well, that's something."

I grimaced. Blaire did not like dust or people who were overly chatty or overly happy, and she hated to be looked in the eye, as if anyone without a PhD was her equal. That was why she was a surgeon. If she were the best—and she was—her bedside manner wouldn't matter as long as she fixed what was broken.

The one thing she couldn't fix was the one person she'd broken.

"Falyn? Table five is asking for their check," Kirby said.

"Oh!" I tapped on the touch screen, and a receipt began to print. I ripped it off and stuck it in the black leather bill presenter before bringing it to a family of four.

"Thank you so much," I said, smiling. "Have a great day."

I checked on my other tables, filled a few glasses, and then approached table three.

"Hi, boys. Are you having the same today or something different?"

They all dipped their heads in unison.

"Same," Dalton said. "You've ruined me for the real stuff."

"Be right back." I spun around, trying to treat them like anyone else who had just come in off the street.

I returned to the bar, put together their Cherry Cokes, and carried the tray to table three with a polite smile.

"Thank you," Dalton said.

Zeke hummed with satisfaction after taking a gulp from his Cherry Coke.

"Did Trex quit?" I asked, making sure not to make too much eye contact with Taylor.

Dalton, Zeke, and Taylor all traded looks.

Then Taylor addressed me, "Trex isn't on our crew. We met him at our hotel."

"Oh," I said. "Are you ready to order? Or do you need more time?"

Zeke squinted at the menu. "You serve breakfast all day?"

"All day."

"What is a crepe?" Zeke asked.

"It's a very thin pancake. Phaedra serves hers filled with a soft hazelnut chocolate. Then she folds it, dusts it with powdered sugar, and then drizzles it with chocolate."

"Yeah, I'll have that," Zeke said.

"Chicken wrap," Dalton said. He handed me his menu, reminding Zeke to hand over his.

After some hesitation, I asked Taylor, "And for you?"

He lowered his menu and looked straight into my eyes. "I want to hang out again."

"Pardon?" For a moment I mused that a second chance might be on the menu.

Taylor sat back and sighed. "I know what I said, but that was when I thought you were just playing hard to get. I didn't actually know you were impossible."

"I'm not … impossible. I'm a local. And you're … not."

Zeke smiled. "Do you have a boyfriend?"

"No."

Dalton backhanded Taylor's arm, and Taylor shot him a death glare.

Taylor let his menu fall to the table. "I didn't mean it when I swore that I'd never ask you out again."

I raised an eyebrow. "You didn't mean to promise me something?"

He thought about that for a moment. "Right. I take it back."

I made a face. "You can't take back a promise. You think I'm going to agree to a second date with a vagrant who takes back promises?"

"You just said we went on a date," Taylor said, a Cheshire Cat grin spreading across his face. His teeth seemed even whiter against the dirt on his face.

"The café is really busy today," I said.

"I know," Taylor said. "Just think about it."

I looked up at the ceiling and then back at him, pointing at him with my pen. "No. Do you want the wrap, too?"

His grin vanished, and he crossed his arms, deflated. "Surprise me."

"You got it." I swiped Taylor's menu and took the order back to Chuck.

"Did he ask you out again?" he asked.

"Yep. I said no."

"Brutal," he said, shaking his head at me.

"He just wants to hang out," I said. "He's not heartbroken or anything."

"If you don't like him, why do you look like you're dying to giggle like a schoolgirl?" Chuck wiped his sweaty brow with his forearm.

"He's from Eakins," I said simply.

"Eakins? Like Eakins, Illinois, Eakins?"

"Yes." I bit my lip.

"Does he know?"

"No, he doesn't know. Phaedra asked the same thing. Why would I suddenly start telling everyone?"

Chuck shrugged. "Just asking. You know, Falyn ... I've offered before—"

"No, Chuck. You're not paying my way to Eakins. You already do too much."

"How much money do you need? Can't be much more now?"

"Nope. I'm almost there. Every time I've gotten close, something's come up."

"Like when you helped Pete buy tires?"

"Yep."

"And when you paid that ticket for Kirby?"

"Yep."

"And when you got sick a couple of years ago?"

"That, too."

"Are you still paying on that hospital bill?"

"No, I paid it off a few months ago. Thank you."

"You should let us help, Falyn. You've helped people, and this is important."

"Yes, it is. That's why I have to do it on my own."

I looked at table three. Taylor glanced over at me, and we locked eyes for a moment.

"Or at least, mostly on my own."

Chuck busied himself again with the soup. "That is going to be one pissed off young man when he figures out what you're doing."

My chest sank in. "I already feel bad enough."

"Good. At least you still have a conscience."

I looked down at my feet, feeling worse by the second. The high I'd felt moments before was completely replaced with guilt. "Did Phaedra go to the back?" I asked.

He nodded. "She's making cheesecakes."

"Oh," I said, knowing it would be a while before I saw her.

The Delaneys waved to Kirby as they gathered their children to leave. Marie carried the twins' carriers, so John could handle their toddler. The girl was being carried over John's shoulder, her little feet kicking wildly as she screamed.

"Whew," Hannah said. "I'm adopting a ten-year-old."

I watched as the Delaneys walked out to their car, parked in one of the angled spaces in front of the Bucksaw. The father fought to get his daughter into her car seat, alternately pleading with her and then scolding her.

"Yeah," I said, distracted.

John secured the girl and then patted his own jeans, saying something to his wife before returning to the bar.

He stopped just in front of me, leaning in. "I'm so sorry," he said. "She asked why we never come in here anymore. I'll try not to come back."

I shook my head. "It's fine. I understand."

"I'm truly sorry, Falyn. For everything," he said again, pulling his wallet from his pocket before jogging outside.

All the air felt like it had left the room with John, and I stood there, unable to move or breathe.

Kirby wandered behind the bar, saying hello to the regulars before leaning over the counter on her elbows. "I didn't think that rush would ever let up." She picked at the corner of a menu and then sighed. "Hey, I'm talking to you. Are you going to tell me what you haven't told me?"

"Not today," I said, snapping back to the present.

Kirby pouted. "So, do you like him? Because ... you're being you but different. You always act weird when a guy tries to pursue you, but you're not running this one off."

"Who?" I asked, my voice higher than I wanted.

Kirby rolled her eyes. "Taylor, stupid."

"Yeah. Why is that?" Hannah asked. "What's with the weirdness when it comes to guys?"

I glowered at her. "Go check your tables."

"Yes, ma'am," she said, turning on her heels.

"I'm serious," Kirby said. "I thought you were just pissed at your parents. Until recently, I didn't realize that you also hated men, and then Taylor happened."

"I don't hate men."

I stole a glance at Taylor. He did the same to me, so I looked away for a moment. With a small smile lingering on his face, he was talking to his crew again.

"I like men. I just don't have time for them."

"No," she said, scratching at a speck on the counter, "it's something else." She grabbed a clean cloth and a spray bottle, and she headed to the main dining area to bus tables.

"Order up!" Chuck yelled, startling me.

I brought a round tray to the window before loading it with the hotshot crew's entrees.

"You okay, kiddo?" Chuck asked.

"I got it," I said, fitting one edge into the crook of my neck as I centered my palm beneath the tray.

"That's not what I meant," Chuck said.

"I know," I called back as I walked away.

The boys were chatting when I approached them, and three pairs of eyes lit up when they recognized the tray of food was theirs.

"Wrap," I said, placing it in front of Dalton.

"Crepe," I said, lowering it to the table before Zeke.

"Denver omelet with jalapenos."

Taylor reached out, and I handed his plate to him.

"The plate is warm," I warned.

"Doesn't bother me," Taylor said with a half smile. Just as I turned, he touched my elbow. "I am capable of just hanging out as friends, you know."

I shot him a dubious look. "I'm a waitress in a popular tourist town. You think I haven't heard that before? That I haven't heard it all before? Listen, you're nice. I like you guys. But I don't need any more friends, especially temporary ones."

I could feel him watching me as I walked away, and I could guess what he was thinking. He'd already proven he enjoyed a challenge, so I was giving him one.

Once they cleaned their plates and sat back against their chairs, I brought them the check. They wasted no time gathering their things and heading out, but Taylor made sure to wait until he could wave to me before leaving.

Kirby bussed their table and brought me a handful of ones and fives and some change for a tip that totaled more than their meals. I shook my head and chuckled quietly. It was the best way to tell a waitress good-bye.

The remainder of my shift was comfortably busy. Hannah and I sat together on the stools near the kitchen end of the bar, counting our tips and listening to Hector's and Chuck's funny stories about their mishaps and near misses throughout the day.

With one hand on her back, Phaedra trudged up to us from the back room, covered in cream cheese, chocolate, and strawberry smears. "The goddamn pies are done."

Chuck hugged her. "Well done, my love. Well done."

He kissed her cheek, and she batted him away.

"How was it? I meant to come out earlier. I got behind."

"We survived," I said.

Kirby smirked. "Taylor came in again today. Left her a big tip."

I rolled my eyes.

"What did it say?" Hannah said.

My nose wrinkled. "Huh?"

Hannah nodded to my stack of cash. "He wrote on one of the bills. I thought you knew."

Kirby rushed to stand next to me as I fanned out my money.

I shook my head. "Nothing."

"It's on the other side, kiddo," Phaedra said, her eyes targeting one of the singles.

I flipped over the stack and found the note scribbled in barely legible print.

COMFORT SLEEP HOTEL

ROOM 201

Kirby laughed. "He gets points for persistence. You have to give him that."

I inhaled, the wheels in my head spinning a hundred miles per hour. Now that I had somewhat of a plan, it was hard to be patient. But being patient was the only way it could work.

"It's not cute. It's obnoxious. But keep seating them in my section, okay?"

"You got it," she said, climbing onto a stool and dangling her feet like a child.

Phaedra patted Chuck's face. "Remember when you were obnoxious, honey?"

"How could I forget?" he said, waggling an eyebrow.

"Please stop," Kirby said, looking ill.

A knock sounded on the door.

Kirby sighed. "He's actually on time for once."

When she didn't move and didn't say anything else, I turned to see Taylor standing in a white hat, a gray hoodie, and navy basketball shorts with flip-flops, holding a laundry basket full of clothes.

"I'll be a son of a bitch," Phaedra said with her gravelly low voice.

"Should I let him in?" Kirby asked.

Everyone looked at me.

"Just … nobody say a word. Let me handle it."

"I feel like this is a joke," Hannah said. "Is she playing a joke on us?"

"No, but it's still funny," Chuck said, trying not to laugh.

I made my way to the front door, not at all in a hurry, stopping just shy of an arm's length away. "What are you doing here?" I asked, trying to seem exasperated.

"Laundry day," he said, grinning from one ear to the other.

"Okay. You still haven't explained why you're here."

"Do you have a washer and dryer?"

"Yes."

"That's why I'm here."

I shook my head in disbelief. "Do people not know how to ask to borrow things where you're from?"

"Illinois."

"I know where you're from!" I growled.

Taylor's smile faded. "Can I borrow your washer and dryer?"

"No!"

He looked both ways, down each direction of the street, and then back at me. "Well ... is there a Laundromat nearby?"

"On Platte Avenue. Just turn left on Platte, off Tejon. It's just before you get to Institute Street. Right across from the supply store," Phaedra called.

I spun around to see her pointing in the correct direction. I shot her a look, and she shrugged her shoulders.

"You wanna come?" he asked. "Laundromats are boring as fuck."

I pressed my lips together and then pulled them to the side, trying not to smile. *This is it.* I reached over and turned the key that was already in the lock. "Come in."

"You sure?"

"Oh, now, you're worried about overstepping?"

"Not really," he said, walking past me. "Up the stairs, right?"

It had to be fate. Taylor was like a stray puppy that I'd fed once, and now, he wouldn't go away. He also happened to be from the exact town I'd been saving money to visit all this time.

I closed the door and cranked the key before facing four identical smirks from my coworkers.

"You coming?" Taylor asked from the bottom of the stairs, still hugging his full laundry basket.

"Well," I said, blowing my bangs from my eyes, "why the hell not?"

CHAPTER SIX

I OPENED THE DOOR for Taylor, watching with a glimmer of amusement while he made a show of glancing around. His shorts sat low on his hips, and he turned his white hat backward, taking in every corner of the room. He was a man I would normally stay far away from, and there he was, beautifully sloppy, standing in my apartment.

"Is this a satisfactory location to do your laundry?" I asked.

He shrugged. "Monumentally better than the Laundromat." He pushed the door close. "Where's your laundry room?"

I gestured for him to follow and then slid open a set of doors situated in the wall between the kitchen and the bathroom. The washer and dryer, probably purchased the same year I was born, were just barely set inside the shallow rectangular closet.

"Still better than the Laundromat?" I asked.

"Yes, but I can go if you want me to."

"Just turn it to whatever setting and pull the dial to start it."

Taylor's appreciative smile was actually a little—okay, a lot—cute. He followed my directions, turning the dial on the washer and pulling. The water began to pour out from the back of the drum. He bent down, grabbed several pairs of jeans, and threw them in.

I retreated to my bedroom, organizing my tips. I added half to the previous day's collection in my wallet and the other half to the shoebox. After stashing both, I changed into a pair of sweatpants and an oversized gray T-shirt.

"Where are your jeans?" Taylor asked.

I stopped in my doorway, taken off guard by his strange question. I pointed to my bedroom. "In there on the floor."

"There's room in the washer," he said, pouring in the laundry soap.

"My jeans don't know your jeans well enough to be washed together."

He chuckled and shook his head while he watched the basin fill with water and suds. "Did I do something to make you hate me? Or is this some kind of test?" He faced me. "Because I'm not trying to get into your pants, Ivy League. I'm just asking to wash them."

I retreated to my bedroom, picking up the wad of denim next to my nightstand. Then I crossed the hall and ducked into the bathroom just long enough to pick through the dirty laundry for the other two pairs somewhere inside the pile.

"Here," I said, handing him the jeans.

"This is it?" he asked, throwing them into the washer.

"Yes, so if you ruin them, I'm screwed." I backed away from him and fell into the chair.

"I won't ruin them. I've been doing laundry for a long time."

"Your mom didn't do it for you?"

Taylor shook his head.

"Good. Moms can really screw kids up that way. You're lucky you never ended up crying over the washing machine because you couldn't figure out how to turn it on."

"Sounds like you know from experience."

"The help did our laundry." I waited for his reaction.

He had none.

"If your parents are so rich, why are you in this shithole?" he asked, pulling off his sweatshirt and throwing it into the washing machine, leaving him in just a thin, too-small T-shirt that read *Eakins Football* in faded letters.

I stared at him for a moment, fighting the inevitable smile creeping across my face. "They made bad choices."

Taylor lumbered to the couch and fell onto it, bouncing a bit, and then he tested the cushions by pushing down on them with his hands. "Like what?"

"None of your business."

He leaned back, crossing his arms.

"What's with all the tattoos?" I asked, letting my eyes glide over the mishmash of colors and shapes that covered his skin down to his wrist.

"We all have them."

"Who's we?"

"My brothers and me. Well, most of us. Tommy doesn't."

"How many brothers?"

"Four."

"Dear God."

He nodded, staring at whatever memory was playing before his eyes. "You have no idea."

"Where are they? Your brothers."

"Here and there."

I liked this game, all questions and no answers, and he didn't seem to mind. Taylor's white T-shirt crumpled in the middle, thin enough to hint at his tan skin and nicely formed abs. Abs—all the assholes had them. Four to six muscles were like a graph chart to show just how big of a douche bag the guy was.

"Are you the oldest?" I asked.

"Yes and no."

"Any sisters?"

Taylor made a face. "God, no."

Either he hated women, or he treated them badly enough not to want to think about them as people. No matter which it was, the longer he was in my apartment, the less I worried about guilt being a problem.

"Want to watch television?" I asked.

"No."

"Good," I said, settling back into my chair. "I don't have cable."

"Got any movies?"

"Phaedra has a box of VHS tapes and a VCR in that closet," I said, casually pointing. "But I haven't hooked it up yet."

"How long have you lived here?"

"A while."

Taylor stood up, groaning as he did, and then he ambled over to the closet and opened the door. He was well over six feet tall and could see everything on the top shelf just fine. He pulled the string to turn on the light and then reached for the dusty VCR, pulling it out along with a mess of cables.

He blew off the dust and then leaned back, looking disgusted. "Pick a movie. I'm going to get this bad boy hooked up."

"Are you bored with the stimulating conversation?"

"To death," he said the words without apology.

Oddly, there was no hint that he was unhappy with the way things were going. He didn't seem annoyed or even put-off, which was a relief. At least he wasn't going to require an exorbitant amount of attention and effort.

"*Aliens*," I said, pointing.

Taylor took the box over to the small television sitting on top of a two-shelf table. He sat the VCR on the bottom shelf and then began unraveling the wires. "Yeah, I like that one."

I wrinkled my nose. "Like it? It's a classic."

"I saw *Sixteen Candles* in there. I figured you'd pick that." He plugged a cable into the back of the VCR and then reached around the back of the television.

"Clearly, you don't know me at all."

"I can't decide if you're trying to hate me or trying to make me hate you."

"Neither."

Taylor made a face but only because he had to reach further to screw the cable into the proper connection. "So, I don't."

"You don't what?"

"Hate you."

"Damn," I teased.

Taylor achieved whatever it was he had been trying to do and sat upright before stretching out his legs and crossing them, leaning his back against the wall beside the TV. "I think you hate yourself enough for the both of us."

I felt my cheeks turn red. He didn't know how close he'd come to the truth.

"Is that a rage coming on?" Taylor said, mistaking my embarrassment for anger.

My arm pressed against the side of the chair as I leaned forward. "You don't have that kind of effect on me."

He blinked. "What do you mean?"

"I'd have to give a shit about you to get angry."

"Oh, are you analyzing now, Ivy League? I thought you said you weren't a psych major."

"Now, you're just being rude."

"Saying you're shit at conversation and that I have a feeling you're a judgmental bitch is rude, but I wasn't going to take it that far. But you are … and you are."

"Ouch." I purposely kept my features smooth.

He shook his head, confused. "One minute, you're reactive, and the next, I can't get a reaction. You're all over the place. I cannot figure you out—like, at all. And I minored in women."

"That must get you so much ass and so many high fives from your friends. But that doesn't impress me."

He paused for a moment. "Do you want me to leave?"

"I don't think so. But you can if you want."

"I don't want. And that's weird for me that I have an opinion, one way or the other."

"I'm intrigued. Continue."

"First of all, I like that you're awkward as fuck and that you're a raging bitch. Girls tend to giggle and run their hands through their hair a lot when I'm around. You've all but told me to fuck off."

"Fuck off."

"See? I like you."

"Maybe I don't want you to like me."

"I know. And I don't, not like that. And I think that's what surprises me the most."

His revelation caught me off guard, but the twinge in the pit of my stomach surprised me even more.

"Listen, Ivy League, I'm here until October. I work my ass off all day. If I'm lucky, I work first shift, so I can eat lunch at the café. You and your hateful-ass mouth have been the highlight of this job. I think you're just being hostile because you think I'm trying to bag you, and clearly, I'm not capable of taming the shrew in this story. So, let's turn the volume up on *Aliens*, so we can't hear that piece-of-shit washer of yours and hang out."

I blinked.

He shrugged. "I don't care about whatever problem you have with your parents. I don't care that you have some sort of fucked-up issue with men. I don't want within five feet of your pussy, and you've gotta know that now because I'd never use the P word if I'm looking to get laid. Girls hate that. I just want to be around someone cool who also owns a washer and dryer and the best collection of VHS tapes I've seen since the nineties."

"Five feet, huh?" I said. I crawled off my chair, across the scratchy carpet, and over to where Taylor was sitting.

He stiffened as I planted my hands on each side of his legs and leaned in, stopping inches from his lips.

"You sure about that?" I whispered.

He swallowed and then opened his mouth, speaking quietly, "Get the fuck away from me. I know full well that touching you would be like putting my finger on a loaded gun."

"Then don't pull the trigger," I dared him, my lips almost grazing his.

He didn't move forward, but he didn't retreat. His body was relaxed, comfortable, with being that close to mine. "I won't."

I sat back on my heels and rested my hands on my knees, thinking about what he'd said. "You sound awfully confident for a guy who keeps coming to see me day after day."

"You're fucking weird—like, weirder than I thought. Did I pass the test?"

"Yes," I said matter-of-factly.

"I might like being around you, but that doesn't mean I'm a fucking fool. And that's a ridiculous test. Any guy is going to go for it if a girl is begging for it like that."

"You didn't."

"I keep telling you, I'm not an idiot. I know what you're trying to do. I just don't know why."

I narrowed my eyes. "You say we can be friends, but you don't keep your word."

"Okay then. I promise to make relentless attempts to bag your ass. How's that?"

I tilted my head, seeing beyond the hint of his smile, his dimple, and his late-night stubble splashed across his defined jawline. I wouldn't find what I was looking for in his words or even in his eyes. Taylor's truth was just out of reach, like my own, so I knew where to look and how to find it. The only way to see into someone's soul was with your own.

"You promise?" I repeated.

"Swear."

"Are you scared of me?" I asked, only half-joking.

Taylor didn't hesitate. "Not even a little. I know exactly what to expect from you."

"And how is that?"

"Because I'm fairly certain that we're the same person."

My eyebrows shot up, unable to hide my surprise at his conclusion, and I offered a single nod. "*Aliens* it is."

"You going to quit busting my balls?" he asked, crossing his arms.

I crawled back over to the chair and sat down, hooking my legs over the arm. "Probably not, but it'll just be run-of-the-mill Falyn bitchery, and it won't be because I'm trying to get rid of you."

Taylor sat on his knees in front of the television, pulled on the knob to turn it on, and then twisted the dial to channel three. "You forgot the movie."

I went to the closet and pulled it from a stack before tossing it to him. He pulled the tape out of its cover and fed it into the VCR's front slot. Once the tape settled in, the movie began to play. For a few seconds, the picture along with the somber violins playing during the opening credits became fuzzy, and then it all cleared up just as Ripley's spaceship appeared in the distance, a tiny speck of white among the darkness.

Taylor walked on his knees to the sofa before crawling up and stretching out.

As I returned to my chair, a tiny part of me wanted to be polite and explain why I was being so hard on him, but I squashed it down to where I kept the old me. Explanations and apologies were a waste for someone like me. Facing forward and remembering to forget were the only things I had, and under no conditions would I ever allow myself to feel—for anyone—and risk any other similar feelings to come to the surface.

Taylor reached down to the crotch of his shorts and adjusted, tugging at the navy fabric. Once he was satisfied with the location of his junk, he pulled down his T-shirt.

I rolled my eyes. He didn't notice.

One arm was propping his head as he sat with his eyes glued on the screen.

Just as the rescue ship crashed and Ripley was apologizing to Newt, Taylor put our jeans in the dryer and started a new load in the washer. He returned to the couch, repeating Newt's line with a perfect young girl's British accent, "'They mewstly come at night … mewstly.'"

I chuckled, but he ignored me, not saying another word until the end credits.

My eyes were heavy. I was feeling the effects of a long Saturday on my feet.

"You're right," he said, standing up. "It's a classic."

"It might take a while to get all those jeans dry," I said.

Taylor opened the dryer door and checked. "Yep, still damp." He turned the knob to reset the time, and then he stretched out on the sofa again, his eyes blinking twice before they closed.

"You can't sleep here," I said.

"Okay. But can I accidentally fall asleep here?"

"No."

He shook his head, his eyes still closed. "I'm even doing your damn laundry. You could at least let me take a nap between loads."

"I'm going to bed soon. You can't be here while I'm sleeping."

"Why not?"

"I'm still not convinced that you aren't a serial killer."

"You think I just wanted to wait to murder you until after we enjoyed a movie together? I hate to break it to you, Ivy League, but I don't need to wait for you to fall asleep to overpower you. You might be scrappy, but I've got at least fifty pounds of muscle on you."

"I'll give you that. You still can't stay here. Just because you don't want to sexually assault me doesn't mean you don't want to rob me."

He shot me a dubious look. "Sorry, but I don't need your retro Zenith. I have a badass seventy-two-inch flat screen on my wall at home."

"Where is home? In Estes Park?"

"Yep. I've thought about moving here a few times, but all my buddies and my brother are living either there or in Fort Collins. But it seems like the Alpine group always ends up here."

"One of your brothers lives in Estes?"

"Yeah." His voice strained as he stretched. "We've always been kind of inseparable. I have two brothers back in Illinois and one in San Diego."

I paused. "Do you ever go home?"

"As much as I can. Between fire seasons."

"So, after October?"

"Yeah. Thanksgiving, Christmas, birthdays. My baby brother got married this past spring, kind of on the fly. They're planning a real ceremony on their anniversary, after the bachelor party and stuff. I'll be going back for that for sure."

"Why?"

"The second ceremony? I guess her best friend was kind of pissed that she wasn't invited to the first one."

"So ... you went to the same college in the same town where you graduated high school?"

"Yes, Falyn. What insult would you like to issue for that?"

"None. It's cute. I imagine that it's a little like high school but with less rules."

"Isn't that what college is anyway?"

"Not really. But I went to Dartmouth."

"Shut up."

I nuzzled my cheek against the arm of the chair, utterly content with how mean we were being to each other. Taylor began tapping at his cell phone, and I relaxed, feeling like an invisible one-hundred-pound blanket was draped over me.

I woke up to the morning sun pouring through my windows. My mouth tasted like a cat had pissed in it while I slept.

"Hey," Taylor said, sitting in the center of the sofa, surrounded by piles of folded clothes. "Do you have to work today?"

"Huh?" I said, sitting up.

"Do you work on Sundays?"

"Not this week. It's my day off," I said, groggy. When my brain began to work again, I blinked and then glared at the man folding my unmentionables. "Why are you still here?"

"I did the rest of our laundry, and then I fell asleep. You woke me up a couple of times though. Do you have bad dreams like that a lot?"

"Huh?"

Taylor hesitated. "You had some pretty gnarly dreams. You were crying in your sleep."

I hadn't had a nightmare in years, not like I had while I was at Dartmouth. My former roommate, Rochelle, would still talk about how I'd terrified her in the middle of the night.

I looked at the delicate cotton in his hands. "Put down my panties. Right now."

Taylor tossed them into the basket with the rest of my panties. Most of them were the discount-store printed variety. On certain pairs, the elastic hung loose in fuzzy strings from the waistline or leg holes.

"This is the last load," he said, gesturing to the basket between his ankles. "Socks and panties."

"Oh my God," I said, rubbing my face. "You're going to make me do the walk of shame in front of all my coworkers and customers."

Taylor stood up. "Isn't there a back door?"

"Chuck and the boys will still see you."

"What time do they open on Sundays?"

"Chuck and Phaedra are pretty much always at the café—from sunrise to sunset."

"How do you have any privacy?"

I blew my bangs from my face. "I didn't need any until now."

"I'll fix it. I know what to do."

Taylor gathered his laundry, fitting it all perfectly inside of the lone basket he'd brought, and waved at me to follow him downstairs. We stood at the bottom in full view of the retirees who always stopped at the Bucksaw on Sundays for coffee, all my coworkers, a few local families, and a table full of tourists.

Kirby stopped in her tracks, and so did Hannah. Phaedra noticed them staring, so she whipped around, her mouth falling open. The loud rumble of converging conversations abruptly silenced.

Taylor cleared his throat. "I didn't touch her. She's too fucking mean."

He passed me, heading for the front door, and I watched him, trying to kill him with my expression alone.

Kirby burst into laughter. She was still cackling as Taylor waved at her before walking out onto the front sidewalk. Phaedra tried not to smile, but her deep wrinkles betrayed her. Hannah seemed just as stunned as I was.

"Good morning, sunshine. Coffee?" Phaedra said, handing me a steaming mug.

"Thank you," I said through my teeth. Then I stomped back up the stairs.

"Falyn?" Phaedra called after me.

I stopped before turning down the hall and looked down at her.

"He's ten steps ahead of you, kiddo."

"I know," I grumbled, taking my coffee to the loft.

I exploded through my door and kicked it shut before leaning against the side of the refrigerator. When I felt angry tears burning my eyes, I set the coffee on the kitchen counter and then rushed to my bedroom, reached for the shoebox, and pulled it onto the bed with me.

The most recent letter was on top of the others, and beneath it was the stack of cash I'd saved so far for a plane ticket. I held the notebook paper to my chest and took a deep breath. The carefully scripted loops and lines informing me of everything I had missed was nearly four months old, and it would only grow older.

I let the thin notebook paper fall to my lap.

Of course it would be Taylor fucking Maddox. The last person on Earth who I want to need is my one quick ticket to Eakins. I pushed the thought from my head. I didn't want a plan or to even think about it.

I just needed to get there. No expectations. No hopes. Just the opportunity to knock on their door. Even if they wouldn't forgive me, maybe I could finally forgive myself.

CHAPTER SEVEN

I WIPED MY CHEEKS, smiling as the dad in *Poltergeist* pushed the television out of the hotel room and onto the balcony. The credits and eerie music began to play, and I scowled at the empty mug of coffee on the carpet next to me.

My fridge contained only a moldy jar of cheese dip, ketchup, and two cans of Red Bull. Phaedra had given me a used coffee maker, but I didn't have any coffee or sugar ... or water if I couldn't afford the bill. I cringed, thinking about having to go downstairs to use the toilet. I would have to clean that restroom on occasion, and although I made a conscious effort not to be a snob about most things, public restrooms made my skin crawl.

I stood up and made my way downstairs to the kitchen. The loud chatter of customers instantly infiltrated my head, especially the squeals and cries of children. They always seemed to hit an octave that stood out to me, grinding inside my brain like a metal fork on a plate.

The water splashed onto my T-shirt as I rinsed the mug. Then I put it into one of three dishwashers.

Hector smiled at me as he rounded the corner, wiping his hands on his apron. "Are you going to get outside and see the world today, Miss Falyn?" he asked.

I sighed. "Are you ever going to stop calling me that?"

Hector just smiled, carrying on with his duties.

Phaedra's face appeared in the food window. "Hey, kiddo. What do you have planned today?"

"Nothing." I took a bite of celery that had been left on the prep table.

Pete slapped my hand as I grabbed for another, and I tried not to laugh.

My grin fell away. "He said I had a nightmare," I said to Pete. He frowned.

"It's been a long time ... since ..." I said, trailing off.

Phaedra came over to stand next to me and gently pulled on one of my tawny waves, moving it away from my face. "You sure you don't have anything planned?" she asked.

"Yes. Why?"

She gestured behind her with a nod. "Because that boy's here, looking for you."

I scrambled to the doors, pushing through to see Taylor standing on the sidewalk outside. He waved to me.

"He likes you," Kirby gushed as I passed her.

Taylor shoved his hands into his jeans pockets, his short sleeves showing off the lean muscles in his arms.

"If you tell me you were in the neighborhood, I'm going to be disappointed," I said, crossing my arms.

He chuckled and looked down. "No. I was bored and came straight over."

"You have the day off, too?"

"I do. Wanna do some stupid touristy shit with me? You listed all that stuff before."

"Are you driving? I don't have a car."

"My truck is over there," he said, turning slightly and gesturing toward a shiny black foreign job with mud tires. He turned back to me, dubious. "How do you get around?"

"Where am I gonna go?" I asked.

Taylor held out his hand, one side of his mouth pulling into a mischievous half smile. "With me."

My first impulse was to say no. I had gotten used to being broody and spitting words that would make any man retreat, but I didn't have to do that with Taylor. My insults had no effect on him, and he'd just keep coming back until it was time for him to leave. If I managed to get him to take me to Eakins, I wouldn't even have to push him away after our return to Colorado Springs. His job and the distance would do it for me.

He flashed his dimple, and saying yes to him was nearly compulsive.

"Just don't do anything stupid, like open my car door."

"Do I look like that kind of guy to you?"

"No, but you don't look like the kind of guy who makes friends with girls either, and it feels like I've got the job."

He pulled me along, looking both ways before crossing the street. "What can I say? You're the opposite of my better half."

"So, I'm so horrible that I make you feel like a better person?" I asked, standing next to the passenger-side door.

He pointed at me. "Exactly."

He reached for the door handle, but I smacked his hand away.

"Don't worry, Ivy League. I wouldn't open your door for you even if I liked you," he said. "You're driving. I don't know where to go, and I damn sure don't want you barking directions at me."

"You want me to drive your truck?" I asked, feeling a bit nervous. I hadn't driven anything in years.

The doors clicked, and Taylor handed me a set of keys—some shiny, some not so shiny. Walking around the front end and then climbing into the driver's seat, I tried not to show fear, but mostly, I didn't want to feel it. I closed the door and pulled on my seat belt, horrified that my hands were trembling.

"Do you even have a license?" he asked.

"Yes. I know how to drive. It's just ... been a while." I sniffed and felt even sicker. "You spent the morning cleaning your truck, didn't you?"

"Smells like new, doesn't she?"

"Isn't it new?"

"*She*. She is not new, no. I bought her last year." He took the keys from my hand and chose the largest one to stab into the ignition.

"Jesus," I whispered. "I really don't think I should drive ... her."

"You'll be fine."

Instantly, the radio blared screamy hard rock.

He twisted the volume. "Sorry."

"No country?" I asked, resting my hands on the wheel at ten and two.

He laughed once. "Country's for dancing and crying. AC/DC is for cleaning your truck."

I made a face. "But ... it's old."

"The classics never get old. Let's go."

I pulled down the gearshift and turned around, slowly backing out of the parking space. A car appeared and honked, and I slammed on the brakes.

Taylor looked at me, his eyebrows shooting up almost to his hairline.

"I desperately want to keep up my cast-iron bitch persona, but I don't think I can do this," I said.

"How long did you say it's been?"

"Five years."

"Why?"

"No car."

"Ever? Or did you wreck yours?"

I stared at him, unable to answer.

He unfastened his seat belt. "You'd better just tell me where I'm going. I'll learn to live with directions from a girl. We can reintroduce you to the road another day."

"Directions from a girl? Shall I assume you'd even ask for them? Or is that too far from the ancient stereotype?"

He stared at me with dead eyes. "Ivy League, stop talking to me like you're writing a fucking paper."

"Let's just do this," I said, climbing over the console.

After jogging around to the driver's side, he climbed up and settled in. "I feel better about this," he said, nodding.

I agreed, "Me, too."

"Where are we going first?"

"Um ... Garden of the Gods. Just over ten minutes away and free parking."

"Not Pikes Peak? You haven't hiked it, have you?" His tone was accusatory. "I've heard the locals don't."

"I have actually," I snapped. "A couple of times. But you can see Pikes from the Garden of the Gods. Trust me. It's really a special place."

"Okay. Where am I going?"

"Take Tejon south to Uintah. Go until you get to thirtieth, and then take West Colorado onto Ridge Road. Just follow the signs."

"You got it," he said, backing out. He slammed on the brakes when another car laid on its horn. "See? It wasn't just you."

I laughed and shook my head as he inched out onto Tejon Street.

The familiar view outside my window hadn't changed much since I was a girl. Colorado was its own Eden, its residents holding tight to preserving the state's natural beauty. The Garden of the Gods was the earth turned on its edge. The views were particularly gasp-worthy. As a child, it had been my favorite local place to visit—not only to see it for myself, but also to watch as others experienced it for the first time.

Taylor was no exception. As we parked, he couldn't stop staring. He said little as we hiked along the formations, breathing in the fresh air and open space. The sky was still a bit hazy from the outlying fires, but it didn't seem to faze him.

An hour after we'd arrived, Taylor sat on a boulder to rest. "This is incredible. I'm pissed I've been here for as long as I have and haven't come here before. I've gotta show the guys."

I smiled, satisfied with his reaction. "Everyone should see this place. I don't know. There's just something about it."

"I walk a lot of miles when I'm on the job, and I'm fucking tired. What's up with that?"

I looked up, squinting from the sun overhead. Beads of sweat had just begun to fall from the nape of my neck down to the top seam of my tank top. "I don't think you're tired. I think you're relaxed."

"Maybe so. All I wanna do is take a nap."

"That's because you were up all night, doing my laundry."

"Not all night. I slept. You drool by the way."

"Oh, that's why you didn't make the moves on me. I thought maybe I snored."

"No. You might actually be the cutest sleeper ever."

I made a face. "Like you've spent a whole night with someone before."

He thought about it. "True."

"So, tell me something I don't know about you," I said, trying not to sound too eager. This was the precarious part. It was the make-or-break moment where I would get information I needed without seeming like I was getting information.

His brows pulled together. "Like what?"

I crossed my arms and shrugged.

He patted the empty space next to him. "My birthday is January first."

"That's kind of cool." I sat next to him, stretching my legs out in front of me. I hadn't realized how tired I was until I sat down. "It's always a big party, huh?"

"I guess."

"I figured you'd talk about your job."

"It's a job. When's your birthday?" Taylor asked.

"Oh, are we doing Twenty Questions?"

He feigned exasperation. "A form of it, I guess."

"It's not just a job. You save lives, homes, entire towns."

He waited for me to answer, unfazed.

"My birthday isn't on a holiday."

He waited.

I rolled my eyes. "May thirteenth."

"Do you have any siblings?"

"Nope."

"Your parents' only child hates them. That sucks."

"Yep."

"Wow. I thought you were going to deny hating them. Do you *really* hate them?"

"I think so." The irony wasn't lost on me that I had answered almost immediately with no *thinking* at all.

"Can I ask why?"

I sighed. The other part of the game I'd started long before Twenty Questions was not to give too much away while still seeming to play along. "I guess you had the perfect childhood."

"Not at all."

"Enough love for your mom to tattoo her name on your arm."

"My brother wanted to, so I had to, too."

"And why is that?"

"We have the same tattoos."

"Like the exact same ones? All of you?"

"Just my brother Tyler and me."

I snorted. "Taylor and Tyler."

He laughed, too. "Thomas, Trenton, and Travis, too."

I raised an eyebrow. "Seriously? You're not serious."

He shrugged. "She liked Ts."

"Clearly. So ... your parents are still in Eakins?"

"Yep."

"What's Illinois like?"

He blinked, unhappy for some reason. "I don't know. Eakins is pretty suburban, I guess."

"Like here?"

"No," he said, shaking his head. "It's really, really small. We have only one grocery store, a few restaurants, and a couple of bars."

"And a tattoo parlor?"

"Yeah. My brother works there—Trenton. He's really good."

"Does he do all of yours?"

"All but one." Taylor held out his arm and pointed to the tattoo that read *Diane.*

"Why not that one?"

Taylor stood up. "That's more than twenty."

He held out his hand to help me up. I pulled on him and then brushed off my pants.

"I don't think so, but we should head back if you want to see other touristy stuff."

He looked around and then shook his head. "No. I'm good with just hiking this trail. Unless you're hungry or something?"

I looked at Taylor. He was a little too sweet, somewhat courteous, and even thoughtful at times, all safely hidden away behind his smart mouth and his tough tattooed exterior.

He cocked his head. "What?"

"Nothing. You're just ... not what I thought ... I think."

"Great. Now, you're in love with me. I'll never get rid of you."

My nose wrinkled. "I am definitely not and never will be."

"Promise?" he asked, smug.

"Yes, and unlike you, I keep my promises."

"Good. Makes things a lot less complicated now that you've been friend-zoned." He playfully pushed me forward, and I pushed him back. "Onward."

We were almost back to the truck as the sun disappeared behind the mountains. The temperature had dropped from sweltering to refreshing, and the sweat that had beaded on my skin was cooling in the light evening breeze.

Somewhere ahead, music was floating in the air, and smells of food tipped off a party.

"Oh," I said, "the fund-raiser is tonight."

"Here?" Taylor said.

"Every year. For the ..." I scanned Taylor from head to toe. "It's the Heroes Gala, raising money for the families of fallen firefighters."

A look of appreciation came over Taylor's face. "That's kind of cool."

Just when the lights and people came into view, I froze. "Shit ... shit."

"What?"

"My parents are there. They attend it every year."

"So, we'll go around it."

"It's dark," I sighed. "We should stay on the trail. People get lost out here."

He grabbed my hand. "We'll hurry past it. My truck's just beyond that boulder."

I nodded, and we rushed toward an enormous white tent with hanging lights, the sound of a generator mixing with excited chatter and laughter.

We had nearly made it when I heard William's voice calling my name. I closed my eyes and felt Taylor squeezing my hand.

"Falyn?" William said again.

We turned, and when William recognized Taylor and then saw our hands, he puffed out his chest, already preparing to lose his temper. Blaire joined us, the swishing of her long gown coming to a halt once she took her husband's arm. The expression on her face was familiar, one I had begun to relish.

"Falyn, dear, what are you doing here?" she asked.

"It's a public place," I said, angry.

By the term of endearment, she had revealed herself. She'd only call me those asinine pet names in front of her friends, the fake ones who she'd ruthlessly trash in the privacy of her home. I wasn't welcome, and she wanted me to leave sooner rather than later.

People were beginning to crowd around my parents, like a small army of judgmental assholes, all listening in to make sure they could hear the juicy details to discuss at the next dinner party.

I began to turn, but William quickly approached. "This has got to stop. You—"

"Dad," I said, my voice saccharine sweet, "you remember Taylor Maddox. He's from Eakins, Illinois."

William blanched.

Blaire touched her fingers to her chest. "Bill," she said, reaching for her husband, "leave Falyn to her friend. Good night, sweetheart."

"We'll discuss this later," William said, turning his back on me.

I pulled Taylor to the truck, desperate to get into the passenger seat. Once Taylor was sitting beside me, I yanked on the seat belt, feeling like I could finally breathe once it clicked.

"You okay?" he asked.

"I think so."

"What was that about?"

I shook my head.

"Falyn," he said, hesitation in his voice, "why do they care that I'm from Eakins?"

"Because they don't want me anywhere near there."

"Why not?"

"Because I could cause a lot of trouble for a lot of people if I go there."

Taylor started the truck, and I peered over at him.

He was staring straight ahead into the darkness. "Did you know I was from Eakins when we met?"

"No."

"Does it have to do with the fire?"

"Does what have to do with what fire?"

He turned to me, glaring. "Are you fucking with me, Falyn? Who are you?"

I wrinkled my nose. "What fire? What are you talking about?"

He faced forward again. "Do you know Trex?"

"The guy who came with you to the café the first time?"

Taylor sighed and then shoved the gearshift into reverse. "We've both gotta work tomorrow. We should call it a night."

He didn't speak again throughout the ride to downtown. When he parked in front of the Bucksaw, he didn't even put the truck into park.

"Th-thanks." I slowly unbuckled my seat belt and placed my hand on the door handle. "It was a good day."

"It was," he said, sighing. Regret was all over his face.

I fished out my keys and unlocked the front door under the lights of Taylor's truck. Once I was inside and the door was locked, Taylor backed into the street and drove away.

I stood in the dim dining area, alone and confused. Eakins had other secrets, more than just mine.

CHAPTER EIGHT

Six days.

Taylor or anyone from his crew, including the now mysterious Trex, hadn't been to The Bucksaw Café in six days. I had gone over what I'd said until my thoughts were sick of themselves. I tapped on the counter with what little nails I had while chewing on a cuticle on my other hand. Most of the time, not having a phone was liberating, but now that I wanted to Google something, I felt an impulsive need to go out and buy one.

"I thought you were going to quit that," Phaedra said, walking by with a tubful of dirty dishes.

I pulled my finger out of my mouth, the skin around my nail white and torn. "Damn it."

Kirby stood by the drink station, picking up clean cloths for wiping down tables even though she hadn't seated anyone in twenty minutes. Only the loyal regulars were in their seats, ignoring the pouring rain outside.

"Do you have your phone?" I asked Kirby.

She pulled it from her apron. "Yeah. Why?"

"I want to look something up. Can I use it?"

Kirby granted my request. The hot-pink case meant to protect her phone felt bulky in my hand. The days when I'd had a cell phone were so far behind me that it felt like a former life, but the screen looked the same. The icon for the Internet was easy to find.

I clicked on it and proceeded to type in the words, *Fire in Eakins, Illinois.*

The first page was full of links to articles about the local college. I clicked on the first one, reading about dozens of college kids who had been killed while trapped in a basement of one of the campus buildings. I shuddered at images of sooty faces, looking just like Taylor's the first day I'd met him. The name Travis Maddox came up more than a dozen times. He was being investigated for being present at the fight. I wondered why, out of all the students present, Travis and one other man were the only two mentioned to be facing charges.

"What is it?" Kirby asked, sensing my unease.

"I don't know yet," I said, looking up to scan my tables.

"Falyn! Order up!" Chuck called.

I set down the phone and breezed by the food window. I had perfected fitting plates onto a tray years ago. Only a few seconds were spent loading entrees before continuing to the dining area.

"Ta-da," I said, standing over my favorite regular, Don.

Don sat up tall, setting his tea down and giving me plenty of room to situate his meal.

"Do me a favor, and cut into that steak, handsome."

He nodded, his shaking hands carving into the thick meat. He hummed a, "Yes," and then brought the fork to his mouth.

I put my hand on his shoulder. "How is it?"

He hummed again, chewing. "You're my favorite, Falyn."

"You're mine, but you knew that." I winked at him and then walked over to the drink station.

The sky was dark outside, and the sidewalks were wet with the intermittent rain that had been falling since mid-morning. Crap weather meant less butts in the seats and less tips in our pockets.

Phaedra brought in a stack of freshly sanitized menus from the back before setting them in a rectangular wicker basket. She crossed her tan arms, her skin leathered from years in the sun. "I'm not going to curse the rain. We needed the rain."

"Yes, we did," I said.

"Maybe that will help your boy with those fires."

"We're going to need a lot more rain than this. And he's not my boy. I haven't seen him in a week."

"He'll be back."

I shook my head, breathing out a laugh. "I don't think so."

"Did you get into a fuss?"

"No. Not really. Kind of. We ran into my parents. Eakins was brought up. There was a misunderstanding."

A knowing smile lit up Phaedra's face. "He figured out you were using him?"

"What? No. I'm not using him," I said, guilt washing over me.

"You're not, huh?"

"I'm ... renting him. He doesn't have to take me if he doesn't want to. I'm not being fake. I'm being pretty damn mean actually."

Phaedra watched me try to talk my way out of the hole my words were digging. "So, why did he quit coming around?"

"I think he thinks I'm somehow involved in an investigation of his little brother."

"What in the Sam Hades? Where did that come from?"

I blew my bangs from my face. "It's a long story."

"They always are."

I felt her watching me as I made my way out to the main dining area.

"More soda?" I asked the woman at table twelve.

She shook her head, waved me away, and I moved on to the next patron.

The sky opened up, and huge drops began dive-bombing the street and sidewalk. They were bouncing off so hard that they scattered after impact, appearing like steam hovering over the concrete.

"It's getting ugly out there," I said to Don. "Want me to call Michelle to have her pick you up?"

Don shook his head. "Don't want her getting the grandbabies out in this. They're my great-grands, you know. They call me Papa."

"I know," I said with a warm smile. "They're lucky ducks. I would have loved to have you as my papa."

He chuckled. "You do. Why in heaven's name do you think I come to visit you every day?"

I gently touched his back with my fingers. "Well, maybe just eat your cheesecake a little slower. Hopefully, the rain will ease up."

I bent down to kiss his cheek, his jowl sinking under my lips. The smell of his aftershave and his scratchy stubble were two of a hundred things I loved about this man.

Several men sprinted along the glass wall and ducked into the door, laughing and out of breath. Taylor squeegeed his glistening arms with his hands while shaking the water from his face.

Kirby pointed at the bar, prompting Taylor to lead Zeke and Dalton to the empty stools in front of the drink station. Taylor and I locked eyes while he passed behind me. I picked up a few dirty dishes and tried not to rush them to Hector before returning to stand next to Phaedra.

"Your boy has the day off," Phaedra said.

I felt my cheeks burn. "Please stop calling him that."

"He likes it," Dalton teased.

Taylor craned his neck at Dalton.

Dalton sank back. "I'm just giving you shit. Damn."

All three men were wearing soaked T-shirts and jeans. Taylor's gray T-shirt had a small red bulldog over his heart with the words *Eastern State* circling around it. He turned his red ball cap backward, and I smiled, knowing he'd deny it if I pointed out that he matched.

"I do kind of like it," Taylor said, his threatening glare vanishing. He elbowed Dalton, who pushed him off.

Phaedra shook her head and held up menus. "You gonna eat or what?"

"We are," Zeke said, clapping his hands and rubbing them together.

Phaedra placed a menu in front of each of them and then left us for the kitchen.

Taylor glanced up at me for only a second before he studied the entrees.

"Drinks?" I asked.

"Cherry Coke," they said in unison.

I breathed out a laugh as I turned to grab cups, and then I filled them with ice.

"Not funny. Shut the fuck up," Taylor seethed, his voice low.

I turned. "Excuse me?"

Taylor's expression smoothed, and he cleared his throat. "Sorry. Not you."

I raised an eyebrow.

"Dalton said you had a nice ass," Zeke said.

"You disagree?" I said, pouring my special cherry concoction into their Cokes.

Taylor made a face, as if I'd just asked the stupidest question in history. "No. I just don't want them noticing."

I set their cups on the bar and handed them straws. "What are you eating?"

"Paninis again," Taylor said, dropping the menu.

I looked to the other two for confirmation.

Zeke shrugged. "We decided before we got here. They're fucking good."

"If they're so good, why haven't you been in for almost a week?" I asked, instantly regretting it.

"Keeping track, huh?" Zeke teased.

"If you like the paninis, you should try Phaedra's cheesecake," I said, ignoring Zeke's jab.

They traded glances.

"Okay," Taylor said.

I left them to put in their order, notifying Chuck, and then I turned to check on my tables. Twelve was almost out of soda, and they were still talking.

Damn it. I'd known she would need more.

Don wasn't quite finished, but he was sitting still, a blank stare on his face. His glasses had fallen down the bridge of his nose, barely hanging on at the tip.

"Don?" I said.

He fell over, hitting the tiled floor hard with his shoulder and head. His glasses slid off his face, flying a few feet across the floor.

"Don!" I yelled, running over to him.

Once I reached him, I fell to my knees and cradled his head with my hands. I leaned over and then looked to Phaedra and Chuck, who had both run out of the kitchen.

"He's not breathing." The reality of what that meant made my heart sink. "He's not breathing! Someone, help him!" I screamed.

Taylor, Zeke, and Dalton all joined me on the floor. Zeke checked Don's pulse and then looked at Taylor as he shook his head.

"Call an ambulance!" Taylor yelled to Phaedra. "Scoot back, sweetheart." He positioned himself next to Don and crossed his hands, one over the other, on the center part of Don's lower chest.

Dalton angled Don's head upward and then pinched his nose, breathing into Don's mouth once, before Taylor began compressions.

I crawled backward several feet until Kirby knelt beside me. Don's glasses were next to my hand, so I snatched them up and held them to my chest, watching the guys working on him. Everyone was quiet, listening to Taylor counting compressions aloud and instructing Dalton when to administer breaths.

Zeke checked Don's pulse, and each time he shook his head, I felt my body sink lower.

Taylor was out of breath, but he took one look at me, and whatever expression was on my face gave him renewed strength. "C'mon, Don!" Taylor said. "Breathe!" he barked to Dalton.

Dalton leaned over, giving a breath, all hope gone from his eyes.

"Taylor," Zeke said, touching Taylor's arm.

Taylor shrugged Zeke off, continuing to press into Don's chest. "I'm not giving up." He looked up at me. "I'm not giving up."

Chuck picked me up off the floor and supported my weight as he held me to his side. "I'm sorry, kiddo."

Just a few minutes after the sirens could be heard, they were loud and right outside the door, the lights casting reds and blues inside the Bucksaw.

Taylor, Dalton, and Zeke let the paramedics take over, one of them patting Taylor on the back. They loaded Don onto the gurney and carted him outside into the rain and then into the ambulance.

Taylor heaved, exhausted after using his entire upper body for so long.

"Is Don going to be okay?" Chuck asked.

Taylor pressed his lips together, hesitant to tell the truth. "I don't know. We never got a pulse. I think he was gone before he hit the floor."

I covered my mouth and turned to Chuck, letting his large arms surround me. I felt other hands on me, but I wasn't sure whose. My knees buckled, and my entire body went limp, but Chuck supported my weight without effort.

"Chuck," Phaedra said, desperation in her voice.

"Go on upstairs, honey," Chuck said into my ear.

"I'll take care of your tables," Phaedra said.

I shook my head and wiped my nose with the back of my wrist, but I was unable to answer.

Taylor tossed his truck keys to Dalton. "You guys go ahead. I'll take mine to go, Phaedra."

"I'll bring it up to you when it's ready," she said.

Taylor peeled me from Chuck's arms and escorted me to the back and up the stairs. Just as he realized neither of us had keys,

Phaedra appeared with a plate in one hand and a to-go cup along with my keys in the other.

"You're amazing," Taylor said as Phaedra unlocked the door.

She pushed it open, and Taylor guided me inside, sitting with me on the couch. Phaedra set his plate and cup on the coffee table and then left my keys.

"You want a blanket, kiddo?" she asked, leaning over and touching my knee.

The sirens blared as the ambulance tore off for the nearest hospital, taking away my friend.

"I should have gone with him," I said, looking up in horror. "Someone should be with him. He's all alone. He doesn't know those paramedics. Someone he knows should be with him."

Phaedra reached out for me. "Chuck is calling Michelle. She's going to meet them at the hospital. Let me get you a blanket."

I shook my head, but she went to the closet anyway. She fetched a threadbare baby-blue blanket, bordered in equally worn satin. She shook it until it unfolded, and then she covered me up to my neck.

"I'm going to bring you some tea. You need anything, Taylor?"

Taylor shook his head, wrapping his arms around me. "I got her."

Phaedra patted his shoulder. "I know."

She left us alone in the silence-filled loft that hovered over the death below. My head and chest felt heavy, my mouth dry.

"You knew he wasn't coming back," I said. "But you kept going. Even though he didn't make it ... you're good at your job."

He looked down on me, his eyes turning soft. "It wasn't about the job, Falyn."

"Thank you," I whispered, trying to find anywhere else to look but his eyes.

"He came in a lot, didn't he?" Taylor asked.

"Yes," I said, my voice sounding far away.

The feeling inside of me was strange. I was so accustomed to feeling numb that feeling anything at all was unsettling. Nestled in Taylor's arms, feeling a myriad of emotions was more than I could stand.

"I need to ..." I began, shrugging from his embrace.

"Breathe?" Taylor asked. He touched my wrist, and then he leaned over to look into my eyes. Once he was convinced I wasn't going into shock, he relaxed back against the sofa. "I'm really pretty comfortable. No expectations."

I nodded, and he reached his arm around me, pulling me gently against his side. I fit perfectly under his wing, his chest warm against my cheek. He rested his jaw on my hair, content.

Comfortable in the silence, comfortable with each other, we just breathed, existing from one moment to the next. The rain tapped against the window, making oceans of the streets and drenching the islands of cars passing by.

Taylor pressed his lips to my temple. My chest heaved, and I buried my chest into Taylor's damp T-shirt. He held me close, letting me cry.

His arms were safe and strong, and even though there was no space between us, I needed him to be closer. I gripped his T-shirt in my fist and pulled him tighter against me. He obliged without hesitation. I cried quietly until I was exhausted, and then I took a deep breath. I waited for the embarrassment to set in, but it never came.

A soft knock on the door announced Phaedra and the mug of tea she had brought back for me. She also had Taylor's cheesecake. "The boys took theirs to-go, too. They said to call whenever you're ready."

Taylor nodded, not relinquishing his grip on me.

Phaedra put the dishes on the table. "Falyn, drink your tea. It'll help." She nodded her head and crossed her arms over her middle. "It always helps me."

I leaned forward and then returned to the security of Taylor's arms, taking a sip. "Thank you. I'll be back down in a little bit."

"Don't you dare. We're slow. I've got it taken care of. Just take the rest of the day off. I'll see you for dinner."

"We'll be down," Taylor said.

Phaedra offered him a small smile of appreciation, the wrinkles around her mouth deepening. "All right then."

She closed the door, and once again, Taylor and I were alone, wrapped in each other's arms under the blue blanket.

"I wasn't prepared for how good this feels," Taylor said. "Every muscle in my body is relaxed."

"Like you've never sat and held a girl before."

He was quiet, so I looked up at him.

"You're full of it," I said.

"I don't really …" He trailed off, shrugging. "It's not my thing. But this is kind of awesome."

"What is your thing?" I asked.

He shrugged again. "One-night stands, angry women, and fighting fires."

"If you weren't sitting here with your arms around me right now, I'd say that makes you kind of an asshole."

He considered that. "I'm okay with that."

"Why am I not surprised?"

He chuckled. "This surprises me. You surprise me."

I smiled, feeling another tear slipping over my lips. I reached up and wiped it away.

"Here," he said, offering his T-shirt.

He touched the cotton to my lips as I looked up at him.

"Why did you stay away?" I asked.

"Because of this. You make me feel weird."

"*Weird?*" I asked.

"I don't know how else to describe it. Any other girl, I could bag and not think twice about it. Not you. It's kind of like that feeling you got as a kid, right before you did something you knew would get you an ass-whipping."

"I have a hard time believing you're that intimidated."

"Me, too." He paused. "Falyn?" He took a deep breath, as if saying my name was painful, and he rubbed his eyes. "Fuck, I thought I wanted to know, but now, I don't think I do."

"Ask me," I said, readying myself to dodge the truth.

"Just tell me one thing." He paused, unsure if he wanted the answer. "Does your connection with Eakins have to do with my brother?"

I sighed, relieved. "No. I just looked up the fire today."

"So, you know about Travis."

"No. I didn't have time to get a good look, and you don't have to tell me."

Taylor rested his chin on my hair, his muscles relaxing again.

I was glad he couldn't see the look on my face. Just because I wasn't involved with the fire didn't mean I didn't have an agenda. "Taylor?" I said with the same hesitation he'd had in his voice.

"Ask me," he said, repeating my earlier response.

"I do want to go to Eakins for a reason. I was hoping you'd take me there. I've been saving. I have enough for a plane ticket. I just need a place to stay."

He took a deep breath and slowly blew it out. "I thought that might be where you were going with this."

I winced. "It's not what you think. I agree, it's a coincidence. But I'm not trying to find out anything about your brother."

"Then tell me."

I chewed on my bottom lip. "What if I prove it to you—that it's not about your brother? Will you consider it?"

Taylor shrugged, confused. "I guess so."

I stood up, leaving him for my bedroom. I pulled the shoebox out of my closet and returned to the sofa, pulling out an envelope and shoving it at him. "The address on your license is on this street."

He looked at the return address, frowning. "This is next door to my dad's house. How do you know the Olliviers?"

I breathed out a laugh, my eyes filling with tears. "Next door?"

"Yeah," Taylor said, handing back the envelope.

I pulled out a photograph and offered it to him. He looked it over—a four-by-six picture of a young girl standing on a sidewalk, leaning against her brother, Austin. Her waist-length platinum-blonde hair was pinned away from her face, her enormous green eyes peering up at the camera over a shy smile. Austin hugged her to him, proud and protective, like a big brother should be.

Taylor handed it back to me. "Those are Shane and Liza's kids. How do you know them?"

I shook my head and wiped a tear that had escaped down my cheek. "It's not important. What is important is that you believe my reason for wanting to get to Eakins has nothing to do with your brother."

"Falyn, it's not that I don't believe you," he said, rubbing the back of his neck again. "It's just ... Shane and Liza are neighbors and family friends. They've been through a lot."

"I get it," I said softly, trying to quell the frustration welling up inside of me. "It's okay. I understand."

Taylor's face seemed to be weighed down with guilt. He started to reach out to me but didn't. "Just ... give me a second. I thought you were undercover or something, to get info on my brother. This is a lot to wrap my head around." He hesitated. "What do you plan to do?"

"I ..." I took a deep breath. "I'm not really sure. I don't want to cause their family any more pain. I just know I want to start over, and I can't do that unless my story with that family ends."

Taylor blanched and then looked away. "You don't have to say anymore. It's all starting to make sense now—why you don't drive, why you've started all over here, away from your family."

"Whatever you think you know, you're wrong," I said, shaking my head. I put the envelope and picture away in the shoebox and closed the lid.

Taylor watched me and then touched my cheek. I recoiled.

"Sorry," he said, pulling his hand back. His eyes gave away his frustration—not with me, but with himself.

"You'd be doing me a huge favor, and I'm willing to do almost anything to get to Eakins."

He sighed, unable to hide his disappointment. "You have priorities. I can appreciate that. God knows I've left plenty of girls behind because of what I wanted."

"Which was what?"

His mouth pulled to one side. "To be the hero."

"Look, I haven't been honest with you. I wish I had been, now that I know you."

"Now that you know me?" he repeated.

"I know it's in your nature, but I don't need you to save me. I just need a little help to save myself."

He breathed out a laugh and looked away. "Don't we all?" He swallowed and then nodded. "Okay then."

I sat up. "Okay what?"

"After my tour here, I'm going to take you back with me."

"Are you serious?" I sniffed.

The skin around his eyes tightened as he thought about what he was going to say. "If you promise to be careful. I don't want you to get hurt, and I don't want them to be hurt either. We can't show up and interrupt their lives."

"That's not what I want."

He stared at me and then dipped his head once, satisfied that I was telling the truth.

"Taylor"—I felt my eyes filling with tears again—"are you screwing with me? You're really going to let me come with you?"

He scanned over my face. "I have one more condition."

My face fell. Of course, there was a catch. This was the part where he was going to ask for sex. He'd already said he didn't want a relationship, and that was the only thing I had to offer.

"What?" I said through my teeth.

"I wanna hike Barr Trail up Pikes Peak. None of the guys will go up with me."

I puffed out a breath of relief. "Pikes Peak. That's your condition?"

He shrugged. "I know you've hiked it before. A few times."

"I'm probably one of the few locals who has."

"Exactly. Will you hike it with me?"

"Really?" I wrinkled my nose, dubious.

He looked around, confused. "Is that stupid?"

I shook my head. "No." I threw my arms around him and squeezed, pressing my cheek against his. His skin was soft, except for the stubbly parts. "It's perfectly reasonable."

His arms snaked around me, his muscles tense. "Not really. You don't know how much hell my brothers are going to give me for bringing a girl home—especially a girl I'm not fucking."

I pulled back, looking at him. "I'm the first girl you'll be bringing home?"

"Yeah," he said, frowning.

"We'll just tell them that we're friends. No big deal." I lay back against him, nestling into his side.

He pulled the blanket up and around me. "Yeah," he said with a sigh, "I'm going to end up punching one of my brothers over this."

"What? Like it'd be the first time?" I teased.

He poked me in the ribs, and I squealed. The sound made him cackle.

He quieted. "I'm sorry ... about what happened to you. And I'm sorry about Don. I tried. I saw the look on your face. I didn't want you to lose him."

"He was a good Papa," I said, leaning my head back against his shoulder.

CHAPTER NINE

"Nope. No more seats left on the Cog Rail," I said, glancing down at Taylor.

He was bent at the waist, grabbing his knees.

"Look," I said.

The peaks and valleys below us were spread out for miles under a blanket of green that turned bluish farther out. We were above the clouds. We were above everything.

Taylor took a swig from his canteen and then let it fall to his hip from the thick green strap hanging from his shoulder and across his chest. He pulled the black fleece pullover over his head that he'd had tied around his waist for most of the climb, and then he returned his Oakley sunglasses back over his eyes.

"It's gorgeous, but so was Lightning Point." He turned toward the building behind us. "There's a fucking gift shop up here? Really?" His breath was still labored, so he took another drink of water. "A gift shop and no way down."

"And a restaurant. I thought you interagency guys were supposed to be in shape?"

"I'm in shape," he said, standing a bit taller. "Almost thirteen miles of uphill rocky terrain, breathing thinner air, isn't part of my daily workout."

"Maybe you should quit smoking," I said, arching an eyebrow.

"Maybe you should start."

"It's bad for you."

"So is that energy bar full of high-fructose corn syrup and saturated fat you ate an hour ago."

I pointed at a gray-haired gentleman posing with his wife at the Summit Point sign. "He's not whining."

Taylor's face screwed into disgust. "He probably drove up here." He put his hands on his hips and took in the landscape. "Wow."

"Exactly," I said.

Both times that I'd hiked Barr Trail were with my parents, and we were some of the only locals who had hiked the Peak once, much less twice. My parents were always passionate about seizing opportunities, and failing to hike a famous trail that was practically in our backyard when hundreds of thousands would travel to experience it would have most certainly been a missed opportunity.

That was back when I had been their Falyn—the girl they felt died the night they'd found me in the bathroom, crouched and sweaty, praying for help I couldn't ask for. But the Falyn they had known didn't die. She never existed, and that was probably what was so hard for them to accept—that they'd never known me at all. Now, they never would.

Taylor and I ambled about the summit. People were talking, but it was quiet. There was too much space to fill with voices. Taylor took pictures of us with his cell phone, and then he asked the older couple we'd spoken about before to take our photo at the summit sign.

"You've got to get a cell phone," Taylor said. "Why not just get one of those pay-as-you-go phones?"

"I save all my money that doesn't go to bills."

"But think about all the pictures you've been missing out on." He held up his phone. "I'm holding these hostage."

I shrugged. "People have forgotten to use their memories. They look at life through the lens of a camera or the screen of a cell phone instead of remembering how it looks, how it smells"—I took a deep breath through my nose—"how it sounds"—my voice echoed over the smaller peaks below—"how it feels." I reached out to touch his upper arm.

Something familiar sparked in his eyes, and I pulled away, stuffing my hands in the front pouch of my hoodie.

"Those are the kinds of things I want to keep, not a photograph."

"When we're their age," Taylor said, gesturing to the older couple, "you'll be glad we have the photograph."

I tried not to smile. He probably didn't mean it the way it sounded to me.

Taylor kicked at my foot. "It was a good day. Thanks for riding my ass all the way up."

"I knew you could do it."

"I'm just glad I did it with you."

We locked eyes for an indeterminate amount of time. I knew I should look away, that it was awkward and weird that we were just staring at each other, yet I couldn't seem to find the desire to look at anything else.

He took a step. "Falyn?"

"Yeah?"

"Today wasn't just good. It might be my best day so far."

"Like … ever?"

He thought for a moment. "What if I said yes?"

I blinked, gripping the strap of my backpack. "We'd better head down."

Disappointment came over Taylor's face. "That's it? I tell you that you're my best day, and all you can say to me is, *Let's go?*"

I fidgeted. "Well … I didn't bring a tent. Did you?"

He stared at me in disbelief and then lifted up his hands, exasperated. "Maybe we can hitch a ride from the Summit House employees?"

I shook my head. "No, but we can hitch from there," I said, pointing toward the highway.

"Hitchhike?"

"Don't worry. I'll protect you."

Taylor chuckled as he followed me out to the road. We walked a good fifty yards with our thumbs out until a red minivan pulled over. The driver appeared, looking just as surprised as I felt.

"Corinne!" I said, recognizing Kirby's mother. "What are you doing up here?"

"Picking up Kostas," she said simply.

Kirby's teenage brother leaned forward, his eyes scanning me and then Taylor. The skin below the American flag bandana covering most of his forehead was smudged with dirt.

"Hi, Kostas," I said.

"Hey, Falyn." His eyes returned to the screen of the Nintendo 3DS in his hands, and he leaned back against his reclined seat, his dirty feet on the dash.

"We just need a ride to the trail head. His truck is parked there."

"Get in," Corinne insisted, waving us inside. "It's going to rain any minute!"

Taylor followed me into the back of the van.

The moment the tires were in motion, Corinne was full of questions. "Kirby told me you had a new friend." She looked at Taylor in the rearview mirror as if a wild animal were in her backseat. "She was kidding that he's a hotshot, right?"

"No," I said, clearing my throat.

The corners of Taylor's mouth turned up, but he managed to suppress a full smile.

Corinne targeted Taylor again and then looked forward, both hands on the wheel. "*Apapa*, Falyn," she scolded with a perfect Greek accent. "What would your mother say?" Her words were free of any accent at all.

"A lot probably."

Corinne clicked her tongue and shook her head in disapproval. "Where is he from?"

"Illinois," Taylor said.

Corinne was unhappy that he had addressed her, so her questions ceased. She slowed in the parking lot, and we directed her toward Taylor's truck. She twisted around to watch us exit the van, glaring at Taylor as if she were trying to cast some sort of Greek curse on him with her eyes.

"Thanks, Corinne," I said. "Bye, Kostas."

"Later," he said, still concentrating on his game.

Corinne pulled away, scowling at Taylor, until she decided it was time to watch the road.

Taylor pressed the keyless entry, and I pulled open the door and climbed in, waiting for him to slide in next to me.

"Who was she?" Taylor asked, peeling off his pullover. His T-shirt inched up as he did so, revealing two of his lower abs.

There has to be four more to go along with them and that gorgeous V leading down to his—

Stop.

"That would be Corinne," I said, blinking, "Kirby's mother."

"Was she speaking English?"

"She's Greek. Kirby's dad was Canadian, I think. Corinne wanted to name her Circe, after a Greek witch. The dad nixed it, thankfully. Kirby was the compromise."

"Way to stick to your guns, Canada. Where is he now?"

I shrugged. "All Kirby knows is that he was a hotshot." I left Taylor with that thought, saying nothing else.

We rode down most of the eight thousand feet from Pikes to the Springs in silence. Taylor turned onto Tejon Street before parking his black behemoth directly in front of Bucksaw's entrance. He climbed out, waiting for me to do the same. Just as my feet touched the asphalt, the sky opened up, and rain began to pour. We ran inside, laughing from exhaustion, surprise, and the embarrassment that had come from Corinne.

Our chuckling died down, an awkward silence becoming the uninvited third presence in the room.

"I'm not bullshitting you," Taylor said. "Is that what your deal is?"

"I don't have a deal. What are you talking about?"

"*Thank you, Taylor. You're my best day, too, Taylor. I'm hopelessly in love with your preciously sculpted abs, Taylor,*" he said, pulling up his shirt to reveal the best thing I'd seen in a while.

I pressed my lips together, stifling a smile. "Are you really still stuck on that? Are you going to cry? Do you need a hug?" I batted my eyelashes and jutted out my bottom lip. He didn't offer any reaction, so I gave in with a sigh. "It was a good day. I sincerely enjoyed every second of it."

"Wow. Don't hurt yourself, Ivy League."

I rolled my eyes and headed for the stairs.

"Hey, we're not finished," Taylor said.

"Then come up," I said.

He followed me, and by the time he had closed the loft door behind him, I was closing the bathroom door behind me.

"I'm going to wash the mountain off of me," I called.

"I'm next!"

Before my hair was fully wet, Taylor was pounding on the door. "Falyn?"

"Yeah?"

"My brother just texted me. He's in town."

"Which one?" I asked, ducking my head under the water.

"Does it matter?" he asked.

"I guess not."

"Tyler, third oldest," he said.

I could almost hear him smiling.

"He's at the hotel now."

"Did you not know he was coming?"

"No. We drop in on each other, unannounced, frequently. Wanna come?"

"To the hotel?"

"To Cowboys."

"Not really."

"Aw, c'mon. You had fun last time, didn't you?"

"I think I'll just stay here."

The door creaked as it opened, and I immediately grabbed the shower curtain, peeking out from behind it.

Taylor crossed his arms over his chest, his inked biceps looking even bigger from lying on top of his fists. "Can I come in? I hate talking to you through the door."

"Whatever."

He slumped his shoulders as he let his arms fall to his sides. "I want you to come. I want you to meet my brother."

"Why?"

He frowned. "What is the big deal? You're going to meet him eventually."

"Exactly."

"He's my roommate in Estes Park."

"So?"

"So ... nothing," he growled, exasperated. "Never mind." He opened the door, but he didn't leave. He slammed it shut and flipped around, a scowl on his face. "Quit it."

"Quit what? I'm just trying to take a shower!"

"Being so ... impervious."

"Impervious? That's a big word for you."

"Fuck off." He opened the door and slammed it behind him.

Not two seconds later, it opened again. "I'm sorry. I didn't mean that."

"Get out of my bathroom."

"Okay," he said. He was comically overwhelmed, looking back at me and at the same time reaching for the knob, missing a few times.

"Get out," I snapped.

"I'm ... going." He finally opened the door and closed it behind him.

I heard the front door slam.

I touched my fingers to my mouth, suppressing the giggle that was desperately attempting to bubble to the surface. I hadn't giggled in a very long time.

CHAPTER TEN

THE HAIR DRYER MADE A HIGH-PITCHED WHINE loud enough to cover the sounds of Kirby letting herself in. When I saw her standing in the bathroom doorway, I yelped.

She lifted her leg and cowered, her hair and hands covering her face. Once she recovered, she stood up, her fingers balled into fists at her sides. "Why are you screaming at me?"

I switched off the hair dryer. "Why are you sneaking into my bathroom?"

She rolled her eyes, smoothing her hair back. "I knocked."

"What are you doing here?" I said, exasperated.

She pointed to her apron. "I just got off work. I came to check on you."

"Phaedra checked on me half an hour ago. I'm fine," I said, turning to brush out the tangles in my hair. From the mirror, I watched her cross her arms, pouting.

"Gunnar's late again. You don't think he's messing around, do you?"

I turned to her, the brush still in my hand. "No. No way. He worships you."

She leaned against the doorjamb. "I know, but we all have our moments. And he's a guy." Her eyes widened with her last word.

"That's no excuse. But Gunnar doesn't need one. He's not cheating."

She looked at me from under her brow, accepting what she already knew. "Then why doesn't he call? Why doesn't he answer his phone?"

"Because he's driving."

"He can't even text?"

"No! Do you want him to come home, alive? You're being ridiculous," I said, turning back to the mirror. "When does he get his truck back?"

"Tomorrow."

"It's about time."

Kirby eyed my small makeup bag. "You going out?"

"I don't know. Taylor's brother is in town, and he wants me to go to Cowboys to meet them."

Her eyes lit up. "That's a good sign! I guess today went well then?"

"Mostly. We saw your mom at the top. She was picking up Kostas."

Kirby made a face. "He is obsessed with that trail. He thinks he's going to Macho Pikachu or whatever in Peru."

"Machu Picchu?" I asked.

She nodded.

"Maybe he will," I said.

"He needs to climb something bigger than Pikes Peak."

"Machu Picchu is almost half the size of Pikes Peak, Kirby."

"Stop acting like Phaedra! Did Mom give you a lift into town?"

"To the trail head. Taylor's truck was there. She doesn't like him."

"He's a hotshot. Of course not."

"She Greeked at me."

"Oh. She must have really not liked him."

"Why do *you* like him?" I asked.

Kirby shrugged. "Just because he's a hotshot doesn't mean he's like my father. Besides, it's hard to dislike someone because he chose a job to save things."

"Things," I said, amused.

"Trees. Homes. People."

"Should I worry that's what's going on here?"

Kirby wrinkled her nose. "He's, like, in his mid-twenties. You think he hasn't come across a damsel in distress before? That's not it. He just likes you."

I opened the cosmetic bag but only stared at the contents.

Blurring lines with Taylor was dangerous. He'd agreed to take me to Illinois. But when? So many things could go wrong between his promise and Eakins. He didn't want my truth now, but what if he required it later? What if there were more conditions?

What if I want more conditions?

Kirby smiled. "Are you wondering if he's worth putting on makeup for?"

I narrowed my eyes. "Get out of my head. I don't understand why he wants me to meet his brother. What purpose would it serve? What would it mean if I did?"

"You need to get out of your own head."

I considered that for a moment. Taylor had been behaving the opposite of what I'd expected from a hotshot, especially one who looked like him. He was all badassery and confidence until I threw him a curveball, and then he'd turned into Jim Carrey.

I had to cover my mouth to stop myself from laughing.

"What's so funny?"

I shook my head. "Taylor, earlier. It's nothing."

Anything more than a chuckle felt foreign in my throat, and Taylor had been the reason for two emotional outbursts. He had held me, made sure I was okay, made plans, and asked me to meet his brother.

For the first time in years, a guy hinting that he was interested in me didn't feel like a violation.

I rubbed on foundation and then ran the mascara wand over my lashes.

After some quick blush and lip gloss, I halfheartedly modeled for Kirby. "Good enough?"

I had made a decent effort at fixing my hair and makeup with the limited tools I had at my disposal, but I still seemed to look the same.

"You look hot. And he's hot. You would make beautiful babies."

My face fell, and I groused at my reflection in the mirror. I was a screwup. Assuming I was going to mess this up, too, was not unreasonable. Taylor had that something about him, more than just charm. He wasn't the asshole he tried to be—at least, not to me.

But is he worth the risk?

"Falyn, go. Stop overthinking it. You spent the entire day together, and you still want to see him. That's saying something, especially for you."

Thinking of the disappointment on his face, I grinned at Kirby. "You make a good point. Wait here for Gunnar."

"Are you sure?"

I grabbed my keys and trotted down the stairs, leaving Kirby alone in the loft.

The muffled music from Cowboys could be heard before I even made it out of the Bucksaw. My heart beat faster, knowing Taylor was less than a block away.

I pushed open the glass door, breathing in the night air. People were passing by in groups, already making their way toward the ridiculously long line snaking down the sidewalk. I wondered if I could slip by even though I wasn't with Taylor.

I sucked in a breath, nerves swirling in my stomach. Something bigger than just a night at Cowboys was about to happen.

CHAPTER ELEVEN

TEJON STREET WAS BUSIER THAN USUAL with both cars and people. Topless Jeeps full of families and young men and women were cruising up and down at negligible speeds, allowing the pedestrians to intermittently jaywalk to get to one destination or another.

Taylor was standing alone in front of the club, looking around with his hands shoved in his pockets.

"Hey," I said.

His eyes lit up. "Hey."

"Are you ready to go in? Or are you waiting on anyone else?" I asked.

He shook his head once, his eyes pouring over me. "Just you."

I arched an eyebrow and then gave the bouncer a nod. "Hey, Darren."

"Falyn," Darren said.

Taylor and I sailed through, not even expected to pay a cover. I wondered what Taylor had done or who he knew that he could bypass the line. He followed me to the same table we'd occupied before.

He looked at me differently, like we were meeting for the first time.

"Stop acting so surprised," I said.

"I'm not surprised at all." He glanced around the room, and then his eyes were back on me. "I'm just trying to figure you out. Want a drink?"

I shook my head.

He simply nodded, staying put.

"You're not going to get one?" I asked.

"Nope."

The air between us felt weird. He was a million miles away but acutely aware of me at the same time. Something was off.

"You know what? This was a bad idea. I'm going to go," I said, standing.

"What was a bad idea?" he asked.

"Coming here."

"Why? Are you bored already?"

"No. I don't know. I guess I'm just tired. It's been a long day." I sat, feeling drained.

"Yes, it has." He looked out on the dance floor and then to me. "I guess you're too tired to dance?"

Dancing with Taylor had been fun. Being in his arms again was tempting. But it had been too long since I hiked Barr Trail. My legs ached from my hip sockets to my toenails. I had done well with walking across the street and halfway down the block to Cowboys.

"I'm pretty tired. Aren't you?"

He thought about it. "I guess."

The guy who had been huffing and puffing at the summit of Pikes Peak this afternoon guessed he was tired? Why is he acting so strange?

"I've seen a lot of good-looking women in this town," he said.

"Congratulations," I deadpanned.

"But you're fucking gorgeous. Has anyone ever told you that?"

"Just you," I said, staring at him like he was nuts. "I forgot to mention I'm the pariah around here." The irony amused me. When we'd first met, I'd sought to stay away from him and his kind when, in reality, he would be more likely to get a bad reputation from hanging out with me.

"Huh?"

"Nothing. Contrary to popular belief, men don't flock to the town whore."

His face twisted to anger. "Who's called you a whore?"

"To my face? Just my parents."

He seemed taken aback by my answer. "That's crazy."

"I agree."

My reaction amused him.

"Any guy in this town not chasing you is an idiot."

"Why?" I asked. I wasn't sure what his angle was, but he was annoying me with his bizarre antics. "There is nothing about me that would justify that statement."

"Well, for one … look at you."

"You just said there are a lot of attractive women here, so I'm throwing a bullshit flag, a big bright yellow one."

"That, right there. Most women don't call bullshit. Most women are willing to forgive ninety-eight percent of it just to see if a guy who might be paying attention to them will turn out to be anything more."

"I'd love to see where you got that statistic. *GQ*?"

"Personal experience. You, however, don't let shit slide. I knew that the second you opened your mouth. You're more than just attractive. You aren't looking for someone, and you need no one. That's hot."

"You're ridiculous

He leaned in, staring at my lips. "What is ridiculous is the sudden urge I have to kiss that smart-ass mouth of yours."

"What?" I said, swallowing.

He took a few steps around the small table, stopping just inches from me. He was so tall that I had to lift my chin to look him in the eyes. Something had changed since the last time we were together. There was a hunger in his eyes, but it was absent of familiarity, lacking any emotion other than lust.

"I've gotta kiss you. Right now."

"Oh. Okay." The words were more absurd than the scenario, but I was so taken off guard by Taylor's behavior that they were the only things I could say.

I knew my mouth was hanging open a bit, but I couldn't snap it shut. I couldn't move. He inched closer to me, his eyes dropping from mine to my lips and then back again.

His hands slipped around my waist, pulling me to him without a second thought, strong and confident. I closed my eyes, waiting for him, unsure if he was hesitating as a request for permission or if silence was good enough. It wasn't until that instant when I realized I wanted Taylor to kiss me, but the moment didn't feel right, he didn't feel right, and that alone was enough disappointment to ruin everything we'd accomplished so far.

Taylor's lips were warm and soft, exactly like I'd imagined. His tongue was in total control, caressing the inside of my mouth. His hand touched my cheek, his thumb gently running along my jawline and down the side of my neck, but it didn't feel like before.

His mouth worked against mine—amazing, perfect—in a way that would make any woman beg for more. He was fucking me with his mouth before we were anywhere near a bedroom. He was telling me with each soft flick of his tongue that he didn't just want me but needed me. All the while, he was tugging at my clothes as if the kiss wasn't enough.

Nothing. I felt absolutely nothing.

The disenchantment was so overpowering, so disgusting, that I recoiled.

Taylor was still committed to the kiss, slow to recognize me pushing against his shoulders. I lowered my chin, pulling away from him. Then I saw Shea, the bartender, standing still behind the bar, watching us in utter confusion and disgust. Realizing I'd just proven my town-whore status after years of trying to buck the label, I did the only thing left to do. I shoved Taylor away and then slapped the shit out of him.

"What the fucking fuck?" I heard Taylor's voice yell, but he hadn't spoken.

"Holy ginger-licker!" Zeke said.

I turned toward Zeke's voice. Taylor was standing next to him. The other Taylor was less than a foot from my face, and in reaction, my upper body jerked back, nearly sending me off the stool to the floor.

Taylor Number Two rushed behind me, interrupting my fall backward. I yanked away from him. I looked from left to right, as if I were watching a tennis match, in total disbelief.

"Falyn," Taylor said through his teeth, "I see you've met my brother Tyler."

"Tyler?" I asked, wiping his lips from my mouth.

"My twin brother," Taylor clarified.

Tyler wasn't exactly happy either. "You know her?" he asked, rubbing the bright red handprint on his cheek.

"Yeah," Taylor said, taking a step toward his doppelgänger. "Tyler, meet Falyn."

The moment my name came out of Taylor's mouth, things began to happen very fast. Tyler looked at me, and Taylor swung, his fist catching his twin square on the same cheek I'd already assaulted. Both men fell to the ground, a blur of punching and grabbing.

Dalton and Zeke were happy to stand back and watch.

"Hey!" I yelled at Taylor's crew. "Make them stop!"

Dalton crossed his arms and shook his head. "I'm not jumping in between two Maddox brothers. I want to live."

A crowd began to form around us, and Darren rushed over. When recognition hit, a similar resignation softened his face.

"Darren!" I yelled. "Do your job!"

Darren's eyebrows shot up. "Have you seen these two fight?"

I shook my head.

"I have. They'll quit when they quit."

"When will that be?" I asked, not sure who was punching whom.

"All right! All right! You're gonna get us arrested, fuck nugget!"

The brothers stood up, bloody, their shirts ripped. I tried to remember what Tyler was wearing when I'd first seen him. I couldn't. They were both wearing T-shirts, one white and one blue. As they stood in front of me, I couldn't tell which one was my friend and which one I'd just kissed. It was unsettling.

I pushed past them, making my way to the exit.

"Falyn!"

A hand cupped my shoulder and whirled me around. There he was, my friend Taylor, in a blue T-shirt with red droplets around his collar and a split lip.

I sighed, touching a place near his eye that looked like carpet burn. "You okay?"

"Yes, I—"

"Awesome. I'm going home."

Taylor followed me outside, interrupting my getaway just a few feet away from the door. "Falyn, whoa. Stop!"

Reluctantly, I stopped.

"I'm sorry, okay? I had no idea that was going to happen."

I crossed my arms. "You have an identical twin brother. How was I supposed to know? You even have the same tattoos!"

"I told you that!"

"But you didn't tell me you also had the same face!"

His shoulders fell. "I know. I should have told you. If I'd known you were coming, I would have given you a heads-up, but ..."

"But what?"

"The twins thing. It's so stupid, and it's worse for us because we look so much alike. He's just my brother. We're not the same person. But when we're together, it's like we're starring in a freak show."

"Whatever. I'm going home."

"Falyn." When I didn't stop or turn around, he caught me by the wrist and pulled me against him. "Falyn."

I looked up at him. His features were so severe that they might even be frightening if I didn't know him better.

"It really fucking bothers me that my brother kissed you before I did."

"What makes you think I would ever let you kiss me?"

"You let Tyler kiss you." His expression softened. "You thought he was me, didn't you?"

I pulled away from him and crossed my arms, pissed that he was right.

"So ... do you still want me to kiss you?"

"If I can slap the shit out of you after, sure."

He thought about it for half a second. "I think it'd be worth it."

I pressed my lips together, trying not to smile. "I'm glad it wasn't you. It was disappointing."

"He's a bad kisser?" Taylor asked, amused.

"No. There was just ... nothing"—I referenced the space between us—"there."

"Huh. Now, I'm curious."

"I'm not kissing two brothers in one night."

Taylor looked down at his watch. "We are now four minutes into tomorrow."

"No."

I walked down to the street corner and pressed the crosswalk button. Taylor followed me, staying quiet until we reached the front door of the Bucksaw.

He chuckled as I turned the key in the lock.

"C'mon. Aren't you a little bit curious?" he asked.

"Nope."

"I am," he said, following me inside.

I shook my head. "I don't exist to satisfy your need for competition with your twin."

"That's not what this is."

"This isn't about you being jealous?" I asked, turning to face him. "It doesn't bother you that you'll be walking back to Cowboys, knowing he kissed me and you got the shaft? I don't want you to kiss me for rivalry or ego."

"Just to get you to Eakins, right?" As soon as the words came out of his mouth, he regretted them. He reached for me. His hand cupped my shoulder, and he brushed my bangs from my face. "I am a royal fucking skag. Sorry. I'm just pissed."

"I knew there would be conditions. I don't want anyone holding anything over my head. I left my parents, Taylor. I can walk away from you."

His brows pulled together. "Don't you think I know that?"

I sighed. "I want to go to Eakins, and I don't want something like petty jealousy getting in the way of that."

He took a step back, his expression changing. As if his anger was just barely contained, he kept his voice low and controlled as he said, "I'm not jealous. I fucking *hate* that his mouth was on yours. I've never felt that heated toward one of my brothers, ever, until tonight. I've been trying to play this off, but whatever this is … it's not petty, Falyn."

I shifted. "It was just a stupid kiss, Taylor. I was overly friendly because I mistook him for you, and it piqued his interest."

Taylor looked away, his jaw working under the skin. "I know it wasn't intentional. Doesn't make me feel any better." He sighed and then rubbed the back of his neck. "I'm gonna … I'm gonna go. You make me feel … not myself."

"Okay. Well, good night."

My casual demeanor only made Taylor more agitated, and he approached me, stopping a few feet away. "I know what I said before, but I like you."

"C'mon, Taylor. You barely know me."

He nodded, pensive. "Not for lack of trying." He backed away and pushed through the door.

The turn in conversation stunned me. In an effort not to screw up, I'd screwed up. My feet slogged toward the back until I heard a quiet low voice in the darkness.

"Hey," Chuck said from the last barstool. He took a drink from a beer can.

"Jesus!" I squealed. "That's the second time someone has scared the shit out of me today!"

"Sorry," he said simply.

"You okay?" I asked.

"Yep. Just had to meet a delivery truck running late. Finally got everything put away. You know how Phaedra is about order."

"Where is she?" I asked, knowing she would usually be at the café to help when a truck came after-hours.

"She's not feeling great. I think she's still shaken up about ole Don. His obituary was in the paper today. The funeral is on Monday. You should go."

"Are you guys going?"

He shook his head. "I'm not. Phaedra was hoping you'd go with her."

I brushed my bangs from my eyes. "Yeah. Yeah, I'll go."

"She's a little worried about you."

"Me?"

"Yeah, you. And now, I am, too. Is that boy bleeding from you or something else?"

I sighed and sat on the stool next to Chuck. The darkness and emptiness seemed to amplify our voices.

"He got into a fight with his brother. They're twins. His brother kissed me. I thought it was Taylor. Taylor punched him. The brother hit back. It's messed up."

"I gather."

"He's going to take me home with him sometime. To Eakins. I think."

Chuck crunched the empty can in his hand. "Does he know?"

"No," I said simply. When Chuck made a face, I raised my hands, palms out. "He doesn't want to know."

"Not that you'd tell him if he did."

"Probably not."

"Falyn—"

"I know. I know. He's going to figure it out eventually."

"That's not what I was going to say. If that's really what you want, Phaedra and I want to help."

I shook my head and stood. "No."

"Falyn," Chuck pleaded.

"We've talked about this. You've already done too much. You've given me a job and a place to live."

"You barely let us do that," he said, arching a brow.

"Thank you for even considering it. But Taylor is the plan."

"He seems like a good kid."

I nodded.

"And you're a good kid. I think he probably deserves to know what he's in for ... and you probably know that, too. I'm sure that's difficult since you've spent so much time not talking about it. But the fact remains the same. If he's going to take you out there, he should probably know to hold your hand."

I thought about that for a moment. "You're worried about him not knowing ... not for him, but for me."

"It's going to be a rough trip, kiddo."

"I hear what you're saying," I said. "I'll sleep on it."

Chuck pressed his lips together. "Good idea."

"Night." I trudged up the stairs. My legs felt like wet noodles, complaining every time I tried to move them.

I wondered if Taylor was as sore as I was. Tomorrow would be even worse—for more reasons than one.

CHAPTER TWELVE

THE END OF THE NEXT SHIFT approached quiet and slow, no low roar of conversations. The only voices breaking the silence were from employees and five customers.

"It's almost September," Phaedra said, scowling at the wet sidewalk and the raindrops streaking down the front windows. "Why in the frickity frack is it raining so much?"

Chuck shook his head. He was caught up with the entrees, having the rare opportunity to venture out into the dining area during dinner hours. "We need the rain, remember, honey?"

Phaedra sighed and headed for the back. "I'm going to make some pies. Kirby, go home."

Kirby huffed in defeat, pulling at her apron strings. "Good thing I have my car back." She grabbed her keys and purse before leaving out the front door.

I plodded behind the bar, looking for something to clean.

"Falyn?" Kirby called.

"Yeah?" As soon as I looked up, I swallowed back the rising panic.

Kirby was standing in front of her hostess podium with Taylor.

"Hey, Tay," I said.

Taylor laughed once, a dozen emotions scrolling over his face, none of them amusement. "Hey, Ivy League."

I noticed one strap over his shoulder. "What's with the backpack?"

He set the pack on a stool toward the center of the bar.

"I brought you something." After a short pause, he tugged on the zipper, pulled out a small white sack, and set it on the bar.

"A present?" I said, trying not to show my nervousness.

"Don't open it until I leave."

"Where are you going?"

"Not work."

"Oh."

"It's raining, Falyn. We're dragging up."

I made a face. "I don't speak hotshot. What does that mean?"

"There's enough moisture on the ground that the local guys can handle the area. I'm leaving."

"But ... you said you were here until October."

He shrugged, defeat on his face. "I can't stop the rain."

I stared at him, speechless. The passing rain clouds were becoming night clouds, darkening the sky.

"Don't give me any shit about your present, okay? For once in your life, don't be a huge pain in the ass."

"Whatever you say," I said, deflated.

"*Whatever* I say?" he said, blinking.

"I guess I'll see you around." I pulled the sack off the counter and put it behind the bar.

"Falyn—"

"It's fine," I said, inexplicably scrubbing the bar with a dry cloth.

He sighed. "We're not doing the stupid misunderstanding thing. I'm coming back. We're going to do what we said we'd do."

"Mmkay."

"Don't do that," he said, his shoulders falling.

I stopped scrubbing and painted on a smile. "If we do, great. If not, I'll figure it out. I'm not your responsibility."

He narrowed his eyes and zipped his backpack closed before slinging it over his shoulder. "You're going to miss me."

"Not at all."

"Yeah, you are. You're pissed because you're going to miss me like hell."

"No," I said, shaking my head and continuing to not clean the counter with the cloth in quick circles. "That would be a total waste of time."

"Stop being a hard-ass," he quipped. "I'm going to miss you, too."

My quick circles slowed.

"That's why I'm coming back next weekend to get you. To take you home. My home. To Eakins."

"What?" I looked up at him, my eyes instantly glossing over.

"I wanted to leave tomorrow, but Chuck said the funeral—"

"Next weekend?" Tears spilled over onto my cheeks in twin streams.

Taylor's expression changed from smug to desperation. "We can go tomorrow. I just thought—"

"No," I said, wiping my face. "No, next weekend is perfect. But"—I pointed at him—"don't promise."

He shook his head. "Fuck no, I'm not promising. I'll promise not to if you want."

I climbed over the counter and jumped on him, throwing my arms and legs around him. "Thank you!" I kissed his cheek. "Thank you."

Taylor chuckled, trying to cover his surprise. His hand settled on the back of my hair, and he pressed his cheek against mine. "I'll see you in a week."

I relaxed my grip on him, and he lowered me to the floor. Out of pure excitement, I slid my hands between his sides and his arms, and I clasped my fingers together, squeezing him. "You make it really hard not to get my hopes up."

"If I disappointed you, I think Phaedra would murder me—right after Chuck slit my throat."

I glanced over to Chuck, who was holding a knife to his own throat and pretending to slice it, not at all teasing.

Taylor leaned over after I released my hold on him, and he kissed my cheek before backing away. "There's a phone in that sack. My number's already in it. Text me your travel info, so I can book the tickets."

I quickly looked back at the bar. "Are you ..." My breath caught. "You're killing me."

"Don't call me Tay. Ever again. Or the deal's off."

I shook my head. "I won't even call you an asshole behind your back."

Reluctantly, he continued toward the door, adjusting the backpack. "Send nudes!" he called back, flashing the peace sign before pushing his way out to the sidewalk.

I looked to Chuck and Phaedra. "I don't even understand life right now. What is going on?"

I ran around the counter and scrambled for the sack before tearing the phone from beneath the layers of tissue paper. I was fairly certain the three bare asses on the wallpaper belonged to Taylor, Dalton, and Zeke even though all three men's faces were obscured as they were slightly bent while they mooned the camera. I choked back tears and covered my mouth.

"Who does that?" I asked to no one in particular. I looked to Phaedra, who had tears in her eyes, too. "I'm going. Next weekend, I'll be in Eakins."

"I'm happy for you, honey," Phaedra said, holding out her arms as she walked toward me. Squeezing me tight, she patted my back. "But if he follows through on his promise, there won't be enough of him left for Chuck to slice after I'm through with him."

She let go of me, and the phone in my hand buzzed. The name on the screen read, *TAYLORBEAST*. I swiped the screen over and read the text.

Stop missing me. It's embarrassing.

I shook my head and slid the phone into my apron. I would return it the moment we were back from Eakins, but his kindness was overwhelming.

For the rest of my shift, it was impossible not to be distracted by images of rolling into town and realizing my own atonement— from a respectable distance—without anyone being the wiser. I'd dreamed about it for so long, and knowing it was just a week away was almost unbearable.

Closing up might take twice as long without Kirby there to help, but we were so slow that I started well before Phaedra flipped the sign and locked the door.

I counted my tips and separated them out for Kirby, locking her portion in the cash register, and then I headed upstairs, waving to Pete and Hector as I passed.

Falling onto my couch, I pulled my new phone from my apron and held it in front of me with both hands. Taylor had sent more texts.

Well crap. Now I miss you. Thanks for being a bad influence.

What time do you get off?

Just text me when you're off.

Waiting sucks.

With my thumbs, I typed on the touch screen.

I hope you weren't driving.

Immediately, three dots appeared, having their own little dance party on the screen. *What the heck does that mean?* Then a message popped up.

Nah, I let Dalton drive.

Oh. It means he's typing.
I typed again, wondering if he could tell that I was replying.

Everyone home safe and sound then?

Yep.

I wasn't sure what to say after that. It had been a long time since I communicated with someone via a phone screen. I was out of practice.

The phone clunked against the coffee table when I set it down, and I decided on venturing out to the thrift store soon to see if they had phone cases. I'd never checked before. Maybe Kirby had an old one I could use.

The phone buzzed again.

What is your travel info?

You're booking now?

As good a time as any.

Are you sure?

Yep.

I typed in my full name and birth date.

Imogene? That's the worst middle name ever.

　　　　?

I can't spell that.

　　　　You just did.

Always making things difficult.

　　　　You can thank my mother for that. What's your middle name?

Dean.

　　　　Easy enough.

That's what all the girls say. Will book tonight.

I put the phone on the table again and then settled back against the couch, propping my legs on the throw pillow. I was getting text messages on a cell phone, and I was going to Eakins, Illinois, in a few days. My life had felt completely different before, and even though it was scary, I'd known it was for the best, and this felt the same.

The room was quiet with muted throbs of bass coming from Cowboys down the block. I thought of Taylor Dean two-stepping, hiking, watching VHS tapes, and doing laundry. I thought about how wonderful life could be if I could add closure to it all.

Just as I began to relax, someone pounded on the door. I jumped up and yanked the door open.

Gunnar stood in the hall, his face red and blotchy, his eyes glistening in the dim light.

My mouth fell open. "Whoa. Are you all right? Where's Kirby? How did you get in?"

"Kirby showed me where they keep the spare key. She won't talk to me, Falyn. I really messed up this time."

"What?"

I watched him as he passed by me and sat in the chair. He put his head in his hands, resting his elbows on his knees.

I closed the door behind me. "What happened?"

He shook his head. "She thinks I'm cheating on her. I tried to explain, but she won't listen to me."

I walked across the room, my arms crossed over my middle. He looked up at me, desperate. "Will you talk to her for me?"

"Sure—as soon as you tell me what's going on."

His eyes fell to the floor. "I lied to her."

"About what?"

"Why I'm always late. It's not because of traffic. I'm only taking ten hours, and I've been working evenings at the school for extra cash."

I shrugged, eyeing him. "Why didn't you just tell her?"

"She wouldn't like it."

"What's the job?"

"It's cash under the table. I'm helping a guy with maintenance on a building just off-campus—trash, lawn, paint, fixing things."

"Okay. Why did you keep that from Kirby?"

He swallowed. "Because it's for the Delta Gamma sorority house."

Unable to keep the laughter from barreling out of my mouth, I pinched my lips together with my fingers.

"I've dug a deep hole here, Falyn. I need your help."

"How am I going to help you? And since when does the UCCS sororities have houses?"

"It's in Boulder," he said, looking exhausted.

"You're driving an hour and a half to Boulder every day for work? Why?"

"Because it's half an hour from Denver, and I wanted to get a closer job for when we move. The opportunity came up, and I took it."

I chuckled. "I bet you did."

Kirby and I were close, but nothing I said would make her ignore the facts.

"It's not funny, Falyn. It's good money, but she's not going to believe me. Please, tell her. You know I love her. You know I wouldn't cheat on her. She knows it, too. She's just mad."

"She also knows you lied."

His shoulders sagged. "She's going to dump me over something stupid." He looked up at me with the most pitiful expression. "Please?"

"I'll talk to her, but I'm not going to promise you anything."

Gunnar nodded and stood before trudging to the door. He twisted the knob, opening the door just a few inches, before he turned to me. "I would never cheat on her, Falyn. She's the only girl I've ever loved."

"Now that, I believe."

He opened the door the rest of the way, revealing a wet-faced Kirby standing in the hall, holding a bottle of wine.

Gunnar's breath caught.

Kirby's bottom lip quivered.

"I just ... I didn't know what else to do," he said.

Kirby threw her arms around him, still holding the bottle. Gunnar lifted her off the floor to keep from bending so far down. He tightly held her, and she buried her face into the crook of his neck.

"You're so dumb!"

"I know," he said.

She leaned back to look him in the eyes and sniffed. "Don't ever lie to me again."

He shook his head. "I won't. This scared me straight."

She kissed his lips, holding the bottle out to me. "I brought this to share."

I grabbed it from her. "You're not old enough to drink."

"I was upset. I snuck it from my mom's cabinet."

She looked at Gunnar, and they practically mauled each other again.

"Take it somewhere else." I pushed Gunnar far enough into the hall, so I could shut the door.

I leaned against the side of the refrigerator and chuckled, looking down at the wine bottle in my hand. Even when they were annoying and dramatic, they were cute.

"Well," I said to no one, "at least I'll sleep well tonight." I was alone. It was safe to enjoy a glass or two.

I screwed off the lid and poured the white moscato into a glass, bringing the bottle with me to bed. It tasted exactly like a twelve-dollar bottle of wine should, too warm and too sweet, but it would do.

I finished off the glass within five minutes and poured another, filling it to the top this time.

Ten minutes later, that was gone, too, and I was pouring another.

So much for only two glasses.

I plugged the phone into the wall and set it on my nightstand, and then I stripped down to nothing before crawling into bed. One of the many good points about living alone was sleeping naked without a second thought. The sheets brushed against my skin as I spread out beneath them and relaxed onto my down pillow.

The phone buzzed on the surface of the nightstand, and I found myself scrambling to pick it up, giggling.

Can't sleep. Wishing I were still in the Springs.

I fought the urge to hold the phone to my chest. Watching Gunnar and Kirby's lovers' spat, followed by three glasses of wine in less than twenty minutes, made me feel oddly sentimental.

I can't either. Gunnar just left.

And Kirby?

Yes. They had a fight.

Young love.

I guess.

Don't be such a hard-ass. It happens.

To whom?

My brother Travis. He fell pretty hard last year. Now he's married before he's legal to drink.

How old is he?

Twenty.

So he was married at nineteen? Weird.

Not really. They're good together.

Oh, so you approve?

If they love each other, sure.

How do you know you love someone at nineteen?

You'll meet them next week. You'll see.

It's a date.

;)

I put away the phone and finished off my glass, feeling everything slowing down. Even my eyes were blinking slower. I stretched out my legs, letting the sheets glide over the tender parts of my skin. I glanced at the phone, grinned, and reached over. I tapped it a few times and held it away from me, waiting until a long tone filled the room.

"You're still up?" Taylor asked, his voice sounding tired but not sleepy.

"This phone buzzes every time you text me, and I'm lying here, naked, in bed," I said, hearing my words slur. "I have this urge to put it between my legs and hope you text me again." I knew how completely inappropriate I sounded, but I didn't give a single fuck.

For a full ten seconds ... there was silence.

"You don't think it'll work?" I asked, impatient for a response.

"Are you drunk?"

I pressed my lips together, attempting but failing to stifle a laugh. "Kirby might have brought a bottle of wine."

"I thought you didn't drink."

"I don't, but I'm alone, so why not?"

"Oh, so you don't drink in public."

"Or in private—if anyone is around."

"I'm conflicted," he said matter-of-factly. "It's tempting to let this play out. Then again, I know you'll hate yourself—and quite possibly me—tomorrow."

"I miss you already," I said, the smile vanishing from my face. "I tried not to like you."

"I knew it," he said, amused. He sighed. "I was a goner on day one. You're fucking mean, and it makes me absolutely crazy. But in a good way."

"I'm mean?" I asked, feeling tears burning my eyes.

"Yes, but ... shit. You're a sad drunk, aren't you? You shouldn't drink alone."

"I'm missing it, all of it," I said softly, touching my fingers to my mouth.

"Missing what?" he asked. "You know, my dad was messed up for a lot of years. He's made up for it. Sometimes, you have to forgive your parents. They don't have it figured out all the time either."

I shook my head, unable to answer.

"Falyn, go to sleep, babe. It's only going to get worse."

"How do you know?"

"My dad was a sad drunk, too."

I nodded even though he couldn't see me.

"Keep the phone to your ear. Lie down, and close your eyes. I'll stay with you until you fall asleep."

"Okay," I said, obeying.

He didn't speak again, but I could hear him breathing. I struggled to hang on to consciousness, if only to know how long he would stay, but it didn't take long for the heavy fuzzy feeling to pull me beneath the surface.

CHAPTER THIRTEEN

A TERRIBLE HANGOVER, Don's funeral, and the countdown to Eakins made the week one of the worst I'd had in a while. Taylor's intermittent texts were always a welcome highlight and helped me pass the time until the night before our flight, but the time in between was agony. He hadn't even mentioned my totally inappropriate late-night conversation, which I appreciated.

The night before our flight to Chicago, I found myself full of nervous energy. Taylor would be picking me up at five thirty a.m. to take me to the airport for our eight o'clock flight.

For the first time in five years, I wished my closet had more of a variety of clothes to choose from. I folded my favorite jeans and set them atop the rest of my things. As a freshman in college, even a weekend trip had called for at least a large rolling suitcase and a carry-on. Now, my things barely filled the rolling carry-on duffel I'd borrowed from Chuck.

Standing over the packed bag, I wrung my hands together, wondering how on earth I was going to fall asleep. It was already eleven o'clock. If I didn't go to sleep right then, I might as well just stay up.

I frowned. Exhaustion did not fit into my fantasy of how the weekend would go.

Someone knocked on the door, and I jumped.

"It's me," a deep voice said from the hall.

I rushed to the door and jerked it open.

Taylor was standing there with a wide grin on his face and a full backpack hanging from his shoulders. "I just figured I'd crash here. Is that all right?"

I threw my arms around him. Time reversed to the last moment we had been together, almost directly below where we now stood. Standing on my tiptoes and squeezing him a bit too tightly made everything a thousand times better. It was as if the last wretched week hadn't happened.

When we parted, he scanned me from head to toe. "I didn't anticipate you wearing that."

I looked down at the thin white tank top I was wearing, barely long enough to cover my navy panties. I tugged it down. "I was just getting ready to go to bed."

"Awesome. I'm bushed," he said, tossing his backpack to the floor. He closed the door behind him.

"I can't believe you're doing this for me. You don't know what this means."

"You've said that a lot this week, but you've yet to tell me why," he said, slipping his arms out from his jacket. He took off his ball cap and tossed it onto the counter.

"I'm working it out in my head. I'm not really sure how I'm going to pull it off."

"I'm not going to ask, but I have no idea how to prepare."

"You don't have to."

He cocked his head. "Whatever it is, Falyn, I want to be with you."

"You will be."

"If you say so," he said, sounding frustrated.

I couldn't blame him for being unhappy. He was doing me a huge favor while being left in the dark about what exactly it was. I hadn't said it out loud for more than five years, and being this close, I was afraid that if I did, I would jinx it.

We both looked around, a sudden awkwardness invading the room.

"Do you ... want some sheets for the couch?" I asked.

"I have a choice? Then you take the couch."

I smacked him on the arm and then shifted nervously. "It's got that, um"—I pointed, my finger making small circles—"that broken bar thing. It's a bitch to sleep on."

He raised an eyebrow, three lines deepening across his forehead. "I remember. So, I guess this means we're having a slumber party." He began walking toward my bedroom.

"Taylor?"

"Seriously, Ivy League, just tell me where to go. I'm fucking tired, and we've got a long day tomorrow."

I held out my hands and then let them fall back to my thighs. "Okay then. The bed. But that's not an invitation for anything else."

Passing him, I switched off the light and pulled back the covers. I crawled into bed, watching his bulky frame fill the doorway. He eyed me as I settled against the mattress, and then he crossed the room, standing next to the bed while he kicked off his Nikes and pulled his T-shirt over his head. His muscles stretched and strained while he unbuckled his brown leather belt and unbuttoned his jeans, and then he pushed them down over his backside and thighs, letting them drop to the floor.

As hard as I tried to seem unimpressed, Taylor was fully aware of the masterpiece that was his body. After all, he was the one who would spend hours in the gym each week to perfect it. Regardless, I wouldn't give him the satisfaction of staring. My facial expressions, my breathing, and my every movement were all at the forefront of my mind. I was wary of the rising level of lust I felt for the mostly naked man in front of me.

The tattoos on his arms extended over the hard slopes of his pec muscles, displaying thick black tribal art, flames, and a skull, all amazingly detailed with beautiful shading.

Not that I was looking.

Stop staring, Falyn.

Down to his gray boxer briefs, Taylor crawled into bed next to me. I turned away from him, feeling my cheeks heat to a bright pink. Without apology, he wrapped me in his arms and pulled me closer to him, my back warming instantly against his skin.

"I wish I could have gone with you to Don's funeral. I know it sucked."

"It was awful," I whispered. "I haven't cried that hard in a long time. I can't imagine how his family must have felt."

"You were family, too. You were the highlight of his day. You seem to be that for a lot of people."

"I'm glad you weren't there. I went through at least one box of tissues. It wasn't pretty."

He hugged me to him. "It gets easier, but it never goes away. It changes you forever."

"You've lost someone?" I asked.

"Let's go to sleep. I don't want to get into it tonight." He relaxed his grip, bent his arm under his head for extra support, and kept his other arm draped over my middle.

I rested my arm on his, lacing my fingers between his. He squeezed and then took a deep breath.

"Falyn?" he whispered.

"Yeah?"

"I know this weekend is important for you. But when we get back, I just want you to know that I don't want to be friends anymore."

My muscles tensed. "Like, you don't ever want to see me again? Or you want to be more than friends?"

"Considering I nearly went crazy from being away from you for less than a week … I think you know what I mean."

Relief washed over me. For the tiny moment that losing him was a possibility, my world had stopped for the second time in my life. Well-thought-out steps had been taken to keep myself from feeling that way, yet there I was, vulnerable.

"You did?" I asked.

"It was ridiculous."

"Is that a condition?"

"No. It's a non-promise." He leaned up, kissed my bare shoulder, and then lay down, melting into the mattress.

I had never slept in the same bed with someone before, not even as a child with my parents. Somehow, lying next to Taylor was the most normal thing in the world, as if it had always been and always would be.

"Good night," I whispered.

But he was already asleep.

"I got it," Taylor said, pulling my carry-on off the conveyor belt.

We had overslept and were running a little late, trying to get through security before they began boarding our flight.

I hopped on one foot to slip on a sandal and then dropped my other shoe on the floor, sliding the strap between my first and second toe and then pulling the back over my heel. Shoes and clothes from the thrift store were always wonderfully worn in. It wasn't the first time I appreciated not having to use the buckle on my three-seasons-old, half-size-too-big Steve Madden sandals.

Even though Taylor was in a rush to get to the gate, he watched me, a patient smile on his face.

"Ready?" he asked, holding out his hand.

I grabbed it. "Yes and no and yes. Stop asking me that. I'm trying to stay calm."

"Haven't you flown before?" he asked as we walked.

I shot him a look. "I've flown all over the world. My parents loved to travel."

"Oh, yeah? Like where?"

"Not Eakins."

He grimaced. "I'm trying to respect your privacy, but I'm getting more and more nervous about walking into this blind."

"For someone so nervous, you sure fell asleep fast."

He squeezed my hand. "You're comfortable."

"Sleeping with you wasn't as bad as I'd thought it would be."

He made a face. "Can't say I've ever heard that from a woman before."

I looked up at the four large screens secured to the ceiling. The flights were listed by city, alphabetically, with the corresponding gate number.

I pointed to the first screen. "Gate six. They're boarding now."

"Shit! Let's go!"

Taylor and I ran, heaving by the time we reached our gate. There was still a long line, but we were both so happy to have made it that we didn't care.

"Damn," Taylor said. "I'm glad this is a small airport. If we were in Denver, we would have been screwed."

After making it down the jetway and all the way back to row twenty, Taylor shoved our carry-ons into the overhead bin and collapsed next to me.

"Fucking hell, Ivy League," he said. "You stress me out."

"Which one of us overslept?"

"That would be me."

"Okay then." I let my head relax back and closed my eyes.

A warm hand slid under mine, and our fingers interlaced.

"Falyn?" Taylor whispered.

"Not yet," I said, looking over at him.

He was leaning his head back, too, his face turned toward me. "You had another nightmare last night."

"I did? Is that why you overslept?"

"What happened to you ... was it bad?"

"It was."

He grimaced. "Is going back going to hurt you?"

"Yes."

He breathed out a puff of air and looked forward. "Then why are we going?"

"Because it has to hurt before it can get better."

He looked back at me, his eyes falling to my lips. "I don't want you to hurt."

"I know," I said, squeezing his hand. "But you'll be with me, right?"

"For as long as you'll let me."

He let his head fall back against the seat. He was fidgeting. "I talked to Tyler. He said you were a fantastic kisser."

"Oh, yeah?" A smug grin curved my lips. "How did that go over?"

"I punched him again."

"Do you ever argue without your fists?"

"Not really. I ..." He looked at my mouth again. "I can't figure out why I can't stop thinking about you. From the moment I looked up from my menu at the Bucksaw, everything has been different."

"I've gathered that Maddox boys just aren't told no very often. You love the challenge. Even Tyler admitted to it."

He shook his head. "No, it's more than that. I saw something in your eyes, something familiar."

"Loss," I said simply.

Taylor blinked, and I turned away from him, pretending to pay attention to the flight attendants' safety instructions.

He shook his head, confused. "What makes you say that?"

"You'll see."

He sighed. "I guess I can't expect you to tell me your shit when I haven't told you mine."

The captain came over the PA system and instructed the flight attendants to prepare for takeoff. Taylor tightened his seat belt and squeezed my hand.

"You don't have to tell me," I said.

"I know," he replied. "But I want you to trust me. So, I'm going to trust you."

I swallowed down the absolute dread threatening to strangle me. There was no telling what he was about to say.

"My little brother Travis is in deep shit," he spoke close to my ear, whispering as softly as he could while still being heard over the noise of the plane. "He was involved in a fire a few months ago."

The plane surged forward, and the entire fuselage rattled until the front wheels left the ground. The wings shifted, and we drifted right, the blinding morning sun shining through our window. Taylor closed the shade and then looked to me for a reaction.

"Is he with the Forest Service, too?" I asked.

Taylor shook his head. "He's a college kid. My brothers and I used to fight all the time—with the locals and later with the college kids who would come to our parties and start fights. One night, Tyler beat this freshman, Adam's, ass at a frat party, and Adam approached him later about taking bets. From there, they started these floating underground fight rings at Eastern."

"Isn't that illegal?"

Taylor breathed out a laugh, amused. "Yes, very. But Adam organized the fights well. No one would know about them until an hour before the fight, sometimes less. We made a lot of money, and we never got caught. Our younger brother Trent fought a few times when he was a freshman, too, but our baby brother, Travis, was the rock star. He was unbeatable. Never lost a fight."

"He sounds lovely."

Taylor lifted his chin, his expression one of pride. "He's a badass."

"Is he okay?" I asked.

His smug smile vanished. "The fights were held in the basements of campus buildings where a lot of kids would be crammed underground. Adam set up a spring break fight. It was the last fight of the year. Travis was set to make a shit-ton of money. Something happened. A fire broke out. A lot of kids didn't make it out. Adam was arrested. I think Travis is being investigated."

"Why?" I asked, dubious.

"I have reason to believe they sent someone here to get information from me, but I can't confirm—at least, not yet. I know they think Travis had something to do with it."

"Who's they?" I asked.

He stared at the floor. "I'm not sure. The local police. Maybe the FBI."

"Did he?" I asked. "Have something to do with it?"

He shifted nervously. "He was getting married that night. In Vegas."

"So, that's why there'll be another wedding. Because they eloped."

Taylor nodded, watching me for a moment. "What if I asked you to come with me? To their vow renewal?"

I narrowed my eyes at him. "I'd say you were trying to change the subject. Just because I don't expect you to keep your promises doesn't mean you also get to lie to me."

He didn't take his eyes from mine. "I am. I'm lying to you. And I'll lie to anyone asking questions."

"You could go to jail."

"I could go to prison."

I pressed my lips together and then exhaled, letting the air fill my cheeks before it escaped. "You're testing me. You still think I'm a spy or something."

"I would go to prison for Travis. I just want you to know that if it came to that, we'd all go down for him, even his wife."

"I believe you. But I'm on your side."

Taylor's eyes fell to my lips, and he leaned in.

I closed my eyes, feeling the warmth of his breath on my face. I wanted nothing more than to let him envelop me like a blanket, feeling him against every inch of me.

"Maybe we should wait," I whispered against his mouth. "We're so close."

"Exactly," he said before pressing his lips against mine.

My lips parted, allowing his tongue to slip inside. Every nerve sizzled under my skin. Begging to be touched by him, my body reacted exactly the opposite of when Tyler had kissed me, when I'd felt nothing. There was no disappointment, no disenchantment. Taylor's soft lips and the way he tugged at me as if he couldn't stand being even an inch away from me another minute made me feel everything, all at once, and I wanted more.

A chime came over the PA system, bringing me back to reality, and Taylor pulled away, breathing hard.

"Sorry," he said, glancing at the people sitting across from us.

The two men seated across the aisle were shamelessly staring.
I sank back into my seat.

"You felt that, right?" Taylor said, keeping his voice low.

I looked up at him. "Promise you'll never do that again."

A grin slowly stretched across his face. "You have my word."

CHAPTER FOURTEEN

TAYLOR PULLED THE RENTAL we'd obtained at the airport into his father's drive. He'd talked most of the way—about his job, the places he'd traveled, his brothers, his cousin, and what he knew of Travis's new wife.

I barely noticed Taylor's father's house. My eyes were trained on the next plot over, the ranch-style brick home set a good thirty yards from the street, its long driveway empty.

Taylor and I had arrived around dinnertime. I watched the sun sinking all the way to the horizon instead of seeing its lights burning out behind a mountain peak. That struck me as a beautiful oddity.

"Home, sweet home," Taylor said, opening his door. "And there he is."

I tore my eyes away from the neighbor's house long enough to see an older gentleman stepping outside.

"Is that your dad?" I asked.

Taylor nodded, smiling at the stout white-haired man waving at us from the porch. It was then when I noticed Taylor had parked the rental behind a silver Toyota Camry, and a young couple stepped out from behind Taylor's father. The woman was holding a small black dog, and the man looked so much like Taylor that, for a moment, I wondered if he were his twin.

Taylor pulled our bags from the backseat, and then we made our way up the steps. He hugged his father and then whom I assumed to be his brother since they looked so much alike.

"Falyn, this is my dad, Jim Maddox."

Jim reached for my hand, and I took it.

"Nice to meet you," I said.

He had the kindest eyes I'd ever seen, next to Chuck and Phaedra. They were patient and a bit excited and curious, too.

"This is my brother Travis and my sister-in-law, Abby."

I shook Travis's hand and then Abby's. Her long caramel hair cascaded over her shoulders, much like mine. She was shorter than me, and Travis was taller than Taylor. Travis was smiling, happy simply to meet me, but Abby closely watched me, taking in every detail, likely wondering what was special about me that had led Taylor to bring me home.

"Well, it's getting late. Let's get you settled in," Jim said.

The screen door complained as he pulled it open, and I followed Taylor inside.

The home was well worn. The carpets looked a lot like mine, and the furniture was so old that each piece had its own story to tell. The hallway opened up into the kitchen with a set of stairs on the other side.

"You two can take Thomas's room," Jim said. "We'll see you back down here for dinner. Abby and Trav cooked."

Taylor arched a brow. "Should I be afraid?"

Abby batted at his arm.

"All right," Taylor said. "We'll put our stuff away and see you in a second. Where's Trent?"

"Chicken Joe's tonight," Jim said.

"He's still doing that, huh?" Taylor said, glancing at me for half a second.

"Just about once a week now," Jim said.

Travis and Abby left us for the kitchen, and Taylor took my hand, guiding me up the stairs and down another hall. He stopped at the last door on the right and twisted the knob, pushing through.

Taylor set the bag down on a loose board, making it creak and reveal itself beneath the carpet.

I hadn't stayed over with friends very often as a child, and leaving for college had been difficult. Moving in above the Bucksaw had been a relief but also stressful. I never did well in foreign places, but the disrepair and decades-old furniture and wallpaper felt like a place I could call home.

My palm fell flat against my forehead. "I can't believe I'm here. They're just next door."

"I can't believe you're here either," Taylor said, reverence in his voice.

The bedroom was decorated with plastic sports trophies, medals, old pictures, and a blanket of dust. The whole house smelled of dinner, stale smoke, and a hint of men's aftershave.

I took a step toward the wall, the setting sun glinting off a portrait of a very young Jim and Taylor's mother, Diane.

"Where is she?" I asked, turning to him. "Your mom."

Taylor rubbed the back of his neck. "She's … not here. She passed away when I was a kid."

My mouth fell open, and I snapped it shut. "Why haven't you told me?"

"It hasn't come up."

"It sure as hell has—at least twice. All that talk about trusting each other, and you failed to mention that you grew up without a mother?"

Taylor let his hand fall to his thigh. "I don't like to talk about it. It's kind of like the twin thing. People see me differently when they know."

"Who gives two fucks and a shit about someone who might think less of you because your mother died?"

He laughed once.

"I'm serious," I said. "You should have told me."

"Why?"

"Because we're friends."

He stared at me, hurt. "Really? We're going to hinge our friendship on sharing? Because I only have a vague idea of why you're here."

"Was it an accident?" I asked.

He shook his head. "Cancer."

"Jesus. That's awful."

He pointed at me. "That look on your face right now is why I didn't tell you." He began unpacking our things, pulling them out of the bags as if he hated them.

"You're lucky I didn't ask your dad where she was. I would never have forgiven you."

He sighed. "I didn't think about that. You're right. I'm sorry."

"You're forgiven."

"I should tell you one more thing," he said.

I braced for it, crossing my arms over my middle.

"My dad doesn't know what I do. He made us promise a long time ago that we wouldn't go into a line of work that could put us into danger. He was in law enforcement, and Mom asked him to give it up before she passed. It's kind of a pact we made with each other."

"So, you applied for a hotshot crew?" I asked in disbelief.

"No. While we're here, Tyler and I sell insurance."

I laughed, incredulous. "You're joking."

"No."

"What does Tyler do?"

"Forest Service, like me."

My mouth hung open. "He's a hotshot, too?"

"Yeah. He's usually on different shifts. Just don't mention it, okay? I don't want to upset Dad."

"You all have a pact to be safe, but your baby brother fought in an underground fight, and you and your twin fight wildfires. What is Thomas? A spy?"

"No, he's an ad exec in California. He's a type-A personality, always doing what he's supposed to do."

"At least one of you is."

He held out his hand. "We should probably go back down."

I stared at his outstretched fingers and then shook my head. "I don't want to give them the wrong idea."

A deep line formed between his brows, and his cheeks flushed red. "Give me a fucking break, Falyn. You're here. Can we stop playing the game?"

"What is that supposed to mean?"

He took a step toward me. "I'm done pretending that you didn't say what you said."

"What?" I squawked.

"On the phone the other night. Granted, you were drunk, but … this isn't just me. I'm not alone in this."

Taylor's family's laughter floated up the stairs and down the hall to where we stood.

"You're right," I said.

Taylor expectantly stared at me.

"We should go downstairs."

The scowl on his face made me wince. He opened the door, waiting for me to lead the way.

Travis was standing behind Abby at the stove, his arms wrapped around her, bending over to nuzzle her neck.

"Can I help with something?" I asked.

They both stopped their giggling and swaying back and forth long enough to look at me, making me regret the interruption.

With the fork in her hand, Abby pointed at a stack of brown glass plates. "If you'd like, you can set the table."

Taylor passed me and picked up the plates, gesturing with his head for me to follow. I grabbed the silverware and trailed behind him into the next room where Jim sat alone.

Taylor set a plate in front of his dad, and I placed Jim's knife and fork down. Abby hadn't set out spoons, but I didn't imagine a soup course would be served. Any home where I felt I belonged wouldn't have courses—or maids or life-changing selfish agendas.

Travis came in, positioning hot pads on the table, and Abby quickly followed, lowering a glass casserole dish with several juicy, heavily spiced pork chops. They were young but clearly in love, always sure to kiss or touch when they passed one another.

Taylor pulled out a chair next to Jim. "Have a seat."

The maroon fabric was stained and faded, but the cushion was nicely worn in, just like Taylor's family.

Jim pushed his glasses up the bridge of his nose. He smiled at me, the slightly swollen skin under his eyes pulling up.

When the bowls of mashed potatoes, white pepper gravy, and snap peas were on the table, Jim nodded. "Looks good, son."

"I got me a good one," Travis said, smiling at Abby.

"Yes, you did," Jim said, winking at his daughter-in-law.

Once Jim took a bite, I picked up my fork and dug in, not realizing the three bites of Taylor's sandwich I'd mooched on the way to Eakins hadn't been enough to tide me over like I thought.

"Oh God, this is good," I said, closing my eyes.

Phaedra was a good cook, and I always ate well at the Bucksaw, but eating from the same menu every day made someone else's home cooking feel like eating out.

"Do you cook?" Abby asked.

Her gray eyes pierced straight through mine into the deepest parts of me. I couldn't blame her for wanting to protect her family from anyone unworthy. They'd been through a lot, and any woman important enough to bring home deserved a thorough evaluation.

"Only some things. But what I cook, I cook well," I said.

"Like what?" She grinned sweetly as she chewed.

"Breakfast foods mostly."

"Does Taylor get up early enough for breakfast?" Travis teased.

"Shut up, asshole," Taylor grumbled.

"I don't know," I said.

Everyone looked at me.

"We're just friends," I added.

Abby's eyebrows shot up, and then she looked to Travis. "Oh."

"Baby," Travis said, "pass me the salt and pepper, would ya?"

Abby reached over and handed the small glass shakers to her husband. He seemed too young to be wearing a wedding band. They both did, yet those rings and their marriage seemed natural, as if they were always meant to love each other, working toward their forever.

"We were friends once," Travis said, unaffected.

Abby pressed her lips together, trying not to smile. "Not that I didn't fight it."

Travis shook his head while he chewed. "Christ, did she ever."

"I'm going to go out on a limb and say you enjoyed the chase," I said.

The room filled with laughter, deep tones from the Maddox boys and Abby's lighter cackles. It made me feel more at ease—the conversation, the laughter, the inflection of the back-and-forth. It felt like the dining area at the Bucksaw.

"So, you can relate?" she asked.

I stopped chewing, mid-bite.

Taylor looked at me, hope in his eyes.

When I didn't answer, he looked to his brother. "So, how did you guys get from there to now?" Taylor asked. "Just ... out of curiosity."

Travis and Abby traded knowing glances. Travis took a bite of pork chop, and Abby rested her chin on her hand, smiling at him, so in love.

"We didn't wait until we worked out our shit," Travis said after he swallowed. "Otherwise, I'd still be chasing her." He leaned over and kissed Abby's cheek. "And thank fuck that's over. Being with her and then without her felt a lot like dying slowly—with a little bit of crazy thrown in for good measure. You'll see."

Taylor shot me a quick side glance and then sawed at his pork chop.

Abby rolled her eyes. "It wasn't quite that bad."

Travis stopped chewing and looked at her. "It was exactly that bad."

Just as Abby reached out to touch her husband's cheek, the front door opened. We waited to see who had arrived, listening to footsteps padding down the hall along with the sounds coming from paper and plastic.

Another Maddox brother appeared, holding a brown sack. Below him stood a tiny girl holding small plastic sacks in each hand. Her platinum hair cascaded in soft waves over her miniature-sized peacoat. Her enormous bright green eyes targeted each one of us, one at a time.

"Olive!" Jim said. "How was Chicken Joe's?"

Bile rose in my throat, and my hands began to tremble. A thin sheen of sweat immediately formed on my skin. I felt like laughing and crying and cheering and collapsing all at once.

"It was good," she said in a voice that matched her small stature. "Cami couldn't come. Twent was 'posed to wash the dishes before we weft, but he fowgot. Cami will be mad, mad, mad."

I breathed out a quiet laugh. She was so articulate, and her sweet little voice made tears sting my eyes.

Taylor noticed my reaction and reached for my hand. "Hey," he whispered, "you okay?"

"She probably had to work, huh?" Travis asked, looking to Trenton.

"Always," Trenton said, readjusting the sack in his arms.

All the air was pushed from my lungs, and salty tears fell down my cheeks. I'd fought to keep my emotions under control for years, but I hadn't been prepared to see her in that moment. Her innocent voice rang in my ears. Of the hundreds of scenarios that had played in my head, Olive walking up behind me with Taylor's brother hadn't been one of them.

Whatever my expression was, Taylor seemed concerned, and he tightly held my hand.

Jim noticed, too, but he forced some small talk. "So, I guess you're not hungry."

"Hi, Olive," Abby said. "What's in the sacks?"

Olive's little legs rushed over to Abby, and she fumbled to open one of the sacks.

"Oh!" Abby said, her eyes bright as she looked back up at Olive. "Yummy! Your mom is going to strangle Trent!"

Travis leaned over to see inside the sack, and he chuckled. "That's a lot of candy, Olive."

"It's not all fow me," she said simply.

Trenton reached for Olive, summoning her back to his side. "We just swung by the store to pick up a few things you were out of, Dad. Liza is home. I'm going to drop off Olive, and then I'm heading to The Red to see Cami."

"Sounds good," Jim said, his fork poking around on his plate. "You guys still liking the apartment?"

"Domestic bliss," Trenton said with a wide grin.

He set the sack down in the kitchen and unloaded a few items. Then he led Olive down the hall by the hand. They were discussing something. He was looking down at her, and she up at him.

I realized I was still turned around, gripping the top edge of the back of the chair.

She was walking away. I felt sick.

"Falyn, are you okay?" Taylor asked, genuine concern in his voice.

I reached for the glass of water and took a gulp. "I think I'm just so tired from not sleeping much last night and then traveling today."

"Take the water with you," Jim said. "Flying dehydrates you. I never sleep well the night before a trip either."

I thanked Travis and Abby for dinner, and then I excused myself from the table, water glass in hand. Taking two stairs at a time, I rushed down the hall and pushed through the bedroom door, setting the glass on the dresser before crawling onto the mattress, curling into the fetal position.

No matter how much air I pulled into my lungs, it didn't seem like enough. My heart was buzzing like a hummingbird in my chest, and my head was spinning. I begged myself to pull it together, but the harder I tried to fight the overwhelmed, panicked feeling, the worse it became.

"Falyn?" Taylor said, slowly opening the door. He was appalled at the sight of me, and he set the plate of leftovers on the dresser by the door. "Christ, you're white as a sheet." He sat next to me, taking my water and brushing my bangs from my face.

"No wonder your parents didn't want you coming here. Whatever you're trying to do, you're not ready for it."

I shook my head.

"Take a drink," Taylor said, helping me up and then reaching for the glass on the dresser. He placed it in my hands.

I took a sip. "I'm okay," I said finally.

"No, goddamn it, you're not okay. This isn't okay."

I took another drink and then blew out a breath. "Really. This is stupid. I'm fine."

Taylor frowned. "In the beginning, I knew that if I let myself get too close, I was going to get burned. I'll be damned if you're not the one trying to keep me at arm's length."

"Maybe I'm the one saving you."

He shook his head. "Quit trying to push me away, Falyn. I'm not leaving. I'm going to stay here until I'm on fire."

"Stop," I said simply. "You need to stop."

His expression softened. "I can't. I've never needed anyone until I met you."

Our eyes met, but I had no words to offer. Taylor made me feel safe, the same feeling I imagined that Kirby felt when walking down a dark alley with Gunnar. It was the kind of safety you might feel with a superhero.

"I need you, too," I whispered.

"I know," he said, looking down.

"No. I don't mean, I need your help. I mean, you."

He looked up at me with hope in his eyes.

His protection didn't make me weak. It just reminded me that I was valued. I wasn't the worthless girl who lived in the reflection of my parents' eyes. Taylor was a hero, but that didn't mean he saw me as a victim. Someone who made you feel safe and strong at the same time could only be a good thing. That wasn't something a girl like me could ignore.

He nodded toward the door. "What was that about? Downstairs."

"I just wasn't prepared."

"For what?"

"For her. I'm okay now."

"You sure?" he asked, touching my knee.

"Why was Olive with Trent?" I asked.

Taylor shrugged. "He watches her sometimes for Shane and Liza."

"Your twenty-something brother, covered in tattoos, watches Olive? How did that come about?"

"Falyn—"

"Just," I snapped, "please answer."

"I'm ... not really sure. Trenton's a good guy. Shane and Trent get along. Since Olive's brother died ..."

"Austin. You can say his name."

Taylor shifted, uncomfortable. "Since Austin died, Shane and Liza have been seeing a therapist. They needed help to get through it, and with Olive to take care of, they were worried about being good parents. They go to therapy together, and then they have a date night twice a month."

"They couldn't find a nice high school girl to watch her?" I asked, my voice growing shrill with each question.

"Trenton would kill anyone who tried to hurt Olive. He'd take a bullet for her. Shane and Liza know that. They won't find a better sitter than Trent. It's weird, I know. But Trent's lost someone, too. Olive is his best friend."

"A little girl is your brother's best friend? You don't find that odd?"

"No, because I know my brother, and I know their story."

I took in a deep breath.

"Falyn, you're not going to go over there, are you? They don't know you're here, and I don't think you can handle it."

I shook my head.

Taylor was quiet for a while, and then he sighed. "You can tell me. My feelings won't change. Was it you?"

"Was it me what?"

"I don't know much about it. I mean ... I only know the little bit Dad and Trent told me. I know it was an accident. I know no one was arrested. I can see you wanting their forgiveness, but, Falyn ... they might not be ready to give it to you."

I didn't have a response.

"Are you the one who ... you know ... the one who hit Austin? Were you driving?"

My eyes filled with tears, and I looked down.

Taylor draped his arm across my shoulders, his hand cupping my upper arm and squeezing me to his side. "It's okay. It was an accident."

"It wasn't an accident," I said, wiping my eyes.

I looked up at Taylor, and his brown irises bounced from one of my eyes to the other.

He hesitated. "What do you mean?"

"It wasn't me. I didn't take their son, Taylor. I gave them my daughter."

CHAPTER FIFTEEN

TAYLOR RECOILED, pulling his hand away.

"You thought I was the one who hit and killed Olive's brother, Austin?" When he didn't speak, I continued, "Now, it makes sense when you mentioned earlier that I didn't drive."

"What the hell are you talking about?" he asked.

"I'm not here because of Austin. It's Olive."

He wrinkled his nose. "Olive?"

"My parents didn't want anyone to know about her because of my father's plans. My father was the mayor in Colorado Springs. He decided to run for governor of Colorado in the next election."

"So, this year," Taylor said, unhappy. "What does that have to do with Shane and Liza ... or Olive? I'm really fucking confused right now. You're saying a lot, but you're not telling me anything."

I wiped a tear that had escaped down my cheek. "She's ... mine."

Taylor stared at me as if I were on fire. "But she's, like ... a kindergartner." He shook his head. "How does no one know about this? I don't understand how you've kept it a secret all this time."

"My parents know. And Phaedra and Chuck know. A lot of people suspect. There've been rumors. A *lot* of rumors."

"Kirby?" he asked.

I shook my head.

"That's why your parents were horrified that I was from Eakins. They didn't want it to come out. They didn't want me to bring you here."

My bottom lip trembled. "They want me to pretend it never happened, that *she* never happened. They held college over my head, saying that if I didn't sign the papers, I would be throwing my life away. And then," I said, almost breathing the words, "I realized it didn't matter. None of it mattered. I'd already thrown my life away because she was gone."

He shook his head. "Falyn, I don't know what's going on here, but"—he cringed, already regretting his next words—"Olive wasn't adopted. She is Shane and Liza's daughter. There's been a mistake."

"You don't believe me?" I asked.

"It's just that ... this is weird as fuck. I mean, what are the odds? She ends up with a couple from Eakins, who live next door to my dad, and then you and I meet and become friends. I don't want to upset you, but this is wrong. I remember when Shane and Liza moved in. They have baby pictures of Olive on their walls, ones of Liza holding Olive in the hospital. They moved in next door when Olive was two. They've never mentioned that she was adopted."

"Exactly," I said, wiping my cheek again and pointing at him. "Exactly. It's too perfect. You and I were supposed to meet. This was supposed to happen."

Taylor's entire face contorted, and he stood. "You're serious. You're really telling me that Olive is your daughter?"

My mouth fell open. "Didn't you see her? Phaedra says she looks just like me. Think about Shane and Liza. Which one does Olive look like, Taylor?"

He thought about that for a moment, his eyes glued to the floor. "She does." He looked up at me. "Same eyes. Same hair. Same nose and lips. The chin is different."

I laughed once without humor. "She has her father's chin."

He blinked, trying to process what I had said. "But their pictures?"

"The pictures of Liza and Olive were taken right outside my hospital room. Go over there now, and look. Liza isn't wearing a hospital gown. I can promise you that. I can take you to the birth center at Saint Francis in the Springs. If the pictures show Olive as a newborn in a hospital, those pictures were taken there."

"It's not that I don't believe you," he said, rubbing the back of his neck. "It's just ... I brought you here. You want to interrupt those people's lives? I'm not okay with that."

I shook my head. "I wouldn't do that."

"You know how I feel about you. I mean, you have to know. I'm not sure there's anything I wouldn't do for you. That sounds pathetically inadequate when I say it out loud," he said, disgusted. "But this is ..." He looked away, his voice trailing off. "We can't do this to them."

"I agree," I said. "I don't want to do anything to them either."

He paused. "What is the plan, Falyn? I don't think Olive knows she's adopted. You're not going to ..."

"No. I just ..." I took a deep breath. "My parents made me believe I had no choice, and I've lived with the decision I made. I'll live with it forever, even now while sitting next door. I know she's already suffered loss. I don't want to turn her life upside down twice."

Taylor looked like he'd been punched in the gut. "They made you give her up?"

"I didn't tell them I was pregnant. I hid it until Blaire found me. I was on my bathroom floor, on all fours, soaked in sweat and trying not to push. I was barely eighteen."

The visual disturbed Taylor, and he shifted his weight, unsettled.

"My mother heard noises coming from my room. She found me and took me to the emergency room." I touched my fingers to my lips. "After Olive was born, I only had a few hours to decide. My parents said if I didn't give her away, I would lose everything. My entire life, I had planned on going to college, having a career, making my parents proud." I choked on my words. "A signature seemed like an easy solution. I didn't understand what I was giving up."

"How could your parents force that on you? That's fucking atrocious, Falyn."

The room grew quiet, and suddenly, it was too awkward to talk.

A sob was caught in my throat, and I swallowed it down. "I went away to college. It's easier to think when someone isn't in your ear all the time. I realized it wasn't what I wanted, but it was too late. I couldn't take Olive from her mother twice. I got sick not long after I started college. I thought it was the stress of everything. So, after a year at Dartmouth, I came home. That's when it happened. Blaire took me to the doctor, and they told me I had developed endometriosis. That was my punishment for what I had done."

Taylor shook his head, confused. "What does that mean?"

"I can't have any more kids."

His eyes fell to the floor as he thought about my words.

"I left my parents because I was surrounded by the things they'd promised, and I didn't want it ... any of it. I realized that anything I took from them was tarnished. It was all something I'd traded my own child for."

Taylor reached out for me, but I pulled away.

"I just wanted to see her," I said. "I can't raise her. I accept that. But I can still be in at least one of her memories. Some days, I think that's the only place where I want to exist."

Taylor shook his head. "No wonder."

"No wonder what?" I said, wiping my cheeks with my sleeve.

"Why you hate your parents so much."

"I hate myself more," I said, only just realizing this as I said the words aloud.

He clenched his jaw. "I can't imagine someone making me feel so alone that I would feel like I had to give up my child."

My eyes stared at nothing as I became lost in the memory. "I held her for just a few precious moments. Her entire body fit in my hands," I said, showing Taylor how tiny she was. "I cried more than she did. I already loved her, and I knew I would never see her again. William wouldn't come into the room. Blaire called him, but he stayed in the hall. He refused to even look at his grandchild, the thing threatening his entire campaign."

I laughed once. "A baby. She was just a baby. Blaire whispered in my ear as I held Olive, as I cried over her, careful not to let the nurses hear. She said, 'It's called sacrifice. It's the most loving thing you can do for her.' And maybe she was right. Olive has a good life with Shane and Liza."

"She does," Taylor said.

"I've made it on my own—from nothing. I could have taken care of her. It would have been hard, but she was mine, and I was hers." I sniffed. "I would have been a good mom."

"No," Taylor said. "You *are* a good mom."

I looked up at him, seeing him with a new perspective and seeing myself through his eyes. It was almost easy not to hate the woman he saw. He'd glued a few of my broken pieces back together in a few weeks. I'd been trying to do that for more than five years.

"You need to stop," I said.

"What?" he said, tense.

"I'm—" I bit my lip hard, punishing myself for my next words. "I'm a mess. I'm nothing, and I'm going nowhere."

Half of his mouth curled up into a smile. "You're with me, right? That's not nowhere."

"You don't want me. I'm a coward," I whispered. "I was more worried about material things than keeping my child."

"You're wrong. I want you more than anything I've ever wanted in my life."

I leaned my head into his chest. He pulled me against him, holding me, while my entire body rattled with overwhelming sobs. The harder I cried, the tighter he held me. He kissed my hair while whispering words of comfort, trying anything to make the pain stop.

"We're here, in Eakins. Somehow, we're going to fix this," he said as I quieted down.

I finally took a deep breath, letting my body melt into his embrace.

"I think it's pretty obvious that I don't just want you." He laughed once, nervous. "I can't stay away from you. That qualifies as need."

I looked up at him, managing a small smile. "You're just trying to be the hero again."

He wiped away a tear from under my eye with his thumb, and then he gently cupped my cheeks in both of his hands. "It's more than that." A line formed between his brows. "I have an idea what it is, but it scares the shit out of me to say it out loud."

I pressed my lips together, seeing the desperation in his eyes. "So, don't say it. Show me."

He slowly shook his head and looked down at my mouth. He inched closer, his breath skipping as he anticipated what was about to happen.

The air between us electrified. Every beat of my heart was banging so loud that I was sure he could hear it. I wanted nothing more than for him to hold me tighter, for us to be closer.

His fingers pressed into my skin as his lips barely grazed mine, but we both startled when someone knocked on the door.

"Falyn?" Abby called from the other side. "You okay? It sounded like you were crying."

Taylor's shoulders sagged, and he took a few steps to turn the doorknob.

Abby's concern was replaced by anger the instant she saw my face. "What the hell is going on?"

"She's okay," Taylor said.

Abby glared at him with accusing eyes. "She's bawling. She's not okay."

Taylor's eyebrows lifted, and he looked at everyone around him. "But it's not because of me. I'd let Travis beat the shit out of me before I made her cry like that."

"I'm okay," I said with an appreciative smile. "We're not fighting."

Travis made his presence known, stepping into the doorway next to his wife. "Since when does a Maddox not fight with his girl?"

Abby tried not to smile, and she nudged him in the ribs with her elbow.

"It's not like I trashed the room or anything," Taylor said.

I wasn't sure what he'd meant, but the mention wiped the smug grin off Travis's face.

Unable to let Taylor take the heat any longer, I spoke up, "We're talking about something else, something that happened a long time ago."

"Oh," Travis said, suddenly enlightened. "Past shit. We know all about past shit."

Abby narrowed her eyes at Taylor. "What did you say to her?"

"Nothing!" Taylor said, defensive.

Abby pointed at him. "You'd better not have brought her here just to make her cry, Taylor Dean!"

"I didn't!"

"What did you say?" Abby demanded.

"That I love her! Kind of." He paused and then turned to me.

My breath caught. "You … what? I'm pretty sure you didn't say anything close to that."

"Well, that's what I've been trying to say for a while," Taylor grumbled.

Abby's mouth fell open, and then she smiled.

Taylor ignored our audience and took a few steps until he was just inches away from me. He scanned my face with such adoration in his eyes that I began to tear up again.

"Don't cry," he said.

"Pussy," Travis said, hooking his arm around his wife.

Taylor took an offensive step toward his taller, younger brother, and Travis leaped back with an amused smile. I stood and gripped Taylor's T-shirt, holding him back. He didn't put up much of a fight.

Abby rolled her eyes. "Just let me know if you need back-up, Falyn. I will kick his ass from here to Sunday."

"Aw, c'mon, Abby," Taylor said. "I just told the girl I love her, and you're makin' me sound like a bag full of dicks."

"You are a bag full of dicks," Abby said. "Stop making her cry."

Taylor's mouth fell open, and then he slammed the door in their faces.

I wiped my eyes and sat on the end of the bed. "Was that for them?"

"Was what for them?"

"The whole I-love-you thing. Does that have something to do with you bringing a girl home you're not fucking?"

Taylor's shoulders sagged, and he knelt in front of me. "Jesus, Falyn, no."

"So … you love me," I said in disbelief.

"You're goddamn right I do," he said without hesitation. "I said, after this trip, we wouldn't be friends anymore." He noticed my expression. "What?"

"That's unfortunate for you."

"That's all you have to say?" he said, wounded.

"I'm a mess, Taylor. Inevitably—"

"You, Falyn, are fucking amazing. I've never been so proud to know someone in my life. And that's saying something. I have a lot of decorated heroes for friends. You were right about how this happened. We were supposed to meet. Just like we did. It can't all be a weird coincidence." His eyes met mine. "I know what you're thinking, but I'm not going to leave you, Falyn. And I'm not going to let you leave me."

"You don't know that."

"You don't have to say it back, but it's too late for me."

Holding back at that point—when Taylor was looking me in the eyes, confessing his feelings—was useless. But the very real fear of good-bye was just under the surface, waiting behind the hope of a happy ending. It had to be. Whether it was me who walked away or the ones I loved being ripped from my grasp, good-bye was nearly all I knew.

"I'm afraid I'll lose you if I say it out loud," I said, hoping my voice was too soft for fate to hear.

"So, you do," he said, surprised. "You love me."

I nodded, wary of his reaction.

He pulled me into his chest and hugged me tight, relieved. "I can't fucking believe it. I have never trusted in this kind of thing before, but it's hard to deny."

"Love?" I asked.

"Before I applied at Alpine, before Shane and Liza decided to adopt—is it crazy to say that this goes way back? That we go way back? Someone knew I'd need to hold your hand before I ever had one."

"That's kind of poetic."

"Roses are red," he began with a mischievous smile.

"Stop," I warned.

"Your eyes are green," he said, tackling me to the bed.

I giggled, not trying very hard at all to push him off of me.

"The most beautiful green I've ever seen."

He stopped tickling me, and I relaxed, breathing hard beneath him.

His smile vanished. "I love you," he said quietly.

"That's a terrible poem. It doesn't even rhyme."

"Yes, it does." He leaned down, touching his lips to mine.

His fingers cupped my jawline, and my lips instantly parted, eager for the same rush that I'd felt when he kissed me on the plane. But this time was different. This time, we were alone.

I gripped the bottom hem of his T-shirt and pulled upward. Taylor reached behind his neck and pulled it the rest of the way. I ran my fingers down his back, and he groaned. It had been years since I touched a man like this, and now that I was, my hands wanted to explore more of him. I reached down to the button of his jeans and unfastened it, the hardness behind his zipper begging to escape.

His mouth left mine and trailed down my neck. His hands lifted my shirt to access the bare skin of my chest and stomach until he was at my waistline. He slipped one hand beneath me, his fingers finding their way to my bra. With his fingers, he unsnapped the clasp, and with the other hand, he released the button of my jeans.

His confident, experienced movements only made me more excited for what would come next. Even though he was exploring my body for the first time, he knew exactly what to do and how to touch me. I had only had one lover, and this was so much better. Not only was the man above me in love with me—not just the idea of me—but by the look in his eyes, I knew he was about to make love to me, which would be something new to him, too.

Taylor pinched my zipper and pulled it toward him, sliding his tongue beneath the fabric. I sighed, feeling my insides tightening, pleading for him. He kissed just behind the metal button as he lowered the zipper, and then he pulled my jeans over my hips. His lips baptized my skin in a line of tiny kisses until he reached my ankles, and then he threw the denim to the floor.

Taylor took his time as he made his way back up, licking my inner thigh with the tip of his tongue. He enjoyed every stretch of my hips every time I writhed beneath him.

The pace at which he undressed me was wonderfully agonizing. He pulled my shirt over my head, and then he slid my bra straps over my shoulders before tossing the white silky fabric to the floor.

The mattress squeaked beneath us as he pushed up and away from me. He stood at the end of the bed, planning what he was going to do to me next, as he pushed his jeans to the floor and stepped out of them. He crawled back onto the bed, hovering above me.

Taylor touched his forehead to mine and sighed.

"What?" I whispered, leaning up to kiss the corner of his mouth.

He lowered himself against me, the only fabric stopping him from entering me was his Calvin Klein briefs and my embarrassingly unsexy cotton panties.

"You were crying fifteen minutes ago. I feel like I'm taking advantage. I'm okay if we just stay like this."

I slowly reached down between us, sliding my fingers down the ripples of his abdomen and beneath the elastic waistband to grip his girth. A low moan hummed in his throat as I tightened my hold and slowly pulled, letting his skin roll over his shaft.

"What if I say please?"

His breath caught, and his mouth slammed into mine, a visceral end to his marginal willpower.

My hands slid around to his backside and then down, his boxer briefs lowering with the movement. As soon as he was exposed, he pulled my panties to the side, touching his skin to mine.

I braced myself, and then I gasped as he slowly rocked his hips forward, working himself inside me. My fingers dug into his back, the mattress creaking in a slow rhythm with each gentle thrust.

Taylor bent down to taste my lips again, groaning in my mouth as he buried himself deep. I crossed my ankles behind him, letting him get closer, sink deeper.

Somewhere on the lower level, his family's intermittent laughter floated up, reminding us both to be quiet. Each time I needed to cry out, Taylor would cover my mouth with his. I wasn't sure how much time had passed, only conscious of the build within me and the push and pull as my body begged equally for more and for release. Taylor provided both, over and over, for hours into the night until I was completely consumed.

Every inch of me felt raw and relaxed as Taylor collapsed next to me, panting and smiling.

"Holy shit, woman. I thought I loved you before …"

I reached down until I found Taylor's fingers, letting them intertwine with mine. "As long as you love me after. Now, that would be something new."

He turned onto his side, propping his head with his hand. "Those aren't words I just throw around. I've never said that to anyone besides family."

"I've only said it to one person until now."

He shook his head. "Just one?"

I looked at the window, the glow from the streetlight outside pouring in. "Olive."

"No one else?"

"No," I said, looking back at him. I touched his cheek. "Just you."

The thought seemed comforting to him, and he relaxed.

My eyes closed, and while Taylor settled in beside me, I willingly let fatigue drag me down beneath the waves of unconsciousness. For the first time in a long time, I wasn't alone in the dark.

CHAPTER SIXTEEN

WAKING UP IN THOMAS'S OLD ROOM in Jim's house, I worried that Taylor would wake up at any moment, and awkwardness would set in. The sun had been up about as long as I had, but Taylor was still asleep next to me, breathing slow and deep.

Birds chirped outside, a perfect blue sky and a few electrical wires the only things visible through the window from where I lay on the bed. It was going to be one of the best days of my life. Whether Olive knew it or not, it was the day I would become a part of her memories, and I could carry that with me forever.

"Baby?" Taylor said. Tightening the arm that had been relaxed across my middle, he pulled me closer to him.

"Yes?" I said, taken off guard by the term of endearment. In my experience, those terms were only used when trying to keep up appearances.

"I'm not sure I can ever wake up without you again." His voice was sleepy but content.

I breathed out a laugh and nuzzled my nose against his neck. "You can."

"I don't want to."

"Estes Park is going to miss you."

"I guess so." He covered my cheek in kisses. "So, what's the plan today? I don't want to be an accomplice to kidnapping before breakfast."

I sighed. "I don't want her to know who I am or why I'm here. I just ... want to see her with my own eyes. This time, I'll be prepared, and I can savor the moment of when I leave a tiny footprint in her life even if I'll be the only one who knows."

"I'll know."

"I know it sounds selfish," I said, covering my eyes with my fingers.

Taylor lifted my chin with one hand, uncovering my eyes with the other. "It's probably the least selfish thing I've ever heard in my life. Olive is next door, and all you want is to be introduced as a stranger, so you can hold on to that moment while she goes on with her life."

I'd never thought of it that way. It sounded sad but honorable. Once again, the woman reflected in Taylor's eyes was someone worthy of forgiveness. No amount of gratitude could ever repay something like that.

"You're just saying that because you have to," I teased.

He smiled, but there was only sincerity in his eyes. "I'm saying it because it's true."

When I didn't respond, he looked down. The sudden change in his mood was disconcerting.

"What?" I asked.

"I want to ask you something even though the answer doesn't matter."

I waited.

"Where's Olive's father? Her biological father?"

I swallowed. "That's a long conversation."

"But you didn't love him?"

I shook my head. It was true. Even before I'd met Taylor, I knew appreciating the attention of an older man—a man who was supposed to be an authoritative figure—was not the same as love.

"Did he ... did he hurt you?" Taylor asked.

I shook my head again. "How important is it for you to know?"

Taylor thought about it for a moment. "I want to know."

I turned away from him. I didn't want to see his face. "He was my teacher, my coach, in high school. He's married. She knows he cheated but not that it was with a student. She doesn't know about Olive."

"Jesus, Falyn. He just left you to deal with it on your own?"

"No. He offered to pay for what he called a solution. I missed the appointment. And the one after that. I never thought he'd leave his wife for me. I never wanted him to. I still don't know why I did it."

"Because you were a kid. Because you had a shitty relationship with your father. There are a dozen excuses."

"There are no excuses. I made choices, and now, I'm living with them."

"But you don't have to live with them alone." Taylor wrapped his arms around me, holding me tight, and buried his face into my hair.

"After today, I'll be okay. I can let her go on my terms."

"Just tell me what you need from me—space, a listening ear, a shoulder to cry on, a hand to hold on to ..."

"Probably all of the above," I said, pulling his arms in toward me until he hugged me to him.

"Anything for you, baby."

I smiled, remembering him saying the same thing outside of the Bucksaw the day we met. Back then, even though it was for show, Taylor had made me feel safe. Now, it was reality, and he was still somehow making everything all right.

"Taylor!" Jim yelled from below. "Breakfast!"

Taylor stood, and he dressed in a T-shirt and jeans before pulling a royal-blue ball cap low over his eyes. "You ready? We're going to kick this day's ass."

After a quick shower, I put on my favorite jeans and a pink blouse I'd specially purchased at the ARC Thrift Store for the day I would meet my daughter again. I wanted her memory of me, however fleeting, to be perfect.

Taylor went downstairs, and I spent a little extra time on my hair and makeup. Then I joined Taylor and Jim at the table. Jim was nearly finished with his breakfast when Trenton knocked twice and swung open the front door, announcing his arrival.

"Good morning, Maddoxes!" Trenton paused to acknowledge me. "And friend." He went into the kitchen where dishes scraped, cabinet doors and drawers slammed, and the refrigerator opened and closed.

"Enough with the friend shit," Taylor said.

Trenton beamed as he sat in a dining chair between his father and brother with a bowl of cereal. "Oh, yeah? Did you seal the deal last night? Trav said you made her cry."

Jim smacked the back of Trenton's head. "Trenton Allen!"

"Ow! What'd I say?" Trenton rubbed the back of his head.

Jim sipped his coffee, trying to smooth the annoyed expression from his face. "Are you feeling better, Falyn?"

"Much. Thank you."

"What's the plan today, Taylor?" Jim asked.

Taylor shrugged, looking to his brother. "What are your plans today, dickhead?"

Jim sighed. "Goddamn it! Can't we have one meal without the language?"

The brothers shook their heads. Jim did, too.

Trenton's spoon raked against his bowl of cereal. "Work."

"Are you babysitting today?" Taylor asked.

Trenton seemed confused. "No. Why?"

Taylor shrugged. "Olive's freaking adorable, and I never get to see her anymore."

Trenton shoveled a bite of Frosted Flakes into his mouth, considering Taylor's comment. "I could ask her if she wants to go to the park, if you're really hell-bent on spending the morning with a five-year-old. I have to be at work later though."

"Six," I said.

Trenton blinked.

"She's six now."

"Right," Trenton said. "She just had a birthday last week. It's going to take me a while to get used to that."

"The park sounds fun," Jim said, eyeing me.

I wasn't sure what he thought he knew, but he was onto us.

"You seem to enjoy spending time with her," I said.

Trenton grinned. "She's a cool little kid." He stood, pulled his cell phone from his pocket, and dialed a number.

"Hey, Trenton," Taylor began, but someone had already picked up the other line.

"Shane," Trenton said. "What's up, buttercup? No. Yeah. Yeah. What's Ew doing today?"

I looked at Taylor and mouthed the word, *Ew?*

Taylor shrugged, unsure of the answer.

Trenton nodded. "Yeah, my brother's in town with his girlfriend. Taylor. Nope, he's still selling insurance. They both are. Up in Colorado. Pussies." He shot a smug grin at his older brother.

Taylor wasn't amused.

Trenton continued his conversation with Shane, "You wanna meet us at the park? Or do you have something going on?"

As Trenton listened to Shane's response, my stomach sank. Shane and Liza would recognize me. If they came to the park, I wasn't sure how they would react that I'd shown up unannounced. "Okay, that's cool. Later." Trenton set his phone on the table. "Shane's at work, and Olive is at home with Liza. He'll call Liza, and he said we could go pick Olive up in twenty."

"Sounds good," Taylor said. "Is Bagby Park still her favorite?"

Trenton smiled. "Yeah."

"All right. I'm going to pick up some smokes, and we'll meet you there."

"Hey," Trenton said, suddenly serious, "no smoking around Olive."

"I know, fuckstick. See you in a bit. See you later, Dad."

Taylor and I stood, and Jim waved good-bye. We walked outside to the car, fingers intertwined. It wasn't the first time Taylor had reached for me, but this felt different. He wasn't just holding my hand. He was offering to be a witness to the day I'd change my future and my past.

I pulled the seat belt across my chest, watching as Taylor twisted the key in the ignition.

"Did you bring your phone?" he asked.

"No. Why?"

"Because you're going to want to take pictures. That's okay. You can use mine."

I shook my head. "No. No pictures. Just memories."

"You sure?" he asked.

I nodded and took a deep breath as Taylor backed out of the drive.

We stopped at the convenience store at the end of the road. Taylor hurried in, bought two packs of cigarettes, and rushed out with them in hand.

I made a face.

He pleaded with his eyes. "I guarantee you, tonight's poker night."

"So, you're going to smoke both packs?"

"Maybe."

I wrinkled my nose, and he chuckled. He kissed my hand before pulling out onto the road and heading for the park.

The drive to Bagby Park was a short trip, just two miles away. Taylor pulled into the small gravel parking area, and I pushed out the door, feeling the small rocks crunch under my feet until I reached the grass.

"Damn, I haven't been on one of those in a while!" Taylor said, pulling me to the seesaw. He straddled one end, waiting for me to sit on the other.

"Don't buck me off this thing. I don't want to waste the day in the ER instead of spending it with Olive."

His expression was one of disappointment, but then he laughed. "You know me too well. Glad there is at least one adult in this relationship."

"Oh, it's a relationship?" I asked.

That caught Taylor off guard. "Um ... well ... yeah. Aren't we?"

"I still have until Monday. You said we were friends until after the weekend."

He arched an eyebrow, unimpressed. "I don't do to my friends the things I did to you last night. Our friendship is officially over."

He sat down, letting his weight take him to the ground as my feet left the grass.

"Fair enough," I said, coming back down to earth.

A slow grin crept across Taylor's face until he was beaming with victory. He popped a cigarette into his mouth. "Holy fuck. Dad said it would happen, but I never believed him."

"What?" I asked.

"I am a one-woman man."

A shoddy red Dodge Intrepid parked next to our rental, and the driver's side door flew open, revealing Trenton. He jogged around the front and opened the passenger side, reaching into the backseat and then plopping a small platinum beauty onto her feet.

My heart leaped the moment Trenton stepped aside, and her angelic face came into view. Liza had braided her hair to the side, and she wore a pair of Mary Janes with thick rubber soles, pretty but also functional for a playdate with Trenton at the park.

She took off at full speed toward the playground, breezing past us as she made a beeline for the swings. I walked with Taylor and Trenton to the nearest bench, and I watched her situate herself. In her sweet tiny voice, she called for Trenton to push her, and tears stung my eyes. The day I had been waiting for was here.

"I'll do it," I said, jumping up.

"Oh," Trenton said. "Okay."

"Is that okay?" I asked Olive.

She nodded her head.

"How high?" I asked as I pulled back on the chains before releasing her.

"High!" she squealed.

I pushed her once and then again.

"Highew!" She giggled.

"That's good," Trenton called. "She says higher, but then she gets scared."

"Do not!" Olive said.

I pushed her, careful to push her enough only to keep her happy. I looked past her to Taylor, who was watching us like a proud father.

Olive let me push her for another ten minutes, and then she asked me to swing with her, so I climbed into the swing next to her. Once I got myself going, she reached out for my hand. We swung back and forth together, giggling at nothing and everything.

She threw back her head, the most wonderful laugh flitting through the air. The whole world fell away, and in that moment, it was just her and me, making the memory I'd dreamed of since she was born.

"Slide!" Olive jumped off the swing to the ground, her little feet already in motion.

Together, we climbed up the ladder, and then I followed her across the bridge to the double slide. We sat side by side, and I looked over at my daughter, her face almost identical to so many of my childhood photographs. Olive pushed off, and I did, too. Our feet hit the ground at the same time. Our eyes met, and we raced around again.

As the hour passed, I chased Olive around the playground, and a peace came over me that I had never felt before. She was happy, and even though I had missed it all, we had that perfect little moment of time, one of just her and me that would hide away in her memory.

All too soon though, Trenton called for her, "Ew! Your mom's home from the store! Time to go."

"Aw!" she groaned. She looked up at me. "Want to come to my house and pway?"

"I wish I could," I said. "I loved spending time with you."

She opened her arms wide, waiting for me. I bent down and gently held her, feeling the strands of her hair in my face and her pudgy little fingers pressing into my shoulders.

"Nice to meet you," Olive said, waving good-bye.

Trenton swept her up into his arms and carried her to the car.

"Bye, wady!"

I tried not to cry as Trenton buckled her in, saving my tears until he pulled away.

"That was the most beautiful thing I've ever seen," Taylor said. "Was it what you wanted?"

All I could do was nod, and then I sat down on the bench, holding myself upright by gripping the edge of my seat.

Taylor sat next to me. He looked upon me with more love and understanding than I'd ever felt. All the while, I let the peace of closure set in. I took a breath and let six years of pain, anger, and shame leave my body as I exhaled.

"Falyn?" he said, his voice thick with worry.

A single tear trickled down my cheek as I looked over at him with a small smile. "She's happy," I said simply. "And I'm happy. I'm not sure what I expected, but this is so much more. I'll never be able to thank you enough."

He brought my hand to his lips. "The look on your face right now? That's all I need."

I threw my arms around him, and he tightly squeezed me.

"Will you tell him?" I asked.

"Trent? No. Today was for you and Olive to make a memory, and then let the rest go."

I released him and then leaned against his shoulder. "I like that."

"I plan to do a lot of things that you'll like. But first, I'm going to sit here with you for as long as you need. Don't feel rushed."

I sighed and hugged his arm, memorizing the playground and the small wooded area about fifty yards behind it. The birds were singing as a slight breeze blew the fallen leaves around on the ground.

"It's perfect," I said.

"Ten minutes ago, watching you and her ... I wish I could have frozen that moment, so we could live in it forever."

"We can. We can live here in Olive's memory. Maybe every time she visits this park, she'll remember our time together."

"I bet she will."

I let my temple relax against his shoulder. "I don't feel rushed. My heart doesn't have room for anything else but you, her, and happiness."

CHAPTER SEVENTEEN

Taylor jumped out of bed just before the sun came up, fumbling around my bedroom and cursing in the dark while trying to find his clothes. Rolling onto my side, I leaned up on my elbow, propping my head with my hand, as I tried to suppress a laugh.

"It's not funny, baby," he said, hopping as he pulled on his jeans. "I'm going to hit Denver traffic if I don't leave in two minutes, and that will make me late for work!"

"Maybe you shouldn't surprise me the night before your shift then?"

He leaped into the bed, and I squealed.

He planted a peck on my lips. "Don't even pretend you weren't fucking ecstatic."

"I was." I leaned up to kiss him again. "Thanks again for dinner ... and the movie ... and everything after that."

With hesitation and regret, he pushed off the bed and away from me to finish getting dressed. He pulled on his boots and then grabbed his phone and his keys. "Call me when you wake up."

"I'm kind of awake."

His frown was barely highlighted from the streetlight outside my bedroom window. "I'm sorry."

"It's okay. Go," I said, glancing outside. "It's snowing. Be careful."

He made a face. "I will kick that snow's ass." He bent down to kiss me once more, but it ended up being three more. He shook his head. "Fuck! I'm gonna miss you. I'm sick of missing you."

"Go to work," I said, touching his cheek.

"I'm going. Call me later!" He hurried out the door, his heavy boots knocking against every step on his way down.

I lay on my back, blowing out a frustrated sigh. I was sick of missing him, too, but we had just returned from Christmas in Eakins and celebrated the New Year and Taylor's and Tyler's birthdays together at their fire station in Estes Park. It was only seven weeks before Travis and Abby's vow renewal in St. Thomas, and then Taylor would be back in Colorado Springs. I hoped. It wasn't that I wished for wildfires, but that was the only thing that would bring Taylor to town.

I relaxed in bed and played on my phone for half an hour and then decided to take a shower, dress for work, and head downstairs. Pete was pulling out ingredients for prep, and I sat on the far counter, watching him work.

"Good morning," I said, letting my legs swing.

Pete dipped his head.

"He spent the night again. I think … I think I love him—like, *really* love him," I said, my eyes widening for emphasis. "I thought I loved him before, but I think that was just the falling part. Every week that passes, I think, *Yep. I love him way more. Maybe I didn't love him before now? Maybe this is love.*"

Pete shrugged.

"Do you have a date for Valentine's Day?"

He frowned and shook his head.

"You should. You're a good guy."

He winked at me and continued working.

"Good morning!" Chuck said, pushing through the swinging doors. "I haven't seen you down here this early in a while, Falyn."

I shrugged. "Couldn't go back to sleep after Taylor left."

Phaedra pulled the small leather pack she used as a purse off one shoulder and shoved it into a bottom cabinet. She brushed her wiry low ponytail off her shoulder. "How was dinner?"

I hopped off the counter. "Amazing, as usual."

"Are you going to up and leave us for Estes Park?"

I shrugged. "He's mentioned it. I said no."

"No?" Phaedra looked to Chuck.

Chuck tied his apron strings behind his back. "He could apply at one of the stations here. If they have a spot open, they'd hire him."

"They don't," I said. "He put a call in a couple of weeks ago."

"Well, he should apply anyway," Phaedra said with her gravelly voice.

"He might."

"He might? He might be the one then, huh?" Chuck asked.

Three pairs of eyes targeted me.

I rolled my eyes. "It's too early in the morning and too early in the relationship to be talking about that nonsense." I picked up a tray and pushed through the double doors. I loaded it with salt and pepper shakers and then brought it back to unscrew the tops.

Phaedra started several pots of coffee, powered on the register, and counted the drawer. She watched me return the full shakers to the tables. Hector arrived as the sun chased the shadows from Tejon Street, and he and Chuck were cracking jokes in the back, being so silly that even Pete was laughing out loud. By the time Kirby arrived, I had everything ready. Every employee at The Bucksaw Café was officially in a good mood.

The morning sun reflected off the white snow piled up on each side of the sidewalk, shining uncomfortably bright even through the transparent solar shades Phaedra had installed specifically to cut down on the glare. In spite of the intense light pouring in, a peaceful feeling seemed to have settled over everyone in the building—or maybe it had always been there, and I was finally free enough to feel it.

"I like it when Taylor stays over," Kirby said, tying on her apron. "He makes my life a lot easier."

"How's Gunnar?" I asked.

"Stressed. He took too many hours this semester, and he's still driving to Boulder, working for the sorority house, which—I have to admit—is a good job for him. His boss works with Gunnar's school schedule, and the girls treat him like a little brother—or so he says."

Just before Phaedra flipped over the sign to show we were open, my cell phone buzzed.

Made it. On time. Love you.

I breathed a sigh of relief. "He made it okay."

"Oh, that's good," Kirby said. "That's not the best drive when it's snowing."

"That doesn't help."

"Sorry," she said. She greeted and then seated the first customers of the day.

I responded to Taylor's text and then slid my phone into my apron before walking over to a table with glasses of water. Tourists—an older gentleman and his white-haired wife—settled in at Don's favorite table. Chuck had had a small plaque made, and Phaedra had replaced the beat-up, rusted Alaska license plate that hung above where Don used to sit. I glanced up at the words engraved in the gold plating.

THIS TABLE IS DEDICATED IN LOVING MEMORY OF

DONALD McGENSEY

The gentleman removed his hat and propped his cane against the wall.

"My name is Falyn, and I'll be your server this morning. May I get you a cup of coffee to start?"

"Yes," he said, opening the menu Kirby had set in front of him. "Half-and-half, please."

"The same," his wife said.

"You got it." I returned to the drink station, pouring them fresh cups of coffee.

Kirby strolled from her podium and around the bar to where I stood. "You have a look."

"What kind of look?"

"A happy look. More than happy. Things seem to be going well with Taylor."

"Yes."

"I have to say, I'm a little surprised that you even gave him a chance. You haven't given any hotshot the time of day since I met you."

"He's different."

"He must be because those are the famous last words of every girl left behind around here, and I would never have thought I'd hear you say them."

"That's not funny," I said.

"Leave her be," Phaedra said, shooing Kirby away.

Kirby offered a cease-fire with a wink, leaving me for her station.

"She's just teasing you," Phaedra said. "We all know that Taylor is one of the good ones."

I loaded the saucers with coffee cups and silver creamer full of half-and-half onto a tray. "He is."

The day passed both quick and slow, seeming to drag on and then the hours flying by near closing time. Now living for the weekends, time in general either passed too fast or too slow. Time seemed to move in fast-forward when Taylor and I were together. There was no in between.

Valentine's Day came and went. Taylor and I both worked that evening, so he stayed in Estes Park, but we more than made up for it that weekend.

I began my mornings and ended my evenings on the phone with Taylor. If I were really lucky, he would get impatient for one of us to have a day off, and he'd drive down to see me, only to have to drive back early the next morning. On the rare occasion when we both had the weekend off, Taylor would drive straight to the Springs early Saturday morning and stay until just before dawn on Monday.

I was looking forward to spending the weekend with him in St. Thomas.

"The second wedding on the island is next Saturday, right? Will Taylor be here Friday night?" Phaedra asked.

I wiped down the last of the tables.

"Taylor leaves Thursday for Eakins. There's a bachelor party on Friday night. I'm flying straight to Saint Thomas on Saturday," I said.

A steady beat of knocking came from the door, and I looked up to see Gunnar standing there, pointing to Taylor standing next to him.

Kirby opened the door, letting them in, and I dropped my rag before throwing my arms and legs around Taylor.

Taylor pressed his lips against mine. "Hi, gorgeous!" he said, lowering me to the floor.

I kissed him again, and then I picked up the rag off the floor. My heart was pounding in my chest as if I'd just run a marathon. It didn't matter how many nights I saw him standing on the other side of the glass. It made me feel the same every time.

Chuck walked through the swinging doors, putting a hand on his round belly. "What time did you leave Estes Park?"

"On time," Taylor said.

Chuck laughed. "You must drive like a maniac. You need to quit that, boy, or you're going to end up launching off a ridge."

I grimaced.

Taylor bent down to kiss me. "I drove a little fast, but I was careful. I was in a hurry to get here."

"It's snowing," I said. "You can't drive fast and careful when it's snowing."

He stood up tall. "Obviously, I can."

Gunnar and Taylor each took a seat on the stools, catching up and cracking jokes with Chuck and Hector. Kirby and I finished our duties, making sure not to leave anything for Hannah the next day.

"You guys coming upstairs?" I asked, drying my hands with a clean rag.

Kirby and Gunnar looked at each other.

Gunnar nodded. "Sure. I just have one paper to write this weekend. It can wait."

We said good-bye to everyone, and then Kirby and Gunnar followed Taylor and me upstairs.

"The good thing about having a girlfriend who doesn't drink?" Taylor was bent over in the kitchen, rummaging in my fridge. He wheeled around with a beer bottle in his hand. He popped the top with a smile and flicked the lid into the trash. "I know she won't drink my stash while I'm gone." He strolled over to the couch, making me bounce when he fell into the cushion next to me.

I leaned into his side, letting that relaxing wonderful feeling that filled the loft when Taylor was there warm me like a blanket.

He stretched his arm over the back of the couch, touching my shoulder with his fingers, and then he held out his bottle to Gunnar. "There are a few more in the fridge."

Gunnar watched him take a gulp and then shook his head. "I'm going to need all my senses to pull off this paper."

Kirby patted his knee.

"I don't miss college," Taylor said. "At all."

"I like school," Gunnar said, gesturing toward Kirby. "I don't like being away from her."

Kirby hugged his arm. "Just keep kicking ass, and we'll be in Denver in no time."

Taylor's eyebrows shot up. "You're moving there together?"

Gunnar looked both proud and excited. "I've just got to get some money saved up and find a place once I transfer."

"Gunnar's applying for the physician's assistant program," I said.

"Oh, yeah? That's fucking awesome, man. Good for you." Taylor held up his beer again, as a toast this time. He looked to me. "What are Phaedra and Chuck going to do when they lose you both?"

Kirby and I traded glances.

"What?" Taylor asked.

"Have you had any luck applying here?" Kirby asked.

"Nope," Taylor said. "But I'm solid at the station in Estes."

"But don't you live with your brother?" she asked.

Taylor set his beer down on a coaster even though the coffee table was scratched and already covered in water rings. "Okay. You two have been discussing. Let's hear it."

I squirmed. "It's just that … it feels wrong to leave Phaedra high and dry after all she's done for me. And I'm not sure I'd like your brother as a roommate. I don't really want to ask him to move out, and we have a perfectly good place here. I can save more if I stay here."

"That's not true. I told you I'd take care of rent."

"And I told you it was fifty-fifty or nothing."

"I'm here, maybe, five months out of the year," he said.

"Until you get hired on here."

"They're not hiring, baby. I've asked—a lot."

"Not yet," I said, pointing at him.

He looked at Kirby and then back at me. "So, what do you propose? I keep up the commute until I'm hired on here? Or that I move here without a job?"

I winced. I knew suggesting either would be an insult. "If I move to Estes Park, you'll be here in the Springs or somewhere else for up to half the year."

"I told you. I have a full-time position at the local station if I want it."

"I can't leave Phaedra and Chuck, not right now. Kirby is leaving soon …"

Taylor blew out a breath, looking away from me. "I don't want to keep doing this. I hate seeing you only on the weekends."

"Should we go?" Gunnar asked.

We both ignored him.

"So, we're at an impasse," I said.

"And what the hell does that mean?" Taylor was more frustrated than angry.

He had been talking about us moving in together since Christmas, and I'd kept giving him excuses—everything from it being too soon to moving expenses.

"I don't have a car. How am I going to get to work if I move into your condo?"

He shrugged. "We'll figure it out. I can drop you off. It's a shorter drive than coming here every weekend."

"We don't have to decide now."

Taylor took a long drink, sucking the beer bottle dry, and then he took it with him to the kitchen. He tossed it into the trash can before opening the fridge to grab another. He twisted off the cap and threw it into the garbage, too, before returning to me in a huff.

"Taylor ..." I began.

"You're not the one who has to make this drive, Falyn."

"You're right," I said. "That is a fair point."

"We definitely need to go," Gunnar said.

"What's your rush?" Kirby asked.

Gunnar's brows pulled together. "When you start agreeing with me the way Falyn just did, shit goes downhill real fast."

She laughed and nudged him, and Taylor and I couldn't help but smile.

He hugged me to him and kissed my hair. "I'll make the drive as long as I have to. It's the time in between I don't like," Taylor said.

"I know. I don't like it either. The silver lining is that, after we get back from Saint Thomas, you'll be working back here in five weeks."

"Maybe. That's never a guarantee. There's no telling where I'll be."

I cocked my head, getting impatient with his negativity. "You said your crew has been here the last three summers."

"Okay, but what about the year I'm not? That's six months I'll be even farther away from you."

"If I live in Estes and you're called somewhere else, you'll be away from me anyway!" I said.

"Not if we're in Estes! I'll take the local position!"

Gunnar stood up.

"Honey," Kirby said, her voice bordering on a whine.

"I'm going to drink one of those beers if we don't leave right now," he said, towering over her.

He reached out, and she took his hand.

"Let's go do something," he said.

"We could go to the hookah bar," she said, standing next to her boyfriend.

Taylor and I glared at each other.

"It is so incredibly stupid for us to be fighting about seeing each other while we're seeing each other," I said.

"See? That's where we're different. I don't think it's stupid to fight for this at all."

I sighed. He didn't see it as fighting over who was moving where and under what circumstances. He felt like he was fighting for us to be together. How could I argue with that?

"Let's go," Kirby said, pulling me to stand. "I think we all need to be outside for a while."

We walked downstairs and stood next to Taylor's truck, watching the snow fall in thick flakes.

"Snow doesn't look like this in Illinois." Taylor held out his hand, letting the frozen white bits melt against his palm. He rubbed his hands together, zipped up his coat, and then popped a cigarette into his mouth.

"I wish we could go to Cowboys," Kirby said, joining Gunnar on the tailgate of Taylor's truck. She swung her feet for warmth.

"You're not twenty-one yet, are you?" Taylor took a deep drag and blew out a puff of thick white smoke. "I could probably get you in."

Gunnar shook his head. "I can't."

Kirby patted his middle. "Not going to chance getting caught, are we?"

"Nope," Gunnar said, pulling her to his side.

Taylor shrugged and continued to smoke. Once he was finished, he pinched off the cherry, rubbed the end along the top edge of his truck bed, and then put the cigarette butt into his pocket. He pulled his knit cap further down to cover his ears, and then he crossed his arms, tucking his hands under them.

"Your nose is red," I said, playfully nudging him.

He only offered a contrived smile, staring down Tejon Street.

Kirby and Gunnar were having their own conversation in the background, and Taylor was lost in thought. I stood next to him, feeling left out of my own party.

"You're being unusually pensive," I said.

Taylor puffed out a laugh. "You know I hate the big words, Ivy League."

"You haven't called me that in a while," I said.

His lips pressed together, making a hard line. "I hate missing you. I hate it more every day."

"I don't like it either."

He turned to me. "Then let's do something about it. Let's figure out a solution."

"You mean, one that includes me moving into your condo."

He sighed. "Okay. We'll talk about it during the week. I don't want to fight."

Gunnar and Kirby's conversation seemed forced, and they made sure not to look in our direction, probably in an effort not to eavesdrop.

"Who's fighting?" I asked. "Just because I'm not giving in to what you want ..."

He craned his neck at me. "That's not it, and you know it."

"It's a big deal, Taylor. We need to think about it."

"Oh. So, it is the moving-in-together part. You're freaking out about it."

"I'm not freaking out. But if I were, it's not an unreasonable emotion to feel."

"No, you're right. I'm just a little more than irritated that you were all fate and meant-to-be in Eakins, and now, you're acting like we're moving too fast."

I arched an eyebrow. "Did you just throw that in my face?" I left him standing alone, sitting next to Kirby on the tailgate.

Taylor began to speak, but the sounds of footsteps crunching against the snow took away his attention.

A small group of teenagers walked toward us, bumping into each other or the buildings or falling off the curb.

"Hey," one of the guys said, smiling, "you got any weed?"

"Nope," Gunnar said before continuing his conversation with Kirby.

Taylor began to respond to my question, but the man knocked on his truck.

"Hey! I'm talking to you!" the man said to Gunnar.

Gunnar and Taylor traded looks.

Then Taylor glowered at the entire group. "Don't touch my fucking truck, kid."

The man puffed out his chest, attempting some form of intimidation, but he was so wasted that he failed to look directly at Taylor. He wasn't completely unfortunate-looking. He had a respectable amount of scruff, and his arms were built nicely enough to fill the sleeves of his flannel shirt.

"Is he high?" Kirby asked.

Gunnar shook his head. "You don't go looking for a fight if you're high. He's just drunk."

Kirby didn't seem fazed as she watched the man sway, waiting for what he might say next.

"Move along," Taylor said.

The man was a couple of inches shorter than Taylor, but he didn't seem to know it. He looked over at Kirby and me. "I'm thinking about crashing your party."

The men behind him laughed, slapping each other on the shoulders and trying just as hard as their bearded friend to stand upright.

Gunnar stepped down off the tailgate, towering over all of them. All three men took a step back.

"You have a giant," the first man said, his chin tipped up.

Taylor's posture instantly relaxed, and he laughed. "Yes. Yes, we do. Now, quit fucking with us, and go back to wherever you came from."

They chuckled among one another and began to move on, but the bearded one paused.

"Don't you work at the Bucksaw?"

I wasn't sure which of us he was addressing. None of us answered.

"I'll come see you," he said, attempting to be flirtatious while struggling to keep his balance.

"No, you won't," Taylor said, his jaw working under his skin.

The drunk laughed, bending at the waist to grab his knees, and then he stood up, pointing at me. "Is she your girlfriend? I'm sorry, man. I won't steal her."

"I'm not worried about it," Taylor said.

"Sounds like you are," he said, using the back corner of the truck bed to hold himself up. Then he flattened his hand on the tailgate next to where I sat.

Taylor glared at his hand. "I don't like you touching my truck. Think about it. What am I going to do to you if you touch my girlfriend?"

"Kill me?" the guy said, trying to stand and back away.

Taylor smiled. "No. I'll beat the hell out of you until you want to kill yourself."

The kid paled but quickly recovered, remembering he had an audience.

He began to speak, but I cut him off, "Hey, Jack Daniel's, you want to keep your face, don't you?"

He frowned at me, more confused than offended.

"Keep walking," I said. "These guys are not going to put up with your shit for much longer."

I glanced over at Taylor, who was staring a hole into the kid's forehead.

The bushy-faced stranger startled, seeming to just notice that our giant was still standing there, and he stumbled off without another word.

Gunnar relaxed. "We'd better get a move on, Kirby. I've decided I'm too tired to go anywhere."

She giggled at him. "We're already an old married couple." She hugged me good-bye. "See you Monday."

I watched the couple walk to their truck while Taylor eyed the group of drunken boys stumbling down the street. He pushed his tailgate closed and then followed me to the Bucksaw.

Once inside, I shook out my hair and rubbed my hands together as I climbed the stairs. Taylor was quiet but trying hard to be in a better mood. I tried to chat about anything other than moving in together in Estes Park. Taylor would nod and smile when appropriate. The longer I talked, the more his smiles seemed forced, and that only made me angry.

When he saw the irritated look on my face, his grin vanished. "C'mon, Falyn. I said I don't want to spend the weekend fighting."

"Just because you're pretending not to be mad doesn't mean you're not upset."

He looked forward, clearly struggling to rein in his temper. "I got a package yesterday."

I quietly waited, too aggravated to give in just yet.

"I told my dad you had a VCR. He sent me a tape." Taylor stood up and went to the counter where he'd left his backpack. He unzipped it and pulled out a VHS tape, holding it up. "*Spaceballs.* Growing up, I used to watch this with my brothers almost every weekend. It was Tommy's favorite."

"Okay," I said. "Let's watch it."

Taylor's eyes brightened, softening my anger. Leaning down in front of the television, he slipped the tape from the sleeve and pushed it into the VCR. When he returned to the couch, he put his hand on my knee, smiling the moment the opening credits began. It was a real smile, something he'd been finding hard to do when around me anymore.

The movie was the perfect distraction, allowing us to spend time together without talking, to sit together without addressing the problem.

Once the ending credits rolled, I left Taylor for the bathroom to take a shower. I pulled the curtain closed, relieved not to be in the same room with him for a while.

Does that mean I'm not ready to move in?

As I rinsed the conditioner out of my hair, I cursed myself for knowing exactly how many times I had thought I couldn't be away from Taylor one more day and how many times I had lain in bed while wishing to God he were with me.

Unbelievable. I was annoying myself.

I rinsed the soap off my skin and stepped out onto the bath mat, wrapping the towel around me. The mirror was fogged, so all I could see was a fuzzy shape that was supposed to be me. It was exactly the way I felt. Everything was blurry.

I slipped an oversized T-shirt and crawled into bed next to Taylor, but he wasn't eager to get my nightgown off of me like usual. Instead, he pulled my back against his bare chest and held me while we both fought the urge to say anything more on the subject.

His body heat seared through my nightgown, and I melted against him. He had already warmed the mattress and the sheets. I wanted him there. Sometimes, I needed it. Going to bed alone after spending even one night with him was miserable.

"Falyn," Taylor said from behind, his voice sounding distant.

"Yes?"

"I just …" He sighed. "I just want to be with you."

"I know. I want that, too."

"Just not as much as I do. Maybe not at all."

"That's not true," I whispered. "We just need a plan, and we'll make one. But it doesn't have to be tonight."

He touched his forehead to the back of my shoulder. "How much longer do you want to wait? Just so I have an idea."

I mulled over his question in my mind. I couldn't say exactly what was keeping me from giving Taylor exactly what he wanted, but I needed more time to find out. "This summer. Can you give me until then?"

"To make a plan?"

"To move."

He pushed himself up on his elbow, hovering over me. "To Estes Park?"

I nodded.

He eyed me for a moment. "You sure?"

"I'm nervous about it."

"Okay, let's talk. What are you nervous about?"

"Change and … I don't know, Taylor. Something feels off. I can't put my finger on it."

Taylor looked wounded.

"It's not you. Or us. Something is just bugging me about it, like it's not right."

"I'll make it right," he said without hesitation. "I just need you to take a leap of faith. Not even a leap. More like a hop."

I touched his face. He had so much hope in his eyes.

"Why do you want me to move in with you? We've been together less than a year, and you've never been in a serious relationship before. You just know?"

"I'm sure that I love you. I'm sure that being away from you drives me insane. That's all I need to know."

"I can't argue that the distance sucks. If you can commute for three more months, I'll hop. That will give Phaedra time to find and train someone."

Taylor exhaled as if the wind had been knocked out of him, and then a small smile curled up his lips. "I'll apply for the station job this week."

He shook his head in awe of my huge gesture. He had no words, so he leaned down and touched his lips to mine, slow at first. Then he touched his hands to my cheeks, and my mouth parted.

We celebrated between the sheets for hours, and halfway into the night, I collapsed next to him. Within minutes, he was asleep. As his breathing evened out, I lay awake, staring at the ceiling. The uncertainty and guilt swirled in my stomach, making me feel sick. I had overturned my life once before and survived.

Why does moving in with my best friend, with the man I love, seem more frightening than leaving my parents while penniless?

I rubbed my temple, feeling as blurry as my reflection in the bathroom mirror. I'd thought maybe if I made a decision, that feeling would go away, but my experiment was an utter failure. The uneasiness became worse. The harder I tried to understand my feelings, the less it made sense. There was something we needed to talk about, something that was still in the way.

Taylor shifted, letting his hand rest on my stomach, and then the answer came. If he stayed with me, Taylor would have to make a sacrifice, one with which I was all too familiar. Family was important to him. He had said it before. He couldn't do what I had done.

Why did I think he could give up the possibility of having his own child?

My stomach sank. He had done so much for me, and I was going to take that away from him.

How can I really love him and allow him to make such a choice?

CHAPTER EIGHTEEN

PETE CHOPPED GREEN PEPPERS while I spoke, nodding occasionally to let me know he was listening. The sun wasn't up yet, and his white apron was already covered in smears of brown and green.

The kitchen was quiet, except for Pete's knife against the carving block. Like a typewriter, he tapped over and over before sliding the pieces to the side when he was finished, only to start again.

I startled when I heard heavy footsteps descending the stairs. Taylor pushed through the double doors, wearing only a pair of gray cotton shorts and untied boots. He froze when Pete pointed a knife in his direction.

Taylor looked at me.

"Don't go near the food," I explained.

Taylor stayed put. "What are you doing?" he asked, crossing his arms to ward off the cold.

I wiped my wet cheeks. "Talking to Pete."

"But"—Taylor held up his hand—"no offense, buddy"—his eyes returned to me—"Pete doesn't talk."

I shrugged. "He doesn't share my secrets, and I don't ask him why he doesn't speak."

Taylor's demeanor immediately changed. "I don't share your secrets either. But that was back when you used to tell me everything."

I hopped down off one of the stainless steel counters lining the wall and waved to Pete before taking Taylor's hand. "Let's go back up," I said, tugging on Taylor's wrist.

"Have you been crying?" he asked. He hesitated and then let me pull him back through the doors and up the stairs.

I could tell by his mannerisms that he knew something was up. I shut the door behind us and leaned against it.

"Falyn," he said, shifting nervously, "is this what I think it is? Because it was just one fucking disagreement. You can't bail on me after one disagreement. And it wasn't even a disagreement. It was a ... passionate discussion. And last thing you said to me last night was that you were moving to Estes. If you're going to freak out about it so much that you're going to dump me, then at least let's talk about options."

"I'm not bailing on you," I said.

His panic was heartbreaking.

"Then what the fuck is going on? Why did you sneak downstairs to talk to Pete at four thirty in the morning?"

I passed him to sit on the couch, using the hair tie around my wrist to pull my hair into a messy bun. "I wasn't sneaking anywhere. I talk to Pete a lot in the mornings when no one is around."

"Not when I'm here," Taylor said, sitting next to me. "What's going on, Falyn? Talk to me."

"I need to tell you something."

He visibly braced himself for whatever I was about to say.

"I can't have children."

He waited for a moment, and then his eyes danced around the room. "I ... know?"

"If we take this further, if we move in together and then whatever comes next ... it will always just be us. I don't think you truly understand that."

All of his muscles relaxed. "Goddamn, woman, you scared me."

"Huh?"

"I thought you were dumping my impatient ass. You were just worried that I wasn't thinking about you not being able to get pregnant down the road?"

"Yes," I said, a little annoyed he was being so flippant about it.

He his head back. "I've already thought about it, baby. No worries."

"That right there shows me you haven't thought this through."

"There are a million ways for us to try to get pregnant. If none of them work, there's adoption."

"No," I said, shaking my head. "You don't get it. I've told you. This was supposed to happen. You can't just screw with the order of things."

"You don't really believe that shit ... about it being your punishment."

I barely nodded. It sounded crazy when he said it out loud.

"Baby, don't you think you've been punished enough?"

Tears burned my eyes. Without any idea what to expect or any way to prepare, I'd assumed this would be an emotional conversation one way or another.

"You're already the best thing to ever happen to me. Stop showing off."

Taylor pulled me in, holding me tight. He kissed my hair.

"What if I told you I don't want to adopt?" I asked, glad that I didn't have to look him in the face.

He hesitated. "I'm ... surprised."

"I know you want kids. I don't want to take that away from you. I've had a lot of time to think about this, and I just can't. I would be too afraid to try to adopt. I'd worry about so many different things, like who gave the baby up and why. What if one of the family members decided to take the child back? I can't chance losing a child twice. I just ... I can't."

"I didn't think about it that way."

"I know."

"I understand. I mean ... we'll cross that bridge when we get there."

"This is something we need to address now. You want kids. I can't get pregnant, and I don't want to adopt. That's a big deal. We can't wait and see, Taylor. Then it will be too late."

"I want you."

Tears welled up in my eyes. "I want you to think about it for a while."

"Jesus Christ, Falyn. Do you really think I have to think about it? No. I'm not giving you up. You're not giving me up."

My face crumpled, and I shook my head. "That right there tells me you're not taking this seriously."

"I hear what you're offering. My answer is no. If we end up being alone but together, I can think of worse things."

I sniffed. "This is why moving in together hasn't felt right. I know better than to let you do this without really thinking it through."

"But it feels right to bail? Fuck that," he said, standing. He paced a few times and then came back.

Kneeling in front of me, he tucked his hands behind my lower back and pulled me toward him until my knees were pressing into his bare chest.

He shook his head. "I'm pissed at you for this, and I love you for this. But you have to know that there's nothing I want more than you."

"What if you regret it?"

He paled, his face falling. "You said you weren't bailing. You're fucking bailing on me. You just want me to be the one to do it."

"You need to think about this ... I mean, *really* think about it."

"Why are you really doing this, Falyn? How about you *really* think about that? It's getting serious, and alarms are going off. Stop, and think about this for two fucking seconds."

"We just need a break. If you still feel the same way later ..."

"Later? When the fuck is later?"

"Taylor," I said, watching him get angrier by the second.

"A break. I'm a grown man, Falyn. What is this? You're putting me in a time-out, so I can think about what you want me to think about, the way you want me to think about it?"

"I know that's how it looks, but I'm just trying to do the right thing. You might thank me later. I'm not trying to stir up trouble for us. I—"

"Don't say it. Don't say it's because you love me, or I'll lose my shit."

He stood up and disappeared into my bedroom. Returning a few minutes later, he wore jeans, socks, and a black fleece pullover with a black-and-gray hat pulled low over his brows, and he bent down to pick his boots off the floor.

"You're leaving *now*?" I was a bit surprised and feeling guilty for it.

Of course he was going to leave. What had I expected him to do? What had begun as good intentions was going downhill fast, and I was already regretting it even though moments before I'd thought that I thought it all through.

He pulled on his boots, shoved his dirty clothes into his backpack, and then slid one strap over his shoulder before swiping his keys off the counter. "That's what you want, isn't it?" he said, holding out his hands. He gripped the knob and then pointed at me. "I'm going to go home, and instead of applying for that job, I'm going to think about this for a week. Then I'm going to come back, and you're going to apologize to me for fucking up the weekend I've been looking forward to for a month." He yanked the door open, and without looking back, he said, "I love you."

The door slammed, and I closed my eyes, wincing at the sound. I fell back against the couch cushion and covered my eyes with my hands. Maybe he was right. Maybe I was pushing him away. Now that he was gone, I felt exactly the way Travis had described the first time I went to Eakins. It was like I was dying slowly with a little bit of crazy mixed in.

"I hate you," I said to myself.

ॐ

Monday morning, I trudged down the stairs, passing on the pancakes for a cup of coffee. It had been a little more than twenty-four hours since I saw Taylor, but I knew no matter how much time passed, the awful feeling that had come over me the moment he left wouldn't go away.

The dining area was empty, except for Chuck, Phaedra, and me. Pete and Hector peeked out from the food window.

Phaedra and Chuck had matching expressions of concern.

"Still hasn't called, huh?" Chuck asked, patting my shoulder.

"He texted late last night," I said.

"Well?" Phaedra asked. "Good or bad?"

"He's still thinking."

"It's your damn fault," Phaedra said. "He didn't ask for an easy out. Sounds to me like he didn't even want it."

"Dear," Chuck said, a hint of warning in his voice.

"She's right," I said. "He might not need it, but he does deserve it."

She grabbed a stack of menus. "Oh, baby girl, he's been good to you. He didn't deserve that." She walked away, clearly angry with me.

I looked sheepishly at Chuck.

"She just wants what's best for you. She hates to see you making things harder on yourself. So ... what did his message say?"

I pulled out my phone and read the text aloud, "*I can't believe you dumped me and ruined our entire weekend over the off chance that I might want to dump you over something you can't control.*" I read the next message, "*To be honest, I haven't really thought about it before, but now that you've insisted there is a real possibility that children are off the table for us, you're right. It's an important decision that I should think about, but you didn't have to kick me to the goddamn curb to make your point.*"

Phaedra returned, impressed with what she'd heard. "He's a smart little shit. I'll give him that."

"What does that mean?" I asked, exhausted. So many warring thoughts in my head hadn't allowed for much sleep.

"He's at least pretending to attempt to be objective."

A scowl compressed my face.

Kirby breezed in, and we all immediately pretended there was nothing wrong. She saw right through our pathetic attempt and grilled me about the weekend every time we had a spare moment to chat.

The Bucksaw was packed for most of the day, a welcome distraction from Kirby's incessant questions and Phaedra's disenchanted expressions. When I wiped down the last table of the day and sat on the stool to count my tips, Kirby pushed me past my limit.

"At least tell me who is mad at whom!" she begged.

"No! Stop asking!" I snapped.

Phaedra crossed her arms. "Falyn, I want you to listen to me. There are thousands of couples out there who are childless by choice. Look at Chuck and me. Granted, we've got you girls, but we've always been happy. You've been honest with Taylor. He knows what he's in for. You can't force him to do what you think is the right thing."

Kirby stared at me like I was on fire. "Oh God, Falyn, are you pregnant?"

"I'm out." I grabbed my things and headed for the stairs.

By the time I finished my shower and crawled into bed, Taylor had texted me. I felt sick, worrying about what he might say, but I read the message anyway.

*Day Two. You don't have to respond. I know you want me
to spend this time being objective, and I want this to be
done, so fuck me if I don't do it the right way, and you
make me start over. Thought about you all weekend.
Yesterday was the first Sunday I've had off in three weeks,
and it fucking sucks that I spent it here without you. I'm
half-missing you, half-pissed at you. Mostly, I'm wondering
how you could think anything would be more important to
me than you. Kids are important, and yes, our relationship
is new. But if it means choosing, I choose you.*

True to his word, Taylor had thought about my proposal all
week, sending me one text every night.

*Day Three. It's only Tuesday. I feel like I'm going to go
out of my fucking mind. You don't have to respond, but I
miss you like hell. It's hard to think about anything else,
but I am, and I still feel the same. This is the longest
fucking week ever, and I'm worried you're just going to tell
me to kick rocks anyway. Are you? Don't answer that.
I'm going to go stay with Tommy for a couple of days to
clear my head.*

On the fourth day, Taylor didn't text. I lay in bed, worrying
until I thought I might puke. Feeling something heavy on my chest,
my emotions were all over the place. I didn't want to lose him, but
if he wanted more, I owed it to him to let him go. That kind of
selfishness would slowly poison any relationship.

Tears fell from the outer corners of my eyes, down my
temples, dripping to my pillowcase with a tiny thud. With my arm
resting on my forehead, my eyes closed, I tried to push it from my
mind, but the fear tore a hole, and it just kept getting bigger.

I looked over at my alarm clock, the red numbers glowing *4:15*
a.m. Just as I reached for my phone, it pinged several times in a
row. I scrambled to grab it from the nightstand.

*It's the fifth day of this bullshit im in San Diego and
maaybe you're right.*

*Maybe a hundred ducking years from now I'll feel fucked
out of having a family and wish i had a sun to play ball*

*with and maybe ill want grandkids maybe I don't deserve
you anyway*

Maybe I'm just drunk

*Fuck it. Fuck all of this. I love you and ive done everything
I'm supposed to until now and I'm further from you than
ive been since we met. That's isnt my fault.*

I typed out a dozen different responses, but I knew he'd been drinking, and he was upset. Trying to reason with him or even apologize wouldn't get me very far, and it might even make things worse. Putting down the phone was the hardest thing I'd done in six years.

For the second time that week, I cursed myself, "I fucking hate you." I covered my eyes.

Just a few hours later, I rolled out of bed, washed my face, brushed my teeth. Then I got dressed before descending the stairs eleven minutes later. I pulled my hair into a messy bun, only to walk back up to get my apron.

I dragged ass all morning, as expected. I was mostly exhausted but also devastated that my intent was lost in the misery we were both in. Still, I had started this mess, and I wasn't about to waffle until Taylor could make the decision for himself.

Just after the breakfast rush, my phone buzzed in my apron. I rushed around the bar to check it, knowing it was Taylor.

*Day Five. Please respond. I'm sorry. I'm so fucking sorry
about last night. I guess technically it was this morning. I'm
sitting here in the airport. Just got off the phone with Dad.
He made a lot of good points that I need to talk to you
about. I'll be in Eakins by tonight. Please go to St.
Thomas. I'll sleep on the floor if you want. My head is
pounding, and I feel like shit, but I wish I felt worse even
though I couldn't feel much worse. I want to see you and
hold you so bad I'm going nuts. All I can think about is
seeing you. No, don't respond. I'm afraid of what you'll
say. Just please be there.*

I ran my index finger along the edges of the phone case, wondering which of his instructions I should follow. Guilt bled from his message, making my guts wrench.

Why did trying to do the right thing end up being so god-awful for us both?

It was just a break, just a week to think about our future, and we were both torn to pieces.

CHAPTER NINETEEN

THE AIR WAS SO THICK when I stepped off the airplane that it felt as if I were wearing it, choking on it, and walking through it. A layer of sweat instantly formed on my skin even though I was wearing shorts and a light blouse.

I readjusted my bag over my shoulder, descended the stairs set outside the plane's front exit, and paused once my feet hit the tarmac. St. Thomas was breathtaking for more reasons than its palpable air. The landscape was full of lush forests with mountains in the distance and palm trees just beyond the concrete.

I pulled out my phone, shooting Taylor a quick text that I'd landed.

He sent a 💜 in reply but nothing else.

The passengers strode in a single-file line to the terminal where we meshed with other travelers until reconvening at baggage claim. I noticed a man standing near the exit, holding a sign with my name on it.

That hadn't happened since I lived with my parents.

"Hi," I said, confused. "I'm Falyn Fairchild."

The man's mouth broke into a bright white grin, a steep contrast with his ebony skin. "Yes! Come with me! Just the one bag?" he asked in a heavy accent, holding out his hand for my bag.

"Who ordered the car?"

"Uh"—he looked down at a paper in his other hand—"Taylor Mad Dox."

"Taylor Maddox?" I said, my surprise making me unintentionally correct him by emphasizing the *ix* pronunciation at the end.

Shock quickly evolved into suspicion. Taylor was either trying very hard to get me back—or for some reason, he was in full groveling mode.

I handed the man my bag, silently scolding myself. Taylor had secured me transportation to the hotel, and I was thinking the worst. He just wanted to make sure I was safe because he couldn't make it to the airport himself.

The driver's steering wheel was on the left side, but we drove on the left side of the road. It took me a while not to panic every time he turned onto a road with oncoming traffic, thinking he was in the wrong lane.

After hills and many, many curvy roads, we finally reached the security gate of The Ritz-Carlton hotel. The driver parked under the covered lobby entrance, and he quickly hopped out to open my door. I stepped out and swallowed hard. The days when I'd stayed in hotels like the Ritz seemed like a lifetime ago.

The light stucco and Spanish-tiled roof as well as the vegetation were impeccably maintained. I returned the smile and wave of a man high in a palm tree, removing coconuts.

The driver handed me my bag, and I opened my purse.

"No, no. It's all been taken care of."

I held out a ten-dollar bill. "But your tip?"

He waved me away with a smile. "Taken care of, madam. Enjoy your stay."

He drove away, and I wandered inside, overwhelmed by the spectacular lobby. I spotted Taylor right away. He was sitting in a chair with his elbows on his thighs, clasping his hands together, while his knee nervously bobbed up and down.

Before I could take another step, he looked up, and a dozen emotions scrolled across his face. He popped up out of his chair and jogged over to me, nearly knocking me over before enveloping me into a hug. I'd never felt so loved and wanted in my life.

"You're here. Thank Christ," he said, overwhelmed with relief. He tugged at me with gentle small squeezes, burying his face into my hair.

When he finally released me, I could see that my earlier suspicions weren't ridiculous after all. His face was weighed down with something, the humidity not the only thing making him sweat.

"You're beautiful," he said.

"Thanks," I said, trying not to sound as wary as I felt.

"God, I've missed you." He hugged me and then kissed my forehead, leaving his lips against my skin for a moment longer. Then he took my bag. "We're in building five, Club Level, with an ocean view." He smiled, but there was sadness in his eyes.

"Club Level?"

"I upgraded. We're in the same tower as Travis and Abby. The room is incredible. I can't wait for you to see it." He gestured for me to follow him outside where a man in a golf cart was waiting.

We sat together in the backseat, jerking when the driver stomped on the gas. Taylor looked over at me, both relief and admiration in his eyes. The golf cart sped along the narrow road for at least two minutes before we reached our building. Taylor didn't speak again even though he looked like he wanted to.

The driver parked and carried my bag across the road and down a stone walk. We passed doors that led to rooms, moving to the side whenever a couple or family would step out, carrying beach bags, towels, or cameras. We ascended a few stairs, and then I followed the men to the room I would share with Taylor.

That thought made me suddenly nervous. We weren't technically together even though it seemed all was well. An important conversation was inevitable, and I wondered if Taylor wanted to get that out of the way now or if he would keep me waiting all weekend.

Taylor took my bag, tipped our driver, and then used his key card to open the door. Fresh flowery smells filled my nose, and my sandals clicked against the tiled floor. The white linen and light décor was sophisticated but cozy, and directly in front of where we stood was a large sliding glass door, the curtains pulled back to expose the full beauty of the Caribbean Sea.

I dropped my bag. "Oh my God," I said, my feet carrying me straight for the door.

Taylor beat me there, sliding open the glass.

I stepped out, hearing songbirds and watching the fronds of the palm trees dance with the breeze that were wafting the smells of the ocean to our balcony. The private beach of the Ritz-Carlton was lined with beach loungers, umbrellas, Hobie Cats, and paddleboats. An impressive sailboat was docked not two hundred yards from swimmers, white paint proudly marking its name, *Lady Lyndsey*.

"I don't think I've seen anything this beautiful before in person," I said, shaking my head in awe.

"I have," Taylor said.

From the corner of my eye, I could see him staring at me. I turned to him, letting his milk-chocolate eyes take in every detail of my face.

"I'm so glad you're here. I was worried. For several days."

"I told you I'd come. You bought the ticket. I wasn't going to stand you up."

"After the other night—"

"You drunk-texted me. There are worse things—like torture, for instance."

A crease formed between his brows. "It's been a long week. I think I fell in love with you more every day. I guess there's some truth to that saying."

"Distance makes the heart grow fonder?"

"Yeah, and so does thinking you've lost the woman you're crazy in love with. When I was alone and even when I wasn't, I said some pretty awful things about you in my head, Falyn. I take them all back."

I wondered what his crew and even his brother must think about me. I could only imagine what he'd said out of frustration.

"I didn't dump you. We took a break, so you could think about something important."

He blinked. "So ... we weren't ... we're still together," he said more to himself than a question. All the color drained from his face, and he backed away from me, sitting down hard in a wicker chair.

"I wasn't clear. Either way, it wasn't fair. It was stupid and cruel, and ... I'm sorry."

He shook his head. "You don't apologize. You definitely shouldn't apologize for this."

I sat next to him. "What I did was shitty, no matter my line of thinking or my intentions. I'm just lucky you love me and that you're more patient than you let on."

He stared at the floor and then smiled up at me. "Let's just pretend last week never happened. Fade out last Friday. Fade in the moment I saw you in the lobby." When I didn't respond, he continued, "I thought about it like you asked, and I don't feel any differently than the night I left."

"You're sure?"

He exhaled like the wind had been knocked out of him. "More now than ever."

"Maybe it was a good thing then? The break?"

"I don't know about that," he said, pushing the table between us back and pulling my chair closer to him. "But there's not a doubt in my mind about how much you mean to me. You're the last woman I ever want to touch."

"I'm sorry," I said, unable to shake the guilt. "I just meant I should have listened to you. You were right about me trying to force it, and even though I didn't realize it, I was probably trying to push you away. I don't want you to leave me even if that makes me selfish."

I leaned in, pressing my lips to his, and I sighed as he wrapped his arms around me.

"It doesn't make you selfish, Falyn. I'm the selfish one. Jesus, I'm sorry, too. I just want to forget about it, okay? Can we do that? It's just you and me. Nothing else matters."

As he held me in his arms, the world was right again. I was never so glad to be wrong.

He pulled away with a frown. "I have to get around. The guys are all in Shep's room, getting ready." He stood up, leading me back into the room by the hand.

I sat on the end of the bed, watching as he opened the closet and pulled out a plastic-covered tux. He held it up, shrugging. "America insisted we go traditional."

"I'm looking forward to seeing you in that."

"Fresh towels are in the bathroom if you want to take a shower before the ceremony. I've already had one, and I feel like I need another one."

"Maybe you should take one with me?" I said, arching an eyebrow.

He dropped the tux and rushed to kneel next to me. "We're okay, right?"

I nodded.

He planted a kiss on my lips. When he pulled away, disappointment flashed in his eyes. "I wish I could. The ceremony is in the gazebo on the beach. Just around the corner and down the stairs."

"See you in ninety minutes," I said, waving to him as he walked backward through the door.

When the door closed, I slipped off my sandals and padded across the tiles to the cold marble floor of the bathroom. The quiet allowed me enough time to think about my awkward reunion with Taylor, and a lump formed in my throat. Colorado Springs was a thousand miles away, and I couldn't seem to hide from the guilt. Instead of seeing it in my reflection in the mirror, it had been in Taylor's eyes.

As glad as I was to see him and to know that he wanted me despite the knowledge that we would never have children, something still felt off. So many questions crowded my mind. Maybe I had hurt him beyond repair. Maybe what I had done to him changed him. Maybe it had changed us.

My shirt stuck to my damp skin as I lifted the bottom hem. The air was so thick that it still covered me, even after I peeled off my clothes.

I tried not to cry while in the shower, scolding myself for finding a way to be melancholy while in a marble bathroom under a shower with high water pressure instead of the antique plumbing in the loft. After a while, I reasoned that my face was wet anyway, and I was alone, so I might as well get it out of my system.

So, I cried. I cried for Olive, for my parents, for what I'd done to Taylor. I cried for not being content before, and I cried because I knew we couldn't get that back. Being the first woman Taylor loved, I had no idea what it must have taken him to admit it to himself—or me. I had destroyed that trust, seemingly for no reason. I cried because I was angry. And then I cried for crying on a beautiful tropical island in a five-star resort.

When I was all cried out, I washed, rinsed, and pulled on the lever, the stream of water disappearing as if it were never there, just like a Caribbean rain shower.

I wrapped the fluffiest white towel I'd ever touched around my chest and stepped out, wiping the moisture from the mirror.

There I was, a blurry mess, but this time, I had puffy red eyes. "Shit." I quickly wet a rag with cold water and held it against my eyes.

When they looked almost back to normal, I combed out my wet hair and then used the hotel blow-dryer. The ceremony was in forty-five minutes. I had taken longer in the shower than I'd meant to.

I rushed around the room, pulling on the maxi dress I'd borrowed from Kirby. The fabric was light and flowy, the empire waist making the V-neckline feel a bit more modest. My favorite part about it was the ombre design, the cream color darkening to pinkie-peach and then a dusty purple. It reminded me of a sunset on the beach, so that had automatically made it an appropriate choice.

I twisted my hair into a sleek, low side bun, and I did my best to put on enough makeup to look a bit more formal. I sucked at being a girl.

When Taylor had said to take the stairs around the corner and down to the beach, I hadn't realized there would be a hundred of them. I took my skirt in my fists and tried not to let my sandals slap against the smooth rock with every step. A small lizard scurried just in front of my feet, and I yelped.

A hotel employee chuckled at me as he passed me, going in the opposite direction. I was glad he was the only witness.

Finally reaching the walkway below, I caught a glimpse of white muslin blowing in the ocean breeze, and I headed in that direction. A handful of white chairs were positioned in front of a white gazebo, white fabric was draped around the pillars, and dozens of roses in muted tones covered the tie-downs.

Jim sat alone in the front row, in the chair closest to the aisle, and I lumbered down the white-sand walkway, navigating it poorly in my shoes. When I finally reached him, he looked up at me with a warm expression.

"You made it," he said, patting the empty chair on his right.

"I did. You're probably surprised, huh?"

"I was hoping."

I grinned, leaning away from him to see his expression. I didn't know him well enough to be certain that he wasn't being a smart-ass. "That's a nice thing to say."

"Hi! I'm here!" a woman said, stumbling past Jim and me before falling into the chair next to me. "Whew!" she said, brushing her long dark curls behind her bare shoulders. She was wearing a white tank top with a long floral skirt. Her big ice-blue eyes overshadowed the intermittent batting of her lashes. She looked like a supermodel, but she moved like an overgrown teenager.

"Yes, you are," Jim said, chuckling. "Rough morning, Ellie?"

"Always. I've been in Shep's room, taking pictures. Hi," she said, one hand letting go of her very expensive camera long enough to greet me. "I'm Ellison, Tyler's friend. Date. Whatever."

"Oh," I said, my body jerking with her firm handshake.

A wry smile sharpened her beautifully bronzed features. "He's a good kisser, isn't he?"

I blinked, completely taken aback by her mention of the mistake-slash-misunderstanding-slash-clusterfuck at Cowboys so many months before.

"That was a long time ago. And an accident."

Jim laughed harder, his belly bobbing. "Those damn boys. I don't know where they got it from. Not from me."

"Not from their mother," Ellison said.

I stiffened at the mention of Jim's late wife, Diane, but he grinned, his eyes lit only with fond memories.

He tapped the gold band on his finger. "She was a good woman. But she would never have caught my attention if she were *all* good."

"The boys definitely get that from you," Ellison said.

I wondered how long she'd known Jim. She seemed familiar enough with him to give him a hard time, but Taylor had never spoken of her.

She reached her arm behind me and squeezed, touching her cheek to mine. "It's so nice to meet the other half of Tyler's other half."

Okay, maybe she's just overly familiar with everyone.

Another woman approached us after taking a few pictures of the gazebo with her phone.

Ellison scooted down, creating an empty chair between us. "Sit here, Cami."

"Oh, thank you," Camille said.

I had the feeling Cami meant more than just giving her a place to sit.

Camille's razored haircut bounced when she sat, and then she tugged at the bodice of her strapless dress. Her arms were covered in dozens of tattoos—large and small, simple and intricate—that ran down to her fingers.

She flashed a perfect smile, and I nodded.

"Falyn," I said.

"I'm Camille."

"Which ..." I began but decided too late that it was an inappropriate question.

"Trenton," she said.

Ellison held up Camille's left hand. "They just got engaged! Can you freaking imagine?"

"I don't ... know what you mean," I said.

Jim laughed. "She means, the thought of marrying a Maddox boy scares her. And she should be worried. She's going to give in sooner or later."

"According to Tyler," Ellison said.

"You are not even fooling yourself," Camille quipped.

Ellison just shook her head, still in good spirits.

After a few minutes, an older couple arrived with another woman. Jim introduced them as his brother, Jack, and his wife, Deana. The woman was America's mother, Pam.

I looked down at my phone, checking the time. It was only ten minutes before the ceremony.

A fifth woman arrived, gripping her clutch and trying her damnedest to appear calm.

"Liis!" Camille said, a hint of panic in her voice. She reacted to Liis's arrival, scooting away from me.

"What?" Ellison said, moving to the last seat in the row. "I thought ..."

Camille seemed to just realize what would come next when she settled into her seat.

Liis stared in horror at the empty seat between Camille and me. Then she quickly sat down and looked forward.

Camille and Ellison traded looks, Camille's cheeks flushing.

Liis was stunning, her shiny black hair a beautiful contrast to her vivid purple dress. It wasn't hard to guess which brother she was with because Thomas had kissed her cheek before cutting across the gazebo's steps.

"Hi, Liis," Jim said, leaning forward.

She did the same, grabbing Jim's outstretched hand. Ellison watched the exchange with a warm smile, but Camille tried her best to ignore it.

Uh-oh. Wonder what that's about?

Music began to play from a few speakers placed on each side toward the front, and the pastor took his place, followed by the men.

The groomsmen were in order by age from youngest to oldest. "Is that Shepley? The best man?" I asked Jim.

Jim nodded, scanning all the boys like a proud father. I could see they were a close family, and I wondered how anyone managed to keep any secrets.

Taylor looked incredible in his tux, but I felt weird thinking that because he looked exactly like Tyler, whose sort-of girlfriend was sitting two seats away from me. Taylor winked at me, and we all chuckled when the other brothers did the same at nearly the same time to their love interests.

The wedding procession began, and I sat back and watched as Travis and Abby renewed their vows, pledging their love to one another. It was beautiful and raw and genuine. They were young, but the way they looked at each other was so touching that it made my heart hurt.

They had a long future ahead of them, a future that included children and grandchildren. As far as I knew, Taylor was the only brother standing who was guaranteed not to have that same chance. There he stood, undeniably happy, as he watched Travis renewing his vows, peeking over at me when his brother said words like *forever* and *always*.

Less than ten minutes after Abby joined Travis in the gazebo, the pastor instructed them to kiss, and we all cheered. Jim hugged me to his side, chuckling and wiping his eyes with his other hand.

I held up my phone to snap a picture as Travis held Abby in his arms, sealing their future with a kiss. I made sure to get Taylor watching them with a grin in the shot.

The wind blew Abby's veil as Travis leaned her back, and the pastor raised his arms.

"I present to you Mr. and Mrs. Travis Maddox," the pastor said, struggling to be heard over the wind, the ocean waves, and the applause and wild cheering from Travis's brothers.

CHAPTER TWENTY

I COULD HEAR NOTHING ELSE but rejoicing as Travis helped Abby down the steps of the gazebo. They rushed past their delighted guests before disappearing behind a wall of tall bushes and palm fronds.

The pastor descended the steps, standing in the aisle. "Mr. and Mrs. Maddox ask that you join them at the restaurant Sails for dinner and the reception. I speak for them when I say thank you for being present on this most special day."

With his hands, he let us know we were free to go, and then Jim stood, prompting everyone else to stand as well. The men stood around with their hands in their pockets while the women gathered their purses and attended to their smeared mascara.

The brothers relaxed, taking the few steps to the front row.

I held up my phone to Thomas and Liis. "Say cheese!"

Thomas stood behind Liis, enveloping her in his arms, and kissed her cheek.

I snapped the picture and then flipped my phone around to show them the result. "Perfect."

Thomas hugged her to his chest. "She is."

"Aw, cute," I said.

Someone tapped on my shoulder.

When I saw it was Taylor, I hugged him, feeling the stiff fabric of his tuxedo beneath my fingers. "Are you hot?" I asked.

"Baking."

"Well, you look intolerably sexy," I said quietly.

His eyes burned when they met mine. "Yeah?"

"There is something to be said about not having all this beauty outside. Makes it easier to stay inside."

Taylor pulled me against him. "I'm flexible. There's a perfectly good beach over there."

Jim clapped his hands and rubbed them together, reminding us other people were around.

But no one was paying attention to our quiet flirtation. Instead, people seemed to notice the palpable tension between Thomas and Liis, and Trenton and Camille.

"Grab your ladies, boys," Jim said. "I'm starved. Let's eat."

Walking hand in hand with Liis, Thomas followed his father, Trenton, and Camille.

"What is all that about?" I asked Taylor.

"Oh, Liis and Camille?"

I nodded.

Ellison leaned in. "They both dated Thomas. It's going to be awkward for a while, but it'll get better."

"Well, you've both kissed the same guy," Tyler said.

Ellison playfully punched him, but the contact still made a thud.

Tyler held his stomach, startled. "Oh!"

Taylor cackled and then interlaced his fingers in mine, and together, we strolled to Sails, the restaurant parallel to our building. The patio was on the opposite side, and the twins sat at one of the empty tables marked *Reserved* for the reception.

Seconds after we sat down, a server approached to take our drink orders.

"Whiskey," Taylor said. "Neat."

"We have a nice Irish Jameson Eighteen."

"Sounds good," he said. He was smiling, but his tone and the skin around his eyes told a different story.

The server looked to me.

"Just a water, please."

"Yes, ma'am. Flat or sparkling?"

"Sparkling," I said. At least that would feel a little more like I was celebrating with everyone else.

Liis and Thomas were across the way, seated with Shepley and America and Shepley's parents. Looking content and in love, Camille and Trenton were chatting with Jim two tables away, completely oblivious of Thomas and Liis at the other table. Whatever awkwardness lived between the two couples must have been one-sided, but I was only speculating.

Taylor pulled off his tuxedo jacket and rolled up the sleeves of his white button-down. He leaned over, pointing to his bow tie, and I helped him loosen it along with his top button.

"Goddamn, I'm glad you're here," he said, leaning the remaining inches to kiss the corner of my mouth. "I was really sweating it until you texted me."

"I told you I would come."

He scanned my face and touched his thumb to my bottom lip. "I want you. Just you. Nothing else. I'm not just content with that, Falyn. You're not part of what I want. You're everything I want. Anything else is a bonus."

I sat back against my chair, trying not to stare. His forearm tensed when he reached up to rub the back of his neck, and I had to cross my legs to control the ache between my thighs. It had been more than two weeks since I felt his skin against mine, and my body was letting me know about it.

"What?" he asked, a coy grin stretching across his face.

"Nothing," I said, looking away as I tried not to smile.

Abby and Travis arrived. Travis held his wife's hand high in the air as her other hand held her bouquet. The hostess announced their arrival over the PA system, and everyone in Sails clapped and cheered. A rock ballad came over the speakers, and Travis pulled Abby out to dance. She looked absolutely beautiful, her elegant caramel waves nearly blending in with her skin that had already been bronzed by the Caribbean sun. The stark white of her dress only made her tan look even darker.

I looked down at my arms, a sad shade of Colorado pale. Whatever time we had left, I committed right then and there to spend it in the sun.

We ate, danced, and listened to the speeches from the best man and maid of honor. We laughed, everyone but me drank, and the men left the covered patio for a bit to smoke the cigars Jim had brought.

Sometime after ten o'clock, Shepley's parents decided to turn in. Jim followed suit not long after.

Eager to be alone, Travis lifted Abby into his arms. She waved her bouquet as he carried her into the night, toward building five. I thought about what would happen once Taylor and I reached our room, and my body screamed at me to make up an excuse for us to leave. I looked over at Taylor having so much fun with his brothers, and I ignored the overwhelming lust building inside of me.

Thomas and Liis were the next to say their good-byes, leaving the middle-born Maddoxes and their cousin with their dates.

An upbeat song came over the speakers, and Taylor pulled me onto the makeshift dance floor, which was only an area of the patio cleared of tables. For the dozenth time that evening, he spun me around, but then he tripped, and we stumbled to the floor. In the few seconds it took for us to fall, despite the many drinks he'd had, he reached out, making sure to hold me inches off the ground while his hip and shoulder banged against the concrete.

"Oh!" his brothers said, all gathering around us.

Shepley, Tyler, and Trenton worked together to help me up.

"You okay?" Shepley asked.

"Yes," I said, watching Taylor struggle to stand upright.

"Are you okay?" Taylor asked me.

"I didn't even hit the floor. Are you okay?"

He nodded, his eyes unfocused. "I can't feel anything at the moment."

Tyler patted his brother's shoulder, hard. "Attaboy."

America shook her head, turning to me. "Want anything besides sparkling water? He's way ahead of you."

"I can see that," I said, smiling when Taylor's brothers took turns pushing him back and forth.

"Okay, okay," Shepley said. "We're all drunk. Quit fucking with one another before someone gets pissed, and a fight breaks out. I don't want to be kicked out of a hotel when we're out of the country."

"This is US territory," Taylor said, weaving. "We're good."

"See?" Ellison said, pointing at Taylor. "He's not too drunk. Partying may proceed."

The boys left for the railing to take a smoke break, and America, Ellison, and Camille joined me at a table.

America rested her arm on top of the back of a chair, looking exhausted.

"You did good," Camille said.

"You planned this?" I asked.

"Every last detail," America said. "Abby wanted nothing to do with it. If I was going to get my dream best friend's wedding where

I was the costar maid of honor, I was going to have to plan it myself. So, I did."

"Impressive," I said.

The pattering of rain prompted the servers to rush to lower the fabric sidewalls and move the tables to protect the guests. The boys didn't move, happily standing in the shower of the warm island rain.

Camille jumped up and rushed to Trenton, hugging him. He twirled her around, and she squealed in delight, letting her head fall back while closing her eyes.

A server approached the boys, offering a glass of water for them to extinguish their cigarettes, and they returned to us. Spatters of rain made translucent specks on the shoulders, chests, and sleeves of their white button-downs.

Taylor sat beside me and lifted my hand to his mouth before kissing my knuckles. "I'm trying to be polite, but all I can think about is getting you back to the room."

"We'll see them tomorrow. It's been a long day. I think they'll understand," I said, unable to even pretend I wanted to stay a second longer.

Taylor stood, bringing me with him. "We're out!" he called.

We walked in a not-so-straight line from Sails to the sidewalk leading back to our building. The waves crashed against the sand less than fifty yards from our path, but it was dark, and all I could see was the sprinkling of lights along the hills across the cove.

Soon, voices could be heard between the sounds of restless water.

"You act as if loving someone can just be flipped off like a light switch. We've had this conversation a dozen times. I want *you*. I'm with *you*."

Taylor froze, and I ran into him from behind.

"Sorry," Taylor whispered, but he wasn't being as quiet as he likely thought. "That's Tommy."

"Shh," I said.

"… missing her," Liis said, "wishing you were with her. And you want me to change everything I trust for that?"

"This is an impossible situation," Thomas responded.

I cringed, feeling guilt and empathy for them both. "C'mon," I whispered. "We shouldn't eavesdrop."

Taylor held up a finger.

"Your payback?" Liis cried. "You've made me believe all weekend that you were falling for me!"

"I am! I have! Jesus Christ, Camille, how can I get that through your head?"

"Oh, fuck," Taylor said. "That's not good."

"Did he just call her Camille?" I asked, horrified.

Taylor nodded, weaving as he tried to stay upright.

"Goddamn it," Thomas said, his voice desperate. "I am so sorry."

"Can we please go?" I asked, tugging on Taylor's arm.

"I am so ... stupid," Liis said. The hurt in her voice could have carried all the way across the ocean.

"Taylor," I hissed.

"I wanna make sure he's okay."

Just then, Thomas emerged from the beach, startled to see us standing there. His features turned severe.

"Hey, man. You all right?" Taylor asked, using me to steady himself.

Thomas's expression softened from anger to concern. "How much have you had to drink?"

"A lot," I said.

"Not that much," Taylor said at the same time.

Thomas glanced at me and then leaned closer to his brother. "Remember what I said. Just sleep it off. You know how you get."

Taylor waved him off, and Thomas patted his brother's shoulder.

"Night." He looked at me. "Make sure he goes straight to bed. No shower. Don't even undress him. Just get him into bed, so he can pass out."

I frowned. I'd seen Taylor drunk before. He had been wasted on New Year's Eve. I was the sad drunk. Taylor just liked to talk a lot—like, until sunrise. But I liked it. He was honest and shameless about his thoughts and feelings on everything. There was no filter, no holding back.

"Falyn?" Thomas said in an authoritative voice.

"I heard you," I said, unappreciative of the order. "C'mon, Taylor, let's go."

Thomas passed us, and I guided Taylor up the never-ending staircase and into our room. He leaned on me to kick off his shoes and then peel off his socks.

"Gross. I think I just need to throw that pair away. They're so sweaty that they probably weigh five pounds apiece."

"Yep," I said, "there's that honesty I love so much."

Taylor looked up at me, something sparking in his eyes, but he looked away, attempting to unbutton his shirt.

"Here, let me help," I said.

He didn't make eye contact while I undressed him, but he couldn't take his eyes off of me while I took off my own clothes. I knelt down in front of him, but he stepped back.

I let my hands slap down to my thighs. "What is going on with you?"

"Nothing," he said, pulling me up to stand. He walked backward, leading me toward the bed.

"Does it have something to do with what Thomas said?"

He shook his head. "No."

I leaned in to kiss him, sliding my hands around his backside. The bed was just behind him, and with one small push, Taylor was lying on his back on the mattress.

I crawled on top of him, and his hands found their way to my hips. He groaned as I sucked on his bottom lip, and his erection formed beneath me as I kissed him.

"Oh my God, this is all I thought about last week," he said.

I sat up. "Not this week?"

"You told me to think about not having kids this week, to really think about it, so I did."

I lowered myself until my breasts were pressed against his warm chest. My mouth made a trail of kisses along his jawline to his earlobe, gently nibbling at the soft skin before pulling away with the slightest suction.

He moaned, grabbing my jaw with both hands, forcing my mouth back to his. I positioned myself over him, but he released me and grabbed my hips, holding me at bay.

"Baby," he said, panting.

I waited, trying to predict what he might say.

"I love you."

"I love you, too," I said, bending down for another kiss.

He sat up, and at the same time, he pushed me so that I was sitting as far away from him as possible while still being on his lap. He swallowed.

"Taylor, what the hell is going on?"

He blew out a controlled breath, his thoughts swimming in the pint of whiskey he'd consumed since dinner. "We should go to sleep."

"What? Why?" I asked, my voice an octave higher.

"Because I need to sleep this off. I shouldn't have had so much to drink."

I shook my head, confused.

Taylor rubbed the back of his neck. "I don't … I don't want you to leave me."

I hugged him. "I'm right here. I'm not going anywhere."

"You promise?" he asked.

I cocked my head.

"Promise me, Falyn. Promise you'll stay."

I shrugged, a bit amused. "Where else am I going to go?"

He touched my face with that look in his eyes, as if he were studying every curve, every line. He sighed, his eyes glossing over. "I didn't know. I thought you … I thought we were … I was pissed at you. I just wanted to get my mind off of it for a night."

I paused. "What night are we talking about?"

"Last week. When I was in San Diego."

I shrugged again. "So, you got drunk?"

The worry that had been in his eyes all day, the dread, even some of the things he'd said now made sense.

My lips parted as the truth set in.

"Baby, I swear to God, I didn't know we were still together. That's not an excuse because I shouldn't have done it anyway."

"What did you do?" I asked, scooting away from him and covering myself with the corner of the comforter. The question had two meanings.

"I went to some dive bar with Thomas. I was upset, and I got as fucking plastered as I could. Thomas left, and I stayed."

"You went home with someone."

"I … the bar was across the street from Thomas's place. She came back with me."

"So, he knows," I said, rolling my eyes at my own words. "Of course he knows. He didn't want you to tell me."

"He didn't believe you'd forgive me."

"I won't."

Taylor's mouth popped open, and then he moved toward me.

I hopped off the bed, yanking the comforter until Taylor stood and I could take it with me. "I admit that what I did was shitty. I have no excuse. It was an awful way to make sure you knew what you were getting into. But you …" I touched my forehead. "You said you were thinking about it. You were thinking about our future and whether you wanted to be with me despite the fact that I'm barren. And you go fuck someone? How exactly did that help your process?"

He stood up, slipped a pair of shorts on, and took a step toward me.

I held out my hand, palm out, and then pointed at him. "Don't touch me."

His shoulders sagged. "Please don't hate me. I thought I was going to go nuts last week. I can't go through that again, Falyn. I can't fucking do it." His voice broke.

I sat down on the bed, staring at nothing in front of me. "Well, I can't either. So, now what?"

He sat next to me. "You can't what?"

"Do this." I looked over at him. "I can't stay with you now. It's not fair for you to even ask."

"You're right. It's not. But I don't give a fuck. I can't lose you again."

"Thomas didn't want you to tell me, but you did anyway. Why?"

"I was going to tell you. I had to before we—"

"You didn't use anything?"

"I can't remember," he said, ashamed.

I made a disgusted face and then wiped away a tear that had escaped down my cheek.

"You promised you'd stay," he said.

"You promised you wouldn't."

"I'm an idiot. That was a stupid thing to do. I admit it. But I didn't go to San Diego to cheat on you. Despite being a complete asshole and trying to distract myself with the first chick who showed me attention, I do love you."

"We were both stupid."

"You were trying to do the right thing. I didn't understand at first, but you were right. It would have been hard for me to make a decision to essentially break up with you if I decided I wanted kids."

I stood up, and he startled.

"What are you doing?" he said, panic in his voice.

"Getting dressed. I think it's safe to say the moment has passed."

I left him for the bathroom, dragging the comforter along with me. I washed my face and brushed my teeth, thankful he hadn't let me go down on him. He would have to get tested for STDs. Just when I'd thought the hard part was behind us, everything had become more complicated.

I dried my face with a towel, and then the tears came. As I cried silently into the lush cloth, everything he'd said and done since I arrived along with the drunk text all made sense. He'd practically admitted it to me then. He had made a huge mistake, but until now, he was the only one who had lost trust. I was just as capable of breaking his heart, and I didn't need to sleep with someone else to do it.

I returned, wearing one of Taylor's T-shirts as a nightgown, carrying the rolled up comforter in my arms. He was still sitting on the end of the bed, his head in his hands.

"I'm going to stay," I said. "We have a lot to work out. But *don't* make me feel like I need to console you. When you're around me, you're going to have to suck it up."

He nodded and pushed himself back until he was at the head of the bed. He watched me fan out the blanket, and then I turned down the covers on my side of the bed.

"Can I hold you?" he asked.

"No," I said simply, lying down and turning my back to him.

I couldn't fall asleep. I heard every noise from his every breath and sigh and every movement he made. The air conditioner eventually kicked on as I stared at the cracks in the walls and then the ceiling. We had spent enough nights together that I knew he wasn't asleep, too, just by the way he breathed, but we lay there, not speaking, not touching, both of us feeling tortured.

CHAPTER TWENTY-ONE

IT SEEMED LIKE I HAD JUST DOZED OFF when the birds outside began to chirp and squawk. Taylor sucked in a deep breath and blew it out, signaling that he was still asleep.

I crept out of bed, put on my swimsuit, cover-up, and hat, and I grabbed my sunglasses and phone before sneaking outside.

"Oh. Hey," Travis said. "Are you going down to the beach?"

I nodded. "You?"

He shook his head. "Headed to Thomas's room before they leave. They have an early flight."

"Oh. Okay. Well, maybe I'll see you later."

"Yeah."

Before I could take another step, Travis said, "Falyn? You make Taylor really happy. He didn't just tell me that the other night, but it's all over his face. Don't let any boneheaded thing he might pull get in the way of that."

My stomach sank. "Does *everyone* know?"

"Does everyone know what?" he asked.

I winced. "Nothing. Congratulations." I passed him, trying not to run down the stairs.

I was the only one on the long stairway and the first one on the beach. The front row of loungers was free, so I picked one in the middle and relaxed.

Ten minutes later, another couple arrived. The sky changed gradually from black to dark blue to light blue, and then a spray of colors was cast across the sky, revealing the ocean and everything else the sunlight touched.

I closed my eyes and listened to the waves and the birds, trying to drown out my thoughts. I breathed in the thick salty air, failing miserably at keeping my focus on the beauty surrounding me and not the ugly visions of Taylor's hands on the woman from California—his lips on hers, kissing and touching her the way he had done to me so many times before, how much she must have enjoyed herself because he was very, very good at those things.

My phone buzzed, and I glanced at the display, swiping when I saw a message from Taylor.

Is that you on the beach?

I turned, quickly locating him on our balcony.

Yes.

Okay. I'll leave you alone. Just wanted to make sure you're okay.

You don't have to.

I don't have to what?

Leave me alone.

Within three minutes, Taylor was standing next to my lounger on the beach, wearing nothing but swimming trunks and sunglasses on his head. He sat down, still panting.

"We have a lot to talk about," I said.

He nodded. "I know sorry isn't enough. Nothing I could say is going to fix it, and I'm going fucking nuts trying to think of something—anything—to make it right."

I faced forward, glad my oversized hat protected me from his stare. "You're right. But you're also not the only one who fucked up here. I recognize that."

He lowered his head, propping his forehead with his hand. "I'm so fucking relieved you're being so levelheaded about this, but I gotta admit, Falyn"—he looked up at me—"it's freaking me out a little that you're this … Zen."

"I don't feel Zen. I feel hurt and angry and betrayed. Our flight leaves at three, and until then, we're here together with your family. Flipping out on you won't solve anything."

He watched me for a moment. "So, what? You're going to dump me as soon as we get back stateside?"

"I don't know."

He sighed. "I'm sorry for hurting you. I'm sorry for betraying you. I'm sorry for making you angry. If you give me another chance, it will *never* happen again."

"I believe you," I said.

He sat on the sand next to me, slipped his fingers between mine, and kissed my knuckles.

After half an hour of silence, Trenton and Camille joined us. Not long after that, Travis came down, alone. He didn't speak and sat two chairs away, staring at the ocean.

"Uh-oh," Trenton said, standing up to walk over to his brother.

Taylor squeezed my hand and then joined the other two men. They chatted quietly but mostly sat in silence, all seeming to stare at the same point in the water.

"I ran into Travis this morning," I said to Camille.

"You did?" she asked. "Where?"

"He was on his way to Thomas's room. Think it has anything to do with that?"

"Thomas?" she paused, pensive. "No," she said. "I don't."

I could tell by the finality in her voice that she was lying. She had dated Thomas before. She knew things, including what had happened in that room.

Travis left abruptly, and Taylor returned to his seat.

"Is he okay?" I asked.

Taylor seemed concerned. "I don't know. He wouldn't say anything."

Camille was pretending not to be listening, so I said exactly what I wanted her to hear.

"For a family who looks so close on the outside, you all sure have a lot of secrets," I said.

Taylor sank back. "I guess so."

"Seems like you're the only one capable of telling the truth." As soon as the words came out of my mouth, I regretted them.

Taylor was wrong. I wasn't Zen. Lashing out and low blows weren't something I'd thought I was capable of, but that didn't seem to be the case at the moment.

Camille turned to me, incensed. "Just because you love someone doesn't mean you have to spill everything you know."

"I guess it depends on who the secrets affect, don't you think?" I asked, still unable to extinguish my anger.

Camille's opened mouth snapped shut, and she found the same spot in the ocean the boys had been staring at before, clenching her teeth. She didn't seem particularly angry with me. It was more like she was frustrated with whatever secret she was keeping.

"So, you know why Travis is upset," I said to Camille. "But you haven't told Trenton because it has to do with Thomas?"

Taylor looked to Camille for confirmation, and she looked to me, desperate for me to stop.

My mouth pulled to the side. "I'm sorry. None of this is directed at you." I sighed. "We all have secrets, Cami. We just have to make sure keeping them doesn't hurt the people we love."

Camille watched me for a long time, and then her eyes returned to the ocean, filling with salty tears.

"What the hell is going on around here?" Taylor asked, his head moving back and forth between Camille and me.

"We should probably get some breakfast and then start packing. We have to leave for the airport by … what do you think? Noon?" I asked.

"Yeah," Taylor said, still concerned over Camille. He stood, holding out his hand for me.

I took it and followed him to Bleuwater, the primary dining venue on the property.

Taylor was quiet, eating his omelet, lost in thought while he chewed.

"Who was she?" I asked.

Taylor stopped chewing.

I wrinkled my nose and shook my head. "Don't answer that."

"She wasn't you."

"Nope," I said before clenching my teeth.

He was waiting patiently as the anger boiled inside of me. He knew as well as I did what was coming.

"Four days? Really?" I hissed.

Taylor stared at his plate.

"Say something," I said.

"There is nothing to say. I have no excuse. I fucked up."

"You said a week. That's what *you* said. You couldn't even make it to your own deadline before you were swiping your player's card in someone else's slot."

He nodded.

"Don't fucking nod at me. Don't just sit there and take it."

He looked up at me. "What do you want me to say? I'm sitting here, scared to death that you're going to kick me to the curb, and there's not a damn thing I can do because we both know I deserve it, Falyn. So, I'm just going to keep my fucking head down."

"How am I supposed to respond to that?"

He opened his mouth to speak and then thought better of it.

I sat back in my chair, fuming, and at the same time, the guilt and anguish in his eyes was hard to watch. He already felt bad. He already knew it was wrong. He was already sorry. I was angry with him for all of those things, too. I deserved a guilt-free moment of anger, and he couldn't even give me that.

I covered my face, unable to finish my meal.

"Do you want me to just get the check?" he asked, sounding miserable.

I could only nod.

"Jesus Christ," he whispered. "Everything was so good. How did we get here?"

Once we finished breakfast, we returned to the room, packed, and then made the jaunt to the lobby for checkout. The entrance was abuzz with activity—people coming and going, employees busy with guests.

"We should have a car waiting outside," Taylor said to the desk clerk.

"All right," she said. "You're all set. I hope you enjoyed your stay at The Ritz-Carlton and that you come back to visit us soon."

"Thank you," Taylor said.

He carried our bags outside and greeted the same driver who had collected me from the airport.

Taylor stared out the window for most of the drive to Charlotte Amalie, and he only spoke when necessary once we reached the airport.

"Two hours early," I said, reading my watch.

Taylor sat next to me at our gate, but he otherwise acted as if I were just another traveler in the terminal. An airplane headed for New York was boarding. We were so early that the monitor above the desk didn't reflect our flight.

I checked my watch several times, curious if he was worried about his family or me or both and if I should try to talk to him about it or leave him to his thoughts.

An infant squalled somewhere behind us, and like so many other times when I'd heard a newborn, something twinged in my chest. Families were all around us, exasperated mothers and fathers trying their best to keep their tired, bored toddlers entertained.

I wondered if Taylor would ever watch children with longing the way I did, if he'd even have to because of our rough start, and if the weekend in St. Thomas was the beginning of our end.

"Taylor," I said.

He pulled his finger from his mouth, spitting out a hangnail. "I'm sorry. I'm not trying to ignore you. I just have a lot on my mind."

"Do you want to talk about Travis?" I asked.

"No, I want to talk about us. Are you just waiting? Are you going to drop a bomb on me when we get home?"

He looked at me, dread in his eyes. "Are you?"

I kept my voice low. "You fucked another woman because you were mad at me, and worse, you don't know if you used protection. I don't know how I feel about it. I don't know how I'm going to feel about it later today or tomorrow or next week. This is one of those things that we're going to have to play by ear."

He peered down at the floor, his knee bouncing.

"What else do you want to talk about?" I asked.

"That's plenty."

I craned my neck, frustrated. "What else?"

"What you said, about all of us having secrets, is true. I don't like it."

"I saw Travis this morning. He was fine."

Taylor's eyebrows shot up. "Before the beach?"

"Yes, as I was leaving the room, he was going to see Thomas."

Taylor thought about that and then shook his head. "Damn it. Something's going on with them. Something big. Nothing good either."

"I think Camille has an idea of what it is."

Taylor narrowed his eyes. "She kept it from Trenton that she was dating Thomas. She didn't tell Trent for a long time. I've always thought there was a bigger reason behind it. I mean ... we all know Cami. Trenton was in love with her for years. No one knew Thomas was dating her, and I assumed it was so we wouldn't jump his shit. Now ... I don't know. It has something to do with Travis, and that makes no sense."

"Travis looked devastated. What would do that to him?"

Taylor shook his head. "Losing Abby. That's about it. He just doesn't give a shit about anything else. Fuck ... do you think it's my dad? Maybe he's sick."

I shook my head. "It wouldn't make sense for Thomas to only tell Travis, right?"

Taylor thought for a long time, and then he sighed. "I don't know. I don't want to think about it anymore. It scares me and pisses me off. Camille shouldn't know more about my family than I do or than Trenton does. That's fucked up."

"You can think about it. It's a distraction," I said.

"From us?" he asked.

I nodded.

His shoulders fell, and he leaned forward, rubbing his temples with his fingers. "Please don't."

I couldn't stand the misery anymore. "I love you. You said once that it's not a phrase you throw around. It's not for me either. I don't like what you did. But I don't like what I did either."

"Just promise me, you'll try."

"Taylor—"

"I don't care. I don't fucking care. We have to fix this."

"I'm not going to drop anything on you. We have a lot to talk about. If we hit a wall, you'll see it coming."

"I do. I see it coming."

"No, you don't," I said, exasperated.

"You don't get it," he hissed, leaning in closer. His jaw worked under his skin. "I have never been so afraid as I was when driving back to Estes from your apartment. I've never felt so lost as I did in the hallway outside Thomas's door, waiting for him to get home. I thought I would feel better when he got there. I didn't. I thought Tommy could tell me something that would make sense of how I felt and my fears, but he couldn't. That feeling has only gotten worse, Falyn. Not until I saw you standing in that lobby did I realize what it was."

I waited. The agony in his eyes made me want to look away.

"It was grief, Falyn. I haven't felt it since I was a kid, but I remember that helpless feeling when you lose someone. No matter how much you love someone, you can't bring them back. No matter how much you scream or drink or beg or pray ... a hole was created when they left. It burns and rots you from the inside out until you stop crying for the pain to stop and start accepting it as the way life will be."

I sucked in a breath, horrified.

"I'm not saying I don't deserve to be left. But I'll do anything if you'll just give me a chance to prove myself to you. Thomas said something to me in Eakins about not sleeping with someone to dull the pain. It's no excuse, but it was a mistake, and I'll learn from it."

I listened to his words and then replayed them in my mind. "I have conditions," I blurted out.

"Name them," he said without hesitation.

"You have to get tested."

"Already scheduled."

"I need time. I can't pretend that nothing happened."

"Understandable."

"I'll need patience from you if and when I have a moment of jealousy and when it takes me a little bit to remember that it was me who set this all in motion and that it's mostly my fault."

Taylor spoke his words slowly, each one emphasized, "This is not your fault. We both fucked up. We both regret it."

"That's about the only thing I know right now," I said.

"No. You know we love each other. And because of that, I know things will get better."

When I nodded, Taylor sat back in his seat, only a bit more relaxed than before. Either he didn't believe his own words, or he thought I didn't. He slid his fingers between mine, and we waited in another awkward silence until our flight was called.

CHAPTER TWENTY-TWO

"I CAN'T DO THIS."

I heard him say the words, but thirteen weeks of work and forgiveness wouldn't allow me to believe it. I sat on a chair in his Colorado Springs hotel room, the beige carpet and drapes mirroring my blank expression.

Taylor sat on the bed with his head in his hands. He wore only a white towel around his waist, his skin still glistening from the shower.

"You checked in two days ago," I said.

He nodded.

"You're going to give up now?" I asked.

He looked up at me, frustration in his eyes. I knew then that I'd lost him. Gone was the longing, the guilt, and the patience.

I stood up, crossing my arms. "What happened to things getting better? To making this work? To forgiveness and loving each other?"

He didn't answer.

"You love me," I said.

"More than I could ever explain to you."

"Then I don't understand!" I said, my volume surprising both of us. My eyes filled with tears. "I've worked on this. I've spent hours and weekends trying to make things better, working it out in my own head that you've had your hands ... and other things ... on another woman. I'm here, taking a chance on everything, ignoring the images in my mind that haunt me every single time we're in bed. And you're just going to quit on me? No," I said, shaking my head, realizing that I was pacing but not stopping myself. "You can't just say it's over. It's not over."

"I didn't," he said, amused. "But this ... this is good. I'm liking this."

I stood in the middle of the room, narrowing my eyes at him. "Then what were you talking about?"

He sighed. "I haven't brought up the commute because ... well ... we were dealing with bigger things, and I was chickenshit." He stood up, cupping my shoulders. "But I still want that, everything we talked about before. I can't keep living apart. I want to at least be in the same city."

I fell to the bed, holding my middle. "I thought you were ending it."

He knelt in front of me. "Fuck no. After the weeks I've been killing myself, trying to make it up to you?"

I shot him a dubious look. "Killing yourself?"

He interlocked his fingers behind the small of my back, smiling. "I didn't say it wasn't enjoyable."

He kissed my cheek, tender and sweet. I leaned into his lips, giggling.

The landline rang, and after a moment of confusion, Taylor hopped up and held the receiver to his ear. "Hello? Yeah, that's me. Who?" When recognition lit his eyes, all the color drained from his face. "I'll, um ... I'll be right down." He hung up the phone.

"Everything all right?" I asked.

"The desk clerk said that a woman is waiting for me in the lounge. Alyssa Davies."

I shrugged and shook my head, having no recollection of the name.

"It's the woman I ... from San Diego."

"She's *here*?" I asked, standing.

"I guess so," he said, rubbing the back of his neck.

"Why?"

He shook his head. "I don't know, baby."

"You were tested," I said, trying not to show the intense panic igniting inside of me.

"Yeah ... no, that can't be it. That's not it."

My heart pounded against my rib cage, making the vessels in my head throb and my fingers tremble.

Taylor's worry vanished, and a contrived smile softened his face. "C'mon. We'll find out together."

I took his outreached hand and grabbed my purse before following Taylor into the hall. We took the elevator to the first floor, and then we found the lounge. Taylor didn't let go of my hand as he paused when he saw a beautiful woman sitting alone at one of the booths along the wall.

He tugged me forward and sat down, scooting across the bench. I sat next to him, looking at the last woman I'd ever expected to meet face-to-face.

"I know you're surprised to see me," she said. "I apologize for not calling first." She glanced at me, blinking and looking down at her folded hands on the table. "But what I have to say needed to be said in person."

Taylor's hand squeezed mine. I wasn't sure he even knew he was doing it.

"Does she ..." Alyssa trailed off.

Taylor nodded. "This is my girlfriend, Falyn. She knows who you are and what happened."

"Well, she doesn't know this," Alyssa said, raising her eyebrows. She pulled a folded paper that looked like it had been wadded up a few times and pushed it across the table to Taylor.

He opened it, read it, and set it down in front of him. I waited, staring at the side of his face. His eyes had lost focus. He was so still that I wasn't sure if he was still breathing.

I had a few ideas about what the paper said, none of them I wanted to be true.

"Pregnant?" Taylor said, swallowing.

All the air was knocked out of me, and my eyes instantly glossed over.

Alyssa sighed. "Fifteen weeks tomorrow. I scheduled an abortion for Thursday."

"You ... do you want me to go with you?" Taylor asked.

Alyssa breathed a laugh, unimpressed. "No. I canceled it."

"So ..." Taylor began. "You're keeping it."

"No."

I rubbed my forehead and then looked down, trying not to scream. This wasn't happening to us, to that baby.

"You're giving it up?" Taylor asked.

"That depends," Alyssa said, putting the paper back into her purse. Her cool demeanor was maddening. "I'm not in the position to raise it. Are you?"

Taylor touched his chest. "You're asking me if I want to keep it."

She folded her hands again. "I'm due December seventh. Shortly after, I have a rather large case that will begin court proceedings. I'm prepared to carry to term and then sign over rights, as I would with a typical adoption."

She's beautiful, confident, pregnant with Taylor's baby, and a lawyer? Could she surpass me in any more ways?

"Stop," I said. "You need to think about what you're doing."

She glared at me. "Excuse me. I respect that you're here for Taylor, but I'm not asking for your opinion."

"I understand that," I said. "But I've been in your position. This is not a business transaction. It's a baby."

"You've—"

"Given up a child, yes. It's not something that ever goes away. Just ... I guess I'm hoping that you make sure it's truly what you want before you decide."

She blinked, for the first time seeing both of us, and then she trained her eyes on Taylor. "I'm leaving it up to you. If you choose to also relinquish your rights, I'll begin the process of looking for candidates for the adoption. A few agencies in San Diego have been recommended to me."

"If you want to keep the baby," I said, "I know Taylor will help you."

He nodded. He seemed a million miles away.

"I don't need anyone's help," Alyssa said, "but I appreciate the offer."

I stood up.

Taylor reached for me. "Where are you going?" he asked.

"Home."

"Just ... give me a second. I'll drive you."

My next words caught in my throat. "You should stay. You two have a lot to talk about."

Taylor began to stand, but I touched his shoulder.

"This decision has nothing to do with me, Taylor. And it's important."

Taylor stared at me, taking deep breaths. "What do you mean, it has nothing to do with you?"

"I mean, it's your decision to make."

He shifted in his seat. "Just remember what you said to me not ten minutes ago."

"I remember. I remember a lot of things. Stay here. You'll regret it if you don't."

I set down the phone he'd given me on the table and then left Taylor and Alyssa behind.

"Falyn!" he called after me.

But I ignored him.

Out of the lounge, I walked across the lobby, passing Dalton on the way.

"Hey, Falyn. You headin' out?" he asked.

I smiled politely and continued through the doors, beginning my trek to downtown. I expected a long walk, but every step I took became more difficult as I fought the urge to sob.

But I would not cry. So many times I'd said—to myself and to Taylor—that we had met for a reason. I'd thought it was so that I could have closure with my past, but sad stories had a funny way of ending the way they'd begun, and the irony of our situation wasn't lost on me. I had given up my child and couldn't have more. Taylor was going to stay with me anyway, and by a snowball of events that had started with me, Taylor would have a child of his own after all.

The streetlights were buzzing, flickering as they reacted to the dim light. Stars were beginning to poke through the twilight sky, and I still had a long way to go. The cars whizzed by, a few full of kids, blaring music and honking as they passed, and I walked alone with the reality of what Alyssa's pregnancy meant sinking in with every step.

Summer was in full swing, and it hadn't rained in weeks. The world was still green but dry. The intermittent wildfires had brought Taylor's crew to the area.

The walk to downtown took longer than I'd thought, and I was out of shape. A dark Mercedes G-Wagon slowed next to me, and the tinted passenger window rolled down, revealing Blaire behind the wheel and no one else in the car. I began to walk again, but she honked.

"Falyn?" she called. "Where are you headed, dear?"

I sighed. "No one can hear you."

"Are you going home?"

"Yes."

"Please let me drive you. We don't have to talk."

I looked down the road and then back at Blaire. "Not a word?" She shook her head.

As much as I didn't want to get in that SUV, my feet were already hurting, and all I wanted was to crawl into my bed and cry. I opened the door and got in.

A victorious smile lit Blaire's face, and she pulled away from the curb.

After just a quarter of a mile, Blaire sighed. "Your father hasn't been well. I don't think this campaign is good for him."

I didn't respond.

She pressed her lips together. "The car is still parked in the garage at the house. Your father drives it sometimes to keep everything in order. Still changes the oil. We would like you to have it back."

"No."

"It's dangerous to walk around alone in the dark."

"I rarely venture out," I said simply.

"But on the off chance that you do ..."

"You said we didn't have to talk."

Blaire parked in one of the many empty spots in front of the Bucksaw. "You have to come home, Falyn—or at least let us move you into an apartment and your father can get you a decent job."

"Why?"

"You know why," she snapped.

"It's always about appearances, isn't it? You couldn't care less about me."

"That's not true. I'm appalled that you live up there in that filth," she said, looking up at the café's second floor.

"Don't you see where keeping up appearances has gotten our family? Your husband is sick. Your daughter wants nothing to do with you. And for what?"

"Because it's important!" she hissed, her hair swaying when she moved her head.

"To you. It's only important to you. I'm not obligated to live a life I hate so that you can feel important."

She narrowed her eyes. "What is wrong with our way of life? Because I want you to go to school? Because I want you to live somewhere that doesn't need to be condemned?"

"When you say it that way, it sounds wonderful. But you can't keep omitting the ugly parts. You can't just erase a pregnancy. You can't hide a baby. You can't pretend your daughter isn't a waitress who doesn't want to be a doctor. Our life is not a highlight reel. It's time you stopped pretending it was."

She inhaled through her nose. "You have always been supremely selfish. I don't know why I expected tonight to be any different."

"Don't come back," I said before getting out of the car.

"Falyn," she called.

I leaned down as the passenger window lowered.

"This is the last slap in the face. If your father loses this campaign because of you, we won't offer to help you again."

"I didn't expect that you would."

I thanked her for the ride and then left her alone, ignoring the sound of my name.

By the time I pushed open the glass door, it was night, and I was exhausted—physically, emotionally, and mentally.

The headlights of the G-Wagon poured through the glass wall as Blaire backed out and then disappeared as she pulled away.

The dining area was dark, and I was alone. I sat on the orange-and-white tiles, lay on my side, and then curled up into a ball before crying myself to sleep.

Someone stabbed a finger into my shoulder, and I winced. The person did it again, and I opened my eyes, raising my hand to protect me from another jab.

My vision sharpened, and I saw Pete standing over me, concern in his eyes.

I wiped my face, sitting up. "What time is it?" I asked, not really expecting an answer.

I twisted the narrow leather band on my wrist to see the face of my watch. It was five a.m. on Saturday morning. Chuck and Phaedra would be arriving at any moment.

"Shit," I said, scrambling to my feet.

Before I could make a dash for the stairs, Pete grabbed my wrist.

I relaxed my shoulders, covering his hand with mine. "I'm okay."

He didn't let go.

"Really. I'm okay."

Pete touched his thumb to his lips, lifting his pinky in the air. "No. I wasn't drinking. The girl Taylor was with in San Diego? She's pregnant."

Pete's eyebrows shot up to his hairline, and he released my arm. I hurried to the stairs, taking them two at a time.

I jumped in the shower, pushing down memories of the previous evening before they could surface.

I was never so glad to be working on a Saturday. It would be busy, and there was a festival this weekend. There was no better distraction than impatient, hungry customers. Without a phone, Taylor would have no way to contact me, other than coming to the Bucksaw, and I knew he was on second shift that day and the next.

I was conflicted, trying not to cry one minute and fighting anger the next. I worried, knowing he was miles away in the burning woods with so much on his mind. Leaving him alone to deal with Alyssa hadn't helped matters any, but I had created the mess we were all in. Taylor had made it worse. But his job wasn't going to change, and neither were our problems. It was time I bowed out for good. One of us had to do it.

I walked down the stairs, tying my still damp hair into a bun at the crown of my head, and I heard Phaedra having a one-sided conversation. I pushed through the double doors and sat on my regular counter in the kitchen, across from the center prep table.

Hector was washing vegetables, keeping his head down, not saying a word. Pete was peeling potatoes, grimacing at me while he worked.

"What the hell is going on?" Phaedra asked.

Chuck was standing behind her with no sign of talking her down. I opened my mouth to speak, but she held up her hand.

"And don't tell me it's nothing, that it's no big deal, or that you just had a bad night because nothing that's nothing is going to make you curl up in the fetal position on a tiled floor for an entire night."

I snapped my opened mouth shut. Phaedra could intimidate anyone, but she had never been so cross with me.

"Spill it," Phaedra demanded.

"When I asked Taylor for the break, he went to San Diego to see his brother. He ended up ... with another woman while he was there. He told me about it in Saint Thomas. We've been working through it."

"And?" she asked, unfazed.

I sucked in a breath, feeling a lump form in my throat. "She came to the hotel last night. She's pregnant."

Audible gasps came from all four of my coworkers.

I quickly wiped away a few escaped tears.

"She's keeping it?" Chuck asked.

I nodded.

Phaedra shifted, trying to uphold her stern demeanor. "What does Taylor have to say?"

"I didn't stick around long after that."

Phaedra held out a set of keys and tossed them to me. I caught them, recognizing the key chain.

"There is also the matter of your parents dropping off your vehicle. You'll have to move it. It's sitting in customer parking."

"What?" I asked.

"I told them you didn't want it," Chuck said. "The key is in the ignition."

I looked down at the shiny metal in my hands. "My car is here? They just left it?"

"Lord, girl. Aren't you listening?" Phaedra asked.

"Where should I … park it?"

Phaedra pointed in the general direction of the street. "Next to where Kirby usually parks. Well? Get goin'."

"Why are you angry?" I asked, wiping my cheek with my wrist.

"I'm not angry, damn it! I'm worried. Beat it. I've got pies to make." She whipped around, wiping her eyes as she marched to the back.

"Want me to move it?" Chuck asked.

I shook my head. "I'll do it."

"Falyn," Chuck said, his voice soft, "Pete finding you on the floor like that is concerning. We wish you'd talk to us."

"It just happened. I haven't had time to talk to anyone."

"You should have called."

"I gave Taylor back the phone."

"Does he know that?"

I nodded.

"So, he knows it's over then."

I gripped the keys in my palm, feeling the edges digging into my skin. "He has something far more important to concentrate on."

I turned for the door, but Chuck called out, "Falyn?"

I stopped but didn't turn around.

"You should let him decide if you're his priority or not."

"It's not that I don't think he would choose me," I said over my shoulder. "It's just that I couldn't live with myself if he did."

CHAPTER TWENTY-THREE

AFTER WORK ON SATURDAY AND SUNDAY NIGHTS, instead of waiting for Taylor to come to the Bucksaw after his shift, I would get into my car and drive. I would keep my foot on the gas pedal until I was too tired to continue, trying to get lost and find my way back again.

Monday, I told myself that Taylor would know better than to show up at my place of work, but at eleven thirty, he and his crew arrived.

Kirby, already knowing what to do, sat them at the back table, and Phaedra took their orders. I did my best to ignore them, but Dalton made it a point to tell me hello.

I remained polite, only seeing Taylor from the corners of my eyes. He was staring at me, waiting for me to see him, but I passed by.

"Falyn! Order up!" Chuck yelled.

My feet moved even quicker than normal toward Chuck's voice. There was no food in the window, so I knew he was allowing me a moment to collect myself. I slipped through the double doors and escaped to my countertop, letting it support my weight as I leaned against it.

"You okay, kiddo?" Chuck asked.

I quickly shook my head. I took a deep breath and then used both of my hands to burst through the swinging doors. If I looked unsure in my decision to end things or showed even a second of weakness, Taylor would be relentless until I gave in. If his post-island actions were any indication, he would never give me a moment of peace.

Taylor didn't try to make a scene. He ate his food and paid his bill, and then they left.

By one o'clock the next day, I thought that I'd seen the last of him, but he arrived for lunch again—this time, with Trex in tow. Phaedra waited on them again.

I passed by their table, and Taylor reached out for me. "Falyn. For the love of Christ."

Even though the desperation in his voice made me want to break down, I ignored him, and he said nothing else. Just a few of the closer tables noticed, but Phaedra frowned.

"Falyn, honey," Phaedra said, "this can't go on."

I nodded, pushing through the double doors, knowing Phaedra was heading to Taylor's table. When she returned, I looked at her from under my brow, ashamed that she had to deal with my problems.

"I told him he can still come in, but only if he promises not to cause a scene. He's agreed not to bother you."

I nodded, hugging my middle.

"Should I tell him not to come back?" Phaedra asked. "I hate to be mean to the poor kid. He looks like a lost kitten."

"I don't think he would take that well. It's just for the summer, right? He can't drive here every day when he's back in Estes Park. By next summer, if they come back, he'll be over it."

Phaedra patted my arm. "I don't know, baby. From where I'm standing, it doesn't look like either one of you will." She scrunched her face. "You sure you can't try to work it out? I know it's a mess, but it might be a little easier to fix it together."

I shook my head and stood up straight before pushing through the kitchen doors and waiting on my tables as if my heart weren't broken.

I lay in bed that night, swearing to banish every memory of Taylor—the way he'd held me, the way his lips had warmed mine, and the way his voice had softened whenever he told me he loved me.

It was better than the agony of mourning him.

That went on for days, and each day he came in, I would tell myself it would get easier to see him. But it didn't.

Just like Taylor had said, I had to accept that the constant ache was going to be a part of my day. I couldn't waste another moment, another tear, on thoughts of him. His life had veered off the path we were on. If he wouldn't let me forget him, I would learn to live with the pain.

∞

May ended, and June began.

The skies grew hazier every day, and reports on television were circulating the globe. The wildfires in our area were at a peak, the firefighters and hotshot crews seeing more occurrences than they had in a decade. Still, Taylor didn't miss a lunch—sometimes, coming in as late as two or three, and other days, hurrying in while covered in soot and sweat.

By mid-July, Chuck and Phaedra were considering banning Taylor from the restaurant, but no one could justify it. He never caused a ruckus, he always ordered a meal, he always paid and tipped well, and he was always polite. He never approached me or even tried to initiate conversation.

Taylor would simply show up, waiting patiently for me to give in.

The Bucksaw had been closed for half an hour, and Kirby and I had just finished our nightly duties when Phaedra broached the subject of how to handle Taylor.

"You can't ban him for loving Falyn," Kirby said, disgusted with our conversation.

"It's just not natural," Phaedra said. "And it damn well isn't healthy for either of them. He's got a baby on the way. He needs to be preparing for that."

I agreed.

"He's a good kid, Phaedra," Chuck said. "He misses her. He'll go back to Estes after the season, the baby will come in December, and he'll be busy."

Kirby pouted. "You're being cruel."

"Kirby," Phaedra warned.

"I have always been honest with him. I want nothing to do with adoption," I said.

"But this is his child!" Kirby screeched.

"You don't understand," I snapped.

"No, you're right. I don't," she said. "But that's because it makes no sense."

"We might be talking about his child, but it poses the same risks as adoption—risks I'm not emotionally capable of taking. She could come back. She could want joint custody or full custody. She could win, Kirby, and she could take the baby to California. I'm not willing to lose another child."

She paused. "What do you mean ... another child?"

I covered my face.

Phaedra put her hands on my shoulders. "Falyn had a baby just after high school. She gave her daughter up."

Kirby stared at me for a long time. "I'm so sorry." Once the shock wore off, her expression twisted into revulsion. "I'm sorry. I really am. But he was willing to forgo a family for you, and you won't even entertain the idea of a family for him?" she asked. "You think you're saving him or whatever, but you're covering your own ass. You're scared."

"Kirby!" Phaedra said. "Enough!"

Kirby hopped off the stool, looking for something to clean. She turned up the volume on the small overhead television in the corner. Looking up at it, she crossed her arms.

"Falyn?" Kirby said, watching the screen.

"Leave her be, Kirby," Chuck said.

"Falyn?" Kirby said again, scrambling for the remote and turning the volume to the maximum level.

The rest of us watched in horror as a female reporter stood in front of tall grass and burning trees not two hundred yards behind her while the words *ALPINE HOTSHOT CREW FEARED MISSING* scrolled across the bottom of the screen.

"That's correct, Phil. The Estes Park crew who have traveled to the Colorado Springs area to help control this fire have not returned or reported in, and officials have listed them as missing."

I rushed to the television, standing next to Kirby. In the same moment, everything I swore to forget came back to me—the way his skin felt against mine, the dimple that sunk into his chin, his laugh, the security I felt in his arms, and the sadness in his eyes when I'd walked away from him in the hotel.

"Cassandra, do officials have an idea where the crew is?" the anchorman asked.

"The last reported communication with the Estes Park crew was at six o'clock this evening, right about the time the two main fires converged."

I grabbed my keys before sprinting out to my car. The moment my seat belt clicked, I twisted the key in the ignition and stomped on the gas.

Less than ten minutes later, Taylor's hotel came into view. I parked and ran inside, immediately seeing Ellison standing with a crowd of firefighters and hotshot crew members from the entire state. She was watching the large flat screen with her mouth covered.

"Ellie!" I called.

She ran to hug me, nearly knocking me over. She squeezed me tight, sniffling.

"I just heard. Any news?" I asked, trying not to panic.

She released me and shook her head, wiping her nose with a tissue she had tucked in her palm. "Nothing. We arrived just after seven. Tyler drove like a maniac. He's out there with the crews, looking for them."

I hugged her. "I know they're okay."

"Because they have to be." She held me at bay, forcing a brave smile. "I heard about the baby. First Maddox grandbaby. Jim's ecstatic."

My face fell.

"Oh God. Oh, no. Did you ... are you not pregnant anymore?"

I stared at her, utterly confused and horrified. She mirrored my expression.

"You're right," she said. "This isn't the time. Let's go sit. Trex is getting updates every half an hour from his people."

"His people?"

Ellison shrugged. "I don't know. He just said his people."

We sat together on the couch in the lobby, surrounded by firefighters, hotshots, and various officials. As the night wore on, the crowd thinned.

My eyes felt heavy, and every time I blinked, it seemed more difficult to open them again. The desk clerk brought us coffee and a plate of doughnuts, but neither Ellison nor I touched the food.

Trex came over, sitting in the chair adjacent to our sofa.

"Any word?" Ellison asked.

Trex shook his head, clearly disheartened.

"What about the rescue team?" I asked.

"Nothing," Trex said. "I'm sorry. My guys only give visual confirmation, and they haven't seen anyone in an hour. The helos are up with spotlights, but the smoke is making it difficult to see." He glanced back at the desk clerk and then shook his head. "I'm going to call them in ten minutes. I'll let you know the moment I hear anything."

Ellison nodded, and then her attention was drawn to the entrance.

Taylor walked in, his skin caked in dirt and soot. He removed his bright blue hard hat, and I stood, my eyes instantly filling with tears.

I leaned forward, my body half-frozen, half-screaming at me to run to him.

Ellison jumped out of her seat and rushed past me, throwing her arms around him.

It wasn't Taylor but Tyler. I'd only felt that much devastation one other time in my life—the moment Olive was pulled from my arms.

Matching clean streaks ran down Tyler's cheeks as he hugged Ellison, shaking his head.

"No," I whispered. "No!"

Tyler rushed over to me. "Taylor's crew was cut off when the fires converged. It's possible that they could have backed themselves into a cave, but ... the temperatures are ... it doesn't look good, Falyn. I tried. They dragged me out. I'm sorry."

He hugged me, and my hands fell limp at my sides.

There were no tears, no pain, no waves of emotion. There was nothing.

And then my knees buckled, and I wailed.

∽

By morning, Ellison was lying on Tyler's lap, asleep, while he sipped his fourth cup of coffee. His eyes had been glued on the television screen, just like mine.

Fresh crews came downstairs, ready for a second search-and-rescue mission. Tyler's team had all trudged in and gone upstairs to catch what sleep they could.

Trex stood at the desk with the woman who had brought us coffee all night. His team had turned in two hours before, waiting until daylight before resuming their air search.

I stood, and Tyler's eyes followed.

"I have to go to work," I said. "I can't sit here anymore. I have to stay busy."

Tyler rubbed the back of his neck, like Taylor would when he was upset or nervous. "I'll let you know the moment I hear something."

"Are you going back out?" I asked.

"I'm not sure they'll let me. I might have punched one or two people before they removed me from the area."

"He's your brother. They'll understand."

Tyler's eyes glossed over, and his bottom lip trembled. His head fell forward, and Ellison touched his shoulder, whispering words of comfort.

I made my way out to the parking lot, moving in slow motion. The drive to the Bucksaw was a blur. I had no thoughts. I didn't cry. Everything was automatic—breathing, braking, turning.

My parking spot was taken, so I parked elsewhere, but by the time I stepped onto the tiles of the dining area, I had forgotten where.

I shuffled across the floor in the same clothes I'd worn the day before, my apron still tied around my waist.

"Dear Jesus," Phaedra said, rushing over and hooking her arm behind me. She escorted me to the kitchen. "Any word?"

Kirby burst through the swinging doors, covering her mouth when she saw me. Chuck, Hector, and Pete stopped what they were doing and stared.

"Nothing. They forced Tyler to ... they called off the search just after midnight. They headed out again this morning."

"Falyn," Kirby said, "have you slept?"

I shook my head.

"All right. Kirby, there's a bottle of pills in my bag, point five milligrams. Bring it upstairs. C'mon, baby girl, you've got to sleep."

I slinked out of Phaedra's grip. "I can't. I have to work. I have to stay busy."

Chuck shook his head. "Honey, you're in no state to wait tables."

"Then Kirby and I can trade for the day." I pleaded with Kirby with my eyes.

Kirby waited for Phaedra's approval.

"Falyn—" Phaedra began.

"Please!" I screamed, closing my eyes. "Please. Just let me work. I can't go upstairs and lie in that bed alone, knowing he's out there somewhere."

Chuck nodded to his wife, and then she dipped her head.

"All right. Kirby, you're on server duty. I'll help."

Kirby pushed through the double doors, going straight over to the tables. I tended to the hostess station, bussing tables and cleaning the floor between customers.

A family came in—a father with tattoo sleeves on both arms, the mother with no tattoos, and two girls and a boy, all three kids under six. The youngest, maybe six months, was snuggled against his mother in a Boba Wrap as he slept, and I choked back the unexpected emotions that seeing him induced.

I seated them at the back table where Taylor had been seated for the last two months and handed them menus. "Kirby will be your server this morning. Enjoy."

I froze when I recognized the man standing by the hostess station as Taylor. Covered in thick mud, he was still wearing all his gear, including his pack and hard hat. The creases next to his eyes were the only skin on his face not covered with soot.

I covered my mouth, stifling a sob.

He took a step, removing his hat. "They said you waited all night at the hotel."

I couldn't respond. I knew if I opened my mouth, all I would be able to do was bawl.

"Is it true?" he asked, his eyes glossing over. He fidgeted with his helmet.

Everyone in the room was staring at the filthy man who reeked of campfire, and then they all looked at me.

As soon as I nodded, my legs gave way, and I fell to my knees, my hand still cupped over my trembling lips.

Taylor rushed to the floor, falling onto his knees, too.

He touched my cheeks, and I hugged him, pulling him to me, grasping at his clothes like he might be taken away from me at any moment. I let the sob break free, my cries filling the café.

He held me as long as I needed, allowing me to hug him as tightly as I wanted. His coat and pack were hard to navigate around, but I didn't pay attention to that. I just grabbed whatever my hands landed on and pulled him against me.

"Baby," he whispered, looking down at me. He wiped my face, probably smudged from the layers of ash on his skin and clothes.

"I'm okay. I'm here."

"Does Tyler know?"

"Yeah. He's the one who told me you were at the hotel. Who knew he would be such a big fucking baby when it came to me?" He smiled, trying to lighten the mood.

"Where have you been?" I asked, shivering uncontrollably.

"We holed up. Let it run over us. Used our fire shelters. Finally crawled out this morning."

I hugged him again and then pressed my mouth on his, not caring that his skin was black with thick soot. He wrapped his arms around me, and everyone in the Bucksaw let out a collective sigh of relief and sentiment.

When I finally let him go, his eyes sparked. "Christ, woman. If I'd known I'd have to have a near-death experience to get your attention, I would have jumped into a fire months ago."

"Don't say that," I said, shaking my head, tears blurring my vision. "Where are Dalton and Zeke? Are they okay?"

Taylor smiled, his teeth gleaming white against his dark face. "Everyone made it out. They're back at the hotel. I came straight over when Ellie told me you'd waited up with them."

Chuck and Phaedra approached, both relieved and happy to see Taylor.

"Take him upstairs, Falyn. Get him cleaned up, so we can make him some breakfast. I'm sure he's half-starved," Phaedra said.

Taylor stood, bringing me with him. "Yes, ma'am," he said, pulling me toward the stairs.

I followed him, still in shock.

When we stepped inside the loft, I closed the door behind me, leaning my back against it. It didn't seem real. All night, I'd thought he was dead, mulling over the idea of truly losing him forever. Now, he was standing a few feet from me, and although the circumstances hadn't changed, everything was different.

"Can you hand me a trash bag? A big one," Taylor said, careful to stand on the tiles in the entrance.

I went to the cabinet under the sink and pulled a large black trash bag from its cardboard box. I shook it out before handing it to him.

Taylor dropped his pack into the sack, and it crashed to the floor. He peeled off his yellow jacket, and then he bent over at the waist to unfasten his boots before pulling them off. Each time he removed a piece of his protective clothing, he'd put it inside the bag.

When he was done, he held the bag closed at the top. "Don't want your place smelling like smoke."

I shook my head. "I don't care."

He grinned. "You will. It doesn't go away for a while. And the black is hard to get out of the carpet. Trust me." Down to his boxer briefs, he tied up the sack and set it outside the door in the hall. "I'm going to take a shower," he said.

I chuckled. Now that he was undressed, his skin was only dirty from the neck up.

He padded into the bathroom, and I heard the shower come on. I covered my mouth, stifling an unexpected sob. He was okay. He was alive and in my bathroom. I thought about what Kirby had said—about the sacrifices he was willing to make and how atrocious I was behaving when it was time for me to take a risk.

I knocked on the open bathroom door, the steam billowing out from above the curtain. The mirror was fogging. Everything was blurry again.

"Taylor?"

"Just wait," he said. "I know what you're going to say. I know what happened last night doesn't change anything. But I've got your fucking attention. I want to talk."

"About what?" I asked.

The faucet shut off, and as Taylor opened the curtain, I grabbed a clean towel from the rack and handed it to him. He dried his face, patted down his chest and arms, and then wrapped the towel around his middle.

"You're not doing this. We love each other. That hasn't changed," he said.

"*How?* How can you still love me? If I deserved it before, I definitely don't now," I said, exasperated.

He shrugged. "I just love you. I don't stop to question whether or not you're worthy. But you can't keep forcing me to make choices that aren't mine."

I had burned him twice. Anyone else would have walked away by now, but he still loved me.

"You're right. You're absolutely right. I know I said I wasn't scared of you. But I lied. I tried not to fall in love with you, but I didn't want to try too hard. Now, we're here, and every time I try to do the right thing, it's wrong. I hurt you, just like I knew I would."

He took a step toward me, interlacing his fingers with mine. He grazed his lips along my cheek until his mouth was whispering against my ear, "No one could have been prepared for this scenario. I don't blame you. I don't want an apology. I just want you to stop the bullshit, Ivy League. You're smart, but you're not always smarter than me."

I looked up at him, the corners of my mouth curling up.

"We've got a baby on the way," he said.

"*You* have a baby on the way."

"No, this is our baby. You have said from the beginning that this was all happening exactly the way it was supposed to. You can't pick and choose. It's either fate, or it's not."

"What if she changes her mind? What if she comes back?"

"Then we adjust. We don't fall apart."

My eyes filled with tears. "I'm afraid. That's a lot to ask."

"I'm not asking." He held the back of my neck and kissed me, tightly closing his eyes, as if it were painful. He held my cheeks and looked straight into my eyes. "You've walked away from me twice, Falyn. I go back to Estes in a couple of months. I'm going to be a dad in December. I'm fucking terrified. But I love you, and that surpasses fear."

Even after months of being apart, being in his arms felt normal, as if it had always been and would always be. I couldn't break his heart again even if it meant being brokenhearted later. I didn't know anymore what the right thing to do was. I just knew that I loved him, and he loved me, too. That was worth all the pain before and all the pain to come.

"Okay. I'm in."

He leaned back, scanning my entire face. "You're in? Which part?"

"Estes Park, the baby—all of it."

A cautious small smile touched his lips. "When?"

"When you go back, I'll go with you."

"Falyn."

"Yeah?"

"I'm having trouble believing you."

"I know. But I promise."

"I have a condition."

I sighed a breath of relief, waiting for whatever he was going to throw my way. "Okay. Name it."

His mouth pulled to the side. "Marry me."

My lips parted, and my breath caught.

Taylor leaned down, touching his thumb to my chin, tilting his head. "Say yes," he whispered against my lips.

"I ... this is not a good time to be making life-changing decisions. We just experienced a traumatic event. I thought you were dead."

"I almost was," he said. He sucked on my bottom lip.

My breath faltered. "When?" I asked, stumbling over the word.

"Why wait?" he said, his voice low and smooth.

He left a trail of kisses from the corner of my mouth to the skin just beneath my ear while reaching around to where my apron was tied in a knot. With two tugs, it came loose and fell to the floor. He backed me up to the door, placing his palms on the peeling white paint on each side of my head.

"Do you love me?" he asked.

"Yes."

"See? It's not hard. Just say yes. Say you'll marry me."

I swallowed hard. "I can't."

CHAPTER TWENTY-FOUR

I REACHED BEHIND ME for the knob before twisting and ducking under his arm. I escaped to the living room, crossing my arms over my middle.

Taylor came out of the bathroom, stopping at the kitchen bar. "You can't?"

I shook my head, pressing my lips together.

"You can't right now or can't at all?" he said. Waiting for my answer was torture for him.

"You're throwing a lot at me all at once. I give you an inch, and you go balls out."

Taylor relaxed a bit, and he breathed out a laugh. "Okay. That's fair."

"I might run away, but you don't know when to quit."

His happiness vanished. "I'm not quitting on you. As long as you love me, I'm going to keep fighting."

"Well," I said, "we're definitely good at that."

He took a step toward me. "I didn't know I wanted it until I said it. But I said it, and now, I want it."

"To get married?" I asked.

He nodded.

"Didn't you hear what I said?"

"Fuck it," he said, shrugging. "Who cares what the logistics are or what your college psych books said or what happened last night? I fucking love you. I want you to be my wife. I want you to have my last name."

A small smile touched my lips. "You do have a pretty great last name."

"Falyn Maddox," he said, each syllable full of admiration and love.

I frowned. "That doesn't sound so great."

He slowly made his way to where I stood, wrapping his arms around me. "I have never exactly fantasized about proposing to a girl, but I damn sure never thought I'd have to beg." He thought about that for a moment and then knelt.

"Oh no, please get up."

"Falyn Fairchild, you are a stubborn woman. You have the mouth of a sailor. You buck every rule anyone lays upon you, and you've broken my heart. Twice."

"This is a terrible proposal," I said.

"Everything that's happened since we met has led to this moment. There is only one woman I've loved before you, and there will never be another after you."

"Unless it's a girl," I said.

Taylor blanched and then stood. "You think it could be a girl?"

"There is a fifty percent chance."

He rubbed the back of his neck, walked away from me, and came back. "I can't have a daughter. I'll kill someone."

I chuckled. "You're right. You do need me—at the very least, for an alibi."

"I'd feel a lot better about it if we made it official."

"I'm not going anywhere."

His face twisted. "You've said that before."

I blew out a breath, feeling like the truth had just punched me in the chest. "I guess neither one of us keeps our promises."

"There is one promise I know I'll keep," he said.

I leaned over, tenderly cupping his face in my hands. "Ask me again."

He blinked. "What?"

"Ask me again."

His eyes glossed over, and he took my hand in both of his. "Will you marry me?"

"Yes."

"Yeah?" he said, beaming.

He crashed into me, kissing every inch of my face. Then his lips landed on my mouth, moving slowly. When he finally released me, he shook his head in disbelief. "You're serious? You're gonna marry me?"

I nodded.

He rubbed the back of his neck. "The worst day of my life has turned into the best day of my life."

"So far," I said.

He kissed me again. This time, he lifted me into his arms and then carried me to the bedroom before closing the door.

We spent the rest of the day in bed, either making love or making plans. I waited to feel panic or regret, but neither came. I had been without him, and then I thought I'd lost him forever. Loss had a way of making everything very clear, and all the things I'd been so worried about seemed insignificant now.

Just before dinner, Taylor's cell phone buzzed, and he climbed out of bed to check it. "Damn it. I got called in."

I sulked. "So soon after what happened?"

He shrugged. "It's the job, baby." He fetched the trash bag in the hall and put on the smoky clothes. "Come with me."

"To wait at the hotel?"

"Ellie will be there. You can hang with her. Tyler's crew was called out, too. I want you there when I get back."

I walked over to the closet and slipped on a T-shirt and jeans, and then I slid my feet into a pair of sandals.

Taylor seemed happy as he watched me wrap my hair into a bun.

"Just let me ..." I said, hurrying into the bathroom to grab a toothbrush.

We rushed downstairs, and I waved to Phaedra before following Taylor out to his truck.

He drove a little too fast to the hotel. At the entrance, he handed me the key card. "Your phone is in the zipper part of my suitcase. Room two-oh-one."

"The same room you were in when we met."

He leaned over to peck my lips, and then I scooted out.

"Be safe," I said before closing the passenger door. "I mean it."

Tyler jogged out, his pack in his hand. He kissed Ellison's cheek, and then he climbed into the shotgun seat.

Taylor punched his arm. "I'm gettin' married, fucker!"

Tyler looked at me, shocked, and then a huge smile broke out across his face.

I nodded to confirm, and Ellison hugged me.

"Let's put out this fire then. Don't want to keep your fiancée waiting," Tyler said, socking his fist straight into Taylor's shoulder.

They waved, and then Taylor pulled away, squealing the tires.

"Oh, those Maddox boys," Ellison said, shaking her head. She put her arm around me. "You really said yes, huh?"

"Am I crazy?" I asked.

"Absolutely," she said. "Why do you think they fell in love with us?"

I looked down the road even though the twins were long gone.

"That's why I know it will work," I said. "You can't really be in love without being a little crazy."

EPILOGUE

THE EDGES OF THE NAPKIN tore easily between my fingers as I waited at the bar for Phaedra to bring me a slice of her famous cheesecake.

I smiled at the low hum of conversation that had made me feel safe for so long. The Bucksaw would always be just that—my home.

"Hannah! Order up!" Chuck yelled. When he caught my eye, he winked. "How are you feeling?"

"Tired," I said. "But happy."

The chime on the door rang, and I turned to see Taylor holding our son on his hip, his free arm hooked around the handle of an infant carrier.

Phaedra set my plate in front of me, but she barely paused before heading to the door. "There are those babies! Come to Granny!" she said, holding her arms out to Hollis.

She carried him to where I sat, and Taylor readjusted the baby bag on his shoulder before bringing over the carrier. Once he set the carrier on the ground, a baby's wails filled the room.

I arched an eyebrow. "Still think taking them to the hotel was a good idea?"

He kissed my cheek. "The guys hadn't seen her yet, and I'd thought it'd be nice to give you a second to chat." He leaned over, pulled the blanket away, and unbuckled the tiny infant. He nuzzled her for a moment before handing her to me.

"It was nice. Thank you," I said, touching Hadley's sweet soft cheek to mine. I hummed a little tune until she settled down.

"I have a confession," Taylor said. "I took off the headband while we were there."

My mouth fell open as I feigned being offended. "But it's so cute!"

"It's ridiculous, baby. Those guys don't care if she's wearing one, especially not one bigger than her head."

I had dressed her in tiny black-and-white houndstooth leggings, a hot-pink shirt, and socks that looked like Mary Janes. Granted, the headband was a bit excessive, but we didn't have many opportunities to dress her up. I mostly focused on keeping her comfortable.

Chuck came out and held out his arms for Hadley. "Just washed my hands."

Phaedra gently pinched a roll of fat on Hollis's arm. "Are you feeding this poor kid?" She kissed his cheek and bounced him a bit. "He's as big as a toddler!"

Hollis rubbed his nose on Phaedra's shirt, and then he rubbed his eyes with his chubby hand.

"Are you getting sleepy, son?" I asked.

He reached for me, and I patted his back while he rested his head on my shoulder. He was his father's son with the same long lashes and warm brown eyes.

Taylor had attended every doctor's and ultrasound appointment Alyssa allowed, and he'd read every book on parenting and newborns he could get his hands on while he was on shift at his new job at the Estes Park station.

The whole time Alyssa had labored and for the half an hour after Hollis was born, Taylor had paced the floor, and I'd watched him from my uncomfortable waiting room chair, rubbing my round belly. The moment we'd entered the room where we met him, the nurse had handed Taylor his son, and it was love at first sight for us both.

Four months after Hollis was born, we'd brought home Hadley. Miracles happened, and Hadley was ours.

"There she is!" Kirby said, grinning and wrinkling her nose at the infant in Chuck's arms. Then she came over to rub Hollis's back in small circles. "His hair grew in dark, huh?"

I kissed the back of his head. "He's all Maddox."

"Lord help us," Phaedra teased.

The door chimed again, and Gunnar breezed in, a big grin on his face.

"Hey," he said, leaning down to take a peek at Hollis. He looked at Taylor. "He's gettin' big! How old is he now?"

"Six months," Taylor said. Like any proud father, he puffed out his chest. "He's going to be a beast."

"Yeah, he is," Gunnar said, walking over to stand next to Chuck. "Aw. She's adorable! Cute headband!"

"See?" I said to Taylor before sticking out my tongue.

I reached over for my fork and cut a piece of pie. "Oh my God, do I miss your food, Phaedra."

"It's here for you anytime," Phaedra said.

Hadley began to wail, and Chuck bounced her up and down before holding her out for Taylor. Hadley squinted her eyes, her whole body shaking while she cried.

"Goodness," Taylor said, leaning down to fetch her pacifier.

Hadley sucked on it for a few seconds and then began to cry again.

"I think she's hungry, baby. I'll trade ya," Taylor said.

I took Hadley in one arm and let Taylor take Hollis from the other. Hollis was already asleep. Taylor handed me a cover-up, and I pulled it over my head with my free hand.

Chuck and Gunnar were instantly trying to find somewhere else to look.

Hadley settled down, and Taylor swayed from side to side as he held Hollis.

Phaedra shook her head. "Good grief. It's like having twins."

"Just about," Taylor said. "Wouldn't trade it though."

He winked at me, and I grinned.

We had matching pairs of dark circles under our eyes, and when Taylor was at the station and both babies woke up during the night, it would be challenging, but we had become pros.

Taylor had been a great boyfriend, but he was the perfect father.

"So, when is the wedding?" Kirby asked.

"As soon as I can fit into the size-six dress that I bought," I said.

Everyone laughed but Taylor.

"You know," he said, "I thought you couldn't be more beautiful than you were when you were pregnant, but I was wrong. I fall in love with you every time I see you holding our kids."

"Easy," Chuck said. "You'll have another one on the way."

Phaedra, Kirby, and Gunnar laughed.

"Wedding first," Taylor said. "Then who knows?"

"I know. We got lucky," I said.

"We've been lucky a lot," Taylor said before kissing me on the forehead. He looked to the others. "We're getting married in Eakins in October. We have a few people from there besides family we'd like to invite."

"Like who?" Phaedra asked.

"Shane and Liza ... and Olive," I said.

Phaedra and Chuck traded glances. "So, you're going to contact them?"

"I'm going to write them a letter," I said. "I have to explain a few things first."

Phaedra seemed concerned. "If you think that's best."

"I'm sure it'll be fine, honey," Chuck said with a smile.

Kirby left to check on the remaining tables, and I finished my slice of pie with one hand, something I'd grown accustomed to. Once I burped Hadley, Phaedra buckled her into her seat.

"Do you have to go so soon?" Phaedra said, forlorn.

"We'll be back," I said, hugging her.

I took a sleeping Hollis from Taylor, and Phaedra kissed the baby's hand.

Taylor picked up the carrier and leaned in to hug Chuck.

"Drive safe," Chuck said.

We waved good-bye, and after securing the children into their seats, we climbed into ours.

Taylor started the truck and reached for my hand. "So much has changed since I first walked into that café."

"That's an understatement."

He held my hand to his lips, and then he lowered it back to the console. "One choice led to all of this. If I hadn't met you, I wouldn't have either of my children. I owe everything that's important to me to you."

With his left hand, he reached across to put the gear in drive. We drove away from the place where we'd met to the place where we were raising our family, holding hands the whole way.

ACKNOWLEDGMENTS

I thank my husband in every book. I can look back on each acknowledgment and see the love and support he's shown me over my career. Jeff helps me so much that at times I joke that his name should be on the cover, too, because without him, there would be no Jamie McGuire books. His presence in my life is just as instrumental to my finishing novels as my creativity or work ethic. Not only does he handle most everything so that I can focus on my career, he is the reason I know how to write about love and why I know men have a soft, sweet, kind side. He is why I know men can be so forgiving and patient.

There are three other people in our household who show patience and love daily—my children. It's hard to have a mom who works in the home. It takes a lot of understanding and respect, and my children have become pros. Thank you, babies.

Thank you to two readers who have become like sisters—Deanna and Selena. You were the first to travel more than an hour to one of my early signings, and it was before anyone knew who I was! I'm so glad that we've become so close, and I cherish our friendship. I love you both.

Danielle, Jessica, and Kelli—Your support has been invaluable. I can't thank you enough for what you do. Not only do you rally the troops on your own time, but you also expect nothing in return. I cherish our friendship as much as I appreciate your dedication.

MacPack! You all, every single one of you, rock my socks. I am in awe of how devoted you are to the cause, and I am eternally grateful. You'll never know just how many times you brighten my day.

Megan Davis—You've never let me down. You are always available, always around to lend an ear or to help in any way you can. You are an amazing friend. The Vegas signing simply would not have been possible without you, and I will never forget your kindness. Thank you.

Teresa Mummert—My sanity thanks you. I don't think there is another person who makes me laugh or look forward to a phone conversation like you do. I consider you to be one of my very best friends, and I'm so grateful you put up with me.

ABOUT THE AUTHOR

JAMIE MCGUIRE was born in Tulsa, Oklahoma. She attended Northern Oklahoma College, the University of Central Oklahoma, and Autry Technology Center where she graduated with a degree in Radiography.

Jamie paved the way for the New Adult genre with the international bestseller *Beautiful Disaster*. Her follow-up novel, *Walking Disaster*, debuted at #1 on the *New York Times*, *USA Today*, and *Wall Street Journal* bestseller lists. *Beautiful Oblivion*, book one of the Maddox Brothers books, also topped the *New York Times* bestseller list, debuting at #1.

Novels also written by Jamie McGuire include *Red Hill*, an apocalyptic thriller; the *Providence* series, a young adult paranormal romance trilogy; *Apolonia*, a dark sci-fi romance; and several novellas, including *A Beautiful Wedding*, *Among Monsters: A Red Hill Novella*, and *Happenstance: A Novella Series*.

Jamie lives on a ranch just outside of Enid, Oklahoma, with her husband, Jeff, and their three children. They share their thirty acres with cattle, six horses, three dogs, and a cat named Rooster.

Find Jamie at www.jamiemcguire.com or on Facebook, Twitter, Tsu, and Instagram.

Made in the USA
San Bernardino, CA
02 June 2015